Published in Great Britain by
L.R. Price Publications Ltd, 2021
27 Old Gloucester Street,
London, WC1N 3AX
www.lrpricepublications.com

Cover artwork by L.R. Price Publications Ltd

Used under exclusive and unlimited licence by
L.R. Price Publications Ltd.

ISBN: 9781739805227

YOUR TIME'S UP HARRY!

# RAVENFALL

## YOUR TIME IS UP, HARRY!

---

## Donald Piasu

# Author's Note

All characters – including the narrator – portrayed in this book are creations of my imagination and bear no relationship to any living person.

The town of Ravenfall is an invention and is not based on any real, existing community in the world!

YOUR TIME'S UP HARRY!

# Introduction

*It's true when it is said that "everyone has a story."*

*Because each of our lives is one great big tale – some parts true, others slightly exaggerated. In every city and every town, you'll find many stories.*

*It's just a shame that, often, the best ones are not always out in the open; they are hidden so deep that you have to dig with your hands, with great effort, clearing away the soil to find the hidden truths. The deeper you dig – or, in your case, the more you read – the more you want to know.*

*Why is it that some people have to hide certain aspects of their life?*

*Because there are stigmas, which everyone suffers at least once in their life; certain things we keep hidden from others – even those who think they know us well. But, nobody truly knows everything about another person.*

*And, in truth, we really don't want to. Because, sometimes the truth you come face to face with is the one thing that can really turn your life upside down.*

*I think it is best to be upfront and completely honest at*

*this stage, by saying that I will give a true and accurate account of what happens in this story – though, as before, I have to lay down some ground rules, some of which you may already know. First, all persons within have been given a pseudonym, to protect their and my family's identity – not that it will spoil the story in any way. The locations have also been changed, along with a few other details. I will let you know about these throughout, and the reasons why.*

# CHAPTER 1

**Friday, 3:05 p.m.**
**Ravenfall – the local high school.**

You can't always choose what you do, or what you're meant to become; it chooses you.

It is often referred to as your destiny. Each of us has a purpose, one way or another.

When you're young, it's natural to fantasize about a dream, since it is the most important decision a person will ever have to make in their life, and it never hurts to keep your options open.

As you grow, life will always throw questions your way, and most of the time you will never have the answers, so you have to always keep an open mind.

One of the most curious questions I had growing up, and one which was only ever asked within my family, was: *"What is the difference between a hitman and an assassin?"*

Most of you out there would probably argue that there isn't one: they both kill for money!

Domestic, political or a simple grudge are all common

reasons, and all have a price tag. That is to say, then, that it is never personal – always financial, no matter what name they choose to go by.

Breaking the word down, "HIT-MAN" is a cold and brutal description for such a lethal profession. Given the choice, I think "assassin" is more appropriately applied to those with a certain skillset. Of course, the term "professional killer" is also a strong designate, though it is not often a calling card to be passed around at social gatherings.

The taking of a life is never a pleasant subject but, surprisingly, it happens every day.

Is it wrong to take a human life, even a life full of terrible sins?

Well, to try and answer this question, it is necessary to tell this story from the beginning. In my case, it is the actual beginning of life.

I am not referring to Genesis, you understand; of course I mean the beginning of human life: a newborn, into adolescence and into adulthood, when life changes. And, so too does the way in which you look at the world!

The coming of a certain age, how you were and what you are yet to become, is the natural state of evolution; a time when discoveries and possible destinies arise with little warning. Being young and ignorant, even of one's own body, you can never tell what you are going to experience from one day to the next. Both outside and inside you change, and the mind struggles with new temptations, leading you toward grave sins, or testing your will to remain pure.

When it came to being a teenage girl, I always played it safe.

Especially when the cutest guy in school cornered me on the last day of term and invited me back to his place alone, away from giggling friends, loitering in the background. Peer pressure can often make young people jump to very rash decisions, but I was as bright as a shining penny, and wanted to remain untarnished.

So, he was out of luck, and my friends were waving me goodbye with some admiration, as I headed out of the main gate, off of school premises, for the last time.

My apologies; I really should have introduced myself: my name is Izzy. The last name I have to withhold, for reasons already explained.

I was seventeen at this stage in my life, riding my bike home whilst contemplating my upcoming future, like any normal teenager.

Though, at this point, I'm sure you must be a little curious – if not concerned – about the question I put forward at the beginning of this chapter: a young girl of seventeen wondering about hitmen and assassins?

It was actually something I used to debate with my sister, whose opinion was thus: *"An assassin isn't just a person with a gun; they are professionals, highly trained and skilled."*

Which makes a lot of sense, since anyone can pick up a gun and shoot another person, even with a blindfold over their eyes.

The assassin is more professional in the "death trade". A lot of work goes into each contract, and thus they are justified in charging more than your average thug.

*"Doing the job right, with complete efficiency, is like doing anything you have a passion for."* This is my father's motto.

When it comes to my family, you get real value for money.

That's right: my family is in the business of "contract killing", for the benefit of those who have not already learnt this from my sister's previous book. I was actually surprised my father allowed the publication to go ahead, seeing as it was about our family's chosen profession… but then, here I am now, talking to you!

Let's get back to the story, now that you are up to date with certain things.

When it came to the end of the school year, there was always a need to celebrate with friends and family. Riding my bicycle down our neighbourhood, I occasionally got the odd wave from our neighbours – our most loyal of customers, when it came to our other trade: meat.

My home, you see, is the local butcher shop in our village; been in our family for four generations now. And, where would any town or village be without a local butcher shop?

Ravenfall, where this story is set, is a quiet, pleasant country village on the outskirts of The Big City: a large, over-populated, crime-filled pond, where the big fish eat the small. Many here – who sought sanctuary from that world – can be found sitting on their front lawn, looking through magazines and drinking themselves to sleep. Ravenfall is the perfect retreat. I don't wish to sound like an advertisement, but our village really is as you first see it, just like in those European movies: nice, colourful gardens and old people wearing floppy hats.

Like most country villages, the locals are quite mindful when it comes to outsiders. If you want to establish yourself within the community, an evening out to the local pub is a good step toward learning who is who – and sometimes what previous life they are escaping. Ravenfall is a sort of haven, where people are able to leave their pasts behind.

There are two types of people you see here: 1. those

looking for a change, and 2. those who have people looking for them. Everyone has a few skeletons in their closet!

This was how it began for my great grandfather, during the First World War, but that's another story for another time; let's get back to the present.

Upon entering the front door to the shop, I usually find my sister Bethany, looking up quickly, eyeing me from behind the counter, then glancing up to the clock. The worst thing about having an older sister is that you always feel they're acting as your warden. Since I hadn't dawdled, even though it was the last day, she kept to the business at hand.

This particular day, we had Mrs. Galloway in, to buy her usual cuts of beef. Holding the door open as she passed by, she smiled and asked me how it felt to have finally finished high school.

"She's going to be very handy to have around here, now she's finished her adolescence," my sister spoke now. "A step into the real world is the next best thing to a summer break!"

If it hadn't been for another customer coming in right then – a Mr. Hollows – I would have bludgeoned her to death with one of our best Cumberland sausages, hanging in the window.

My father had also come out from the back to greet Mr. Hollows, who was there to purchase a goose. My father beckoned with his finger for me to follow him to the kitchen. I was happy to leave my sister to attend to Mr. Hollows, who was a true patron of our business.

It may shock you to know that our family is well respected in our community, even if our history is stained in red. It doesn't make us sociopaths.

I don't lie to my friends; I just don't tell them everything about my family's business, and they never really ask questions about being the daughter of a butcher.

Walking into the kitchen, I found my mother chopping vegetables at the kitchen table, looking up and smiling as we entered. "How was the last day, dear?"

I merely shrugged, coming over and sitting down opposite, taking a piece of raw carrot from the bowl and popping it into my mouth, catching a slight disapproving look my way.

"I can't say that I'm going to miss the place. I'm just a little anxious about my final results," I said earnestly, letting my school-bag drop from my shoulder to the floor beside me.

"You worked very hard this semester, so I'm sure everything is going to be okay," my mother said, getting up and taking the bowl over to the sink.

My father was standing at the fridge, getting a glass of milk. "I have to go pick up a lamb for the shop in a moment. I'd like you to come along."

I took the statement in, then looked over to my mother, who just looked back, thoughtfully. This was unusual; he had never asked me before – it was usually my sister who went with him to the farm, to fetch the meat.

"I've just got back from school. I need to change and check my emails, as some college offers might have already come in."

Taking a big sip from the glass, he wiped away the white moustache from his top lip and went over to join my mother at the sink. "You can see to that later... and going online with your friends."

His tone then became serious: "As for you going out to The Big City for your celebration party, I think it's best you keep to the village tonight; there's been some trouble over there."

I had seen this coming, and was not prepared to concede without a fight. "There's always trouble! But it's got the hottest nightclubs anywhere and this is a special night; it only comes round once in a lifetime." I looked to my mother for support.

"You can celebrate here, with your family, so we don't have to worry about you. Invite your friends to come over," he said, placing his empty glass in the sink, causing Mother to catch him harshly by the ear like a naughty boy, running the tap and placing the glass back in his hand.

"What your father is saying is that we don't think you should be going there at night. It's risky. Even being in a group, predators find you easy targets!" I could hear the usual concern in my mother's voice.

Most of you out there, with the usual maternal or paternal instincts, would no doubt agree – probably even adopt the same diplomatic approach.

"Everyone else is going! How's it going to look if I don't turn up – the only senior?"

My father quickly finished drying up and put the glass back in the cupboard, with Mother eyeing him very carefully; she liked things to be done a certain way in her kitchen. My father was head of the business, but she was queen of this domain!

"They are just going to have to accept that you have parents concerned for your wellbeing," he said firmly. "Now, go and get ready. I'll be out back, waiting in the truck."

I looked to my mother once more, but she wasn't going against my father's wishes. So, I picked up my bag and made my way upstairs.

Closing my bedroom door, I threw my bag at the wall

and collapsed forward onto my bed, rolling over onto my back, to look up at the ceiling.

*How I hate being in a family of killers! Evil-doers, plotting terrible things every minute of the day.*

As you've probably gathered, this is so far not your typical story.

Our family never meant to become who we are; like most people in life, circumstances shape our destiny. But then, we each have a choice whether to accept it or not.

At that very moment, the one thing which had been nagging at my brain the whole day had returned to my thoughts. Coming to the end of the school year, no longer being looked upon as a child, surely meant certain changes. Though, so far, I was still being treated as a child.

Quickly, I changed out of my uniform and looked to the collage of photographs spread over my bed: a lot of good memories of childhood, actually – but all were of Ravenfall. There were a few shots taken on the odd family holiday, but not one had ever been taken of just me, away from home on an adventure. My parents, as you've probably gathered, are very protective.

Some children would be using this upcoming break to go away and enjoy their youth, to be free and have fun, but in my case I was still thinking about the future which lay ahead for me now.

I would be at home more if I didn't decide to go to college – something I hadn't as yet discussed with my parents. And if I did, there was the question of something which had bothered me greatly.

*Would I be the one to finally break the family legacy?*

When it comes to family, so many are pressured into making decisions based on an obligation of following in their parents' footsteps – some strange hereditary gene, one would argue. As teenagers, we've all made certain judgements at one time or another. But, I have truthfully never been ashamed of our family history.

However, there has always been one question which has taxed me, even in regard to my family.

*How is it for us – or any person – to decide who lives and who dies?*

This is something I questioned my father about once. He said that our actions are only fulfilling the decisions of others; we do not seek to justify them, as a vigilante might. Usually, their motives are based on some means of freeing themselves from their own demons. Truthfully, I didn't understand this at the time, until I started listening secretly at my father's office door, whilst he deliberated with my mother and sister over the assignments offered. If you knew the sort of people we are asked to eliminate – the pain and suffering they have caused to others – you might secretly give us your blessing.

Or, you might argue they should only be judged by God.

Well, let's leave religion for now.

The question, from the point of right or wrong, good or bad, is something I struggled with terribly, and this made my decision to join the family business a difficult one.

My parents had never talked with me about it, as neither had my sister, Bethany. I've never felt alienated from any of them, but I knew they all had one advantage over me; they had the answer I was still searching for: *What was it like deciding to kill someone?*

That which lies in our hearts, motivating us to kill and wipe evil from the world, is not necessarily bad – it's a calling, a responsibility, a service; a necessity to vanquish those who are evil. If our objective – the outcome – is a sane and just one, then how can our actions be evil?

How many of you truly know the evil that some people do in this world?

Well, I suppose you have your own opinions and ideas of how such people should be dealt with. And, by the end of this story, each will have their own opinions about me and my family.

Or, maybe you wish to close the book right now?

Well, *each to their own* is all that I can say at this stage.

God gave us free will to do as we please, so I leave it to you, at this point, to decide whether to continue, or to close the book right now.

But every story – even that of a life – has to be told. So, a book never really stays closed, and a life never really ends – as long as there are those who remember our words.

# CHAPTER 2

### Friday 4:10 p.m.
### Ravenfall – the churchyard.

We all enter this world at birth, and begin our lives much as a pen writes words, or sketches images on paper and in books. And each is given its own heading or title.

A person cannot choose their own name, however, just as they cannot choose their nature. You are given a name at birth, and it is immortalized in stone upon your death.

There is a lot more to life and death than people realize. Death comes to us all, but in two ways: when it matters to someone, and when it doesn't.

But, how can a death not matter to somebody? Surely, the worst pain a person ever feels is the loss of a loved one? It's a wound which doesn't ever completely heal, even over time.

Every day, people are struck by tragic events. Many lives are lost, and there are always those left behind to wonder if it was unjust, or perhaps incomprehensible.

Uncle Harry stood by the graves of his daughter and son-in-law.

The dates of their passing were the same day – but sadly they had not passed together, as man and wife.

Lowering himself down onto one knee, he placed fresh flowers carefully on the mound, feeling the tears wanting to well up once more.

It had only been a month since the funeral of his daughter. He had cried unashamedly, in the presence of most of the town's people, who had come along to pay their respects.

All about us can be found the good, whom God chooses to bless with his wisdom and mercy: friends, neighbours and loved ones. When it comes to a close community, nothing brings it together better than a tragedy.

Looking at her gravestone, he could feel a deep pain rising in his heart; regrets haunted him: unspoken words he should have said when he had the chance. At least then he might find some solace, instead of ruing matters left unresolved, of which only the dead were now free.

I, myself, would like to believe that when you are finally laid to rest, you are not completely separated from this world. I believe that the spirits of loved ones have not left us altogether, as from time to time there is always that slight feeling of a warm, supportive hand on our shoulders, when we need it the most. They still watch over us, even in death, until we are reunited once again. Those who look back over our shoulders, or speak freely from the heart may be laughed at, but only by those who never felt the touch, and do not see clearly with their heart. Each of us is free to believe what we like.

Normality is like a safety cloak in our society: it protects us from the horrible stains and beliefs which disfigure or influence people's views. Those who live by the law, and by the word of God, believe their life to be good, and that any misfortune befalling us is God's will – or just dumb fucking luck. But, it could also be a means to stop everyone going mad, when everything we hold precious crumbles between our fingers – though we try to pick up the pieces, we're not always able to put them successfully back together. What we once had is gone, and we have no other choice than to accept it and live on.

Rising back to his feet, Uncle Harry looked at the other grave, with a regret less sympathetic.

In this harsh world, not all are strong, or fortunate enough to hold onto faith; desperate times often lead to rash decisions which, when discovered, can cost a man greatly for his sins.

Martin, his son-in-law, had been out of work and down on his luck, which is an unfortunate occurrence for most people. But, not all choose to turn to crime out of desperation. Martin had made subsequent choices which ruined his family; he had turned against and stolen from his neighbours and friends, and had paid dearly for his sins.

Looking up to the sky, Uncle Harry had managed to say at least one prayer.

*The darkest sins are secrets between man and God!*

Walking out of the large, metal gates back into Ravenfall town square, Uncle Harry gave his eyes another wipe with his handkerchief, then pocketed it again − straightening himself up, now that he was back in the public eye.

So far, his normal daily routine was going like clockwork. He'd got up fairly early that morning, skipped breakfast and settled for coffee. Being the end of the week, he wanted to get some provisions and bare essentials in, to cover him over the weekend.

The village was busy that afternoon, with people going about their normal business, and most seemed to be in a buoyant mood.

He walked first to the greengrocers and bought some potatoes and leeks, along with a punnet of strawberries; fruit is always good to keep a man healthy. Over the past few weeks, he'd cut back a lot on the alcohol and smoking.

It is strange how, in particular moments of grief, a person can suddenly choose to transform, for either better or worse.

He had responsibilities now, to the last surviving

members of his family: the two grandsons his daughter had given birth to, with her last, dying breath. As there were no other relatives on his daughter's side, and Martin's only brother was currently serving time in prison, Harry had been awarded custody.

As a parent, he hadn't been much of a supportive father toward their mother Laurie, so he was determined to try and make an effort for his grandchildren's future. Now with little ones, he was finding his time – the hours in the day – a little pressed these days. But they were not a burden. He had made his choice, and would stand fully by his word.

Looking across the street, he thought for a moment he'd seen a familiar figure in one of the shop windows.

Entering the hardware store, he moved around one of the aisles and recognized the small figure standing by the rat-poison shelves: a small, grey-haired lady.

"I didn't think my eyes were deceiving me!" He looked down at the twin boys, Olivier and Andrew, in the stroller, then up to his newly-appointed housekeeper, Mrs. Sykes.

When his own father had died, Uncle Harry had taken over the family business of construction, and managed to maintain the family manor in which he had been raised. Harry's was the finest house in the whole village, which meant that it took some looking after. So, since he still had a business to run, he had taken on Mrs. Sykes as a housekeeper and nanny.

"I was just getting some more rat killer for the basement," she said, holding up a box. "I think I heard some more little pests scurrying around down there, last night."

Harry bent down and smiled at the two toddlers, who just sat quietly, looking back at him – which was a rarity, particularly when he was left in charge of them. I guess it just took a woman's touch when it came to handling children.

"I don't know how effective that stuff can be. It's like those vermin have become immune and just eat it up now, as though it were mere sustenance," he chuckled.

She smiled and moved over to the counter, to pay the young girl at the till, who smiled warmly at Harry, handing back the change with a nod to Mrs. Sykes. Leaving the store together, he asked the housekeeper if she wanted to take a lift home with him, but she had some more shopping to do.

The temperature was starting to drop a little, and he didn't like the thought of the youngsters catching cold. Whatever else they needed, they would make do with whatever was at home.

Leading her back to his vehicle – a very large Land Rover – he enquired as to how the new carpet was coming along, in the upstairs master bedroom.

"I left the workman with your man Victor; hopefully it should be finished by the time we get back," she said, assuredly.

Since it was now summer, the house was getting a good airing out. He had placed his full trust in her to see that the work was done properly.

I myself could not see why a grown woman would want to clean and take care of other people's houses – it's not really a career I would have chosen. Not that I'm a stranger to light housework! Some would have thought it unusual for a housekeeper to take on a second role. But, during her time at the house, she had grown very fond of the twins, and accepted live-in based employment, so that she could assist Harry more in taking care of them.

"I noticed that the clothes in the guest room are still piled up on the bed," she said, inquisitively. "Are you going to get around to seeing they get collected for goodwill, or did you want me to attend to it?"

Harry hadn't gone into that room since the day his daughter had passed. The clothes had been freshly cleaned, but never put away.

"In truth, I'm reluctant to part with them. There's not much left I have to remember my daughter by, and I thought that the children—"

"Well, I think little mementoes are important, but really I think that photos and keepsakes are more meaningful," she said, reaching into her pocket for her handkerchief. "It's a shame to have them just sitting around, when somebody else – someone in need – could be making good use of them."

Harry was not offended by the statement; his own daughter would probably have said the same thing. He said that he would get them bagged up that day.

He still had pictures, and some of the jewellery he had taken from the hospital, to give to the children when they were older. As for Martin, he had only the one wedding photograph.

He had wanted so much to keep the bad history away from the twins – and at least he still had some time before they started asking questions. How was he to go about explaining their parents, and how they died? Perhaps they would never need to know the truth. A lie and a secret are not really the same thing, after all.

But, then again, even this village was too small for secrets. And, those who grew up here often discovered that secrets find their way out.

Stopping briefly outside the flower shop, Mrs. Sykes wanted to pick up some fresh daisies, while Harry carried on walking to where he had parked. Uncle Harry, of course, knew that she had a liking for fresh flowers, which were usually displayed about the house, leaving a pleasant perfume in every room.

The roads and traffic weren't busy that day, so it was a clear shot over to his vehicle, as he fumbled in his pocket for the keys. Behind him, Mrs. Sykes was making her way over. She stopped abruptly as a car suddenly rounded the corner, sounding its horn.

Harry looked back, as the car carried on along its way, leaving Mrs. Sykes a little flustered, attending to the children, who were themselves unfazed by the incident. Moving away again, Uncle Harry started back toward them, wanting to find that driver and give him a good piece of his mind about the speed limit.

Suddenly there came a loud noise, almost like a firework: a high-pitched eruption, which shook the ground beneath his feet. A great, yellow and orange spark had ignited, expanding in the blink of an eye. There came a great force from behind, as the Range Rover exploded, lifting him forward, off of his feet and into the air. Simultaneously, there were cries all around, as there followed breaking sounds, and shards of glass started to fill the air around everyone. Harry felt as if his whole body was being spun around and around in the air, until finally he felt it collide with the ground. Everything was pitch black within seconds.

Mrs. Sykes had reacted protectively toward the children, covering them with her body. She now stood once more, to find the whole street's surface covered with pieces of glass. Black smoke and flames were rising from what had once been Harry's vehicle.

Suddenly, there came screams from across the pavement, where people were crying and holding their heads, cut and bleeding from the glass of the café's front window. Some had taken in the fact that something terrible had just happened, while others just stood in a state of shock.

Harry couldn't move, as though he was stuck to the ground. His whole body was going numb, and his eyes would not function. All he could do was stare into the darkness, waiting. When you are so close to death, you can only but wonder who is coming to help. *This is it: time to meet my Maker – or just suffer the burning flames.*

At moments like this, your family – your whole life – might play out in front of you.

Dying is a part of living. It happens to everyone, and it makes you appreciate life more, and regret all the simple things you took for granted.

There is an old Native American saying:

*The only way man will truly inherit the Earth is when he*

*is six feet under it!*

# CHAPTER 3

**Friday 4:30 p.m.**

**Ravenfall – the farmyard.**

When my father invited me to join him on his visit, to go and pick up a lamb from one of the neighbouring farms, I had been a little put out at first – especially since I was now staying at home that night, while all my friends would be celebrating their liberation in The Big City.

As we drove along the dirt track, however, I suddenly realized that I was about to witness an event which could help answer the question I had been pondering beforehand.

The opportunity to see my first slaughtered animal was nothing I had ever anticipated before, but as we drove up to the farm in my father's truck, I could feel a slight rush of adrenalin.

Was it wrong to feel this way? No, it was a new experience, that's all.

Even my father noticed a slight change in my body language, as we drove past some cows grazing in a field. "Are you feeling alright?" he asked.

I recognized the tone to be one of slight concern, but I took a breath and casually looked out of the window, taking in the landscape – not to mention the horrid smell of fertilizer.

"Do animals have a good life before they are led to slaughter?" I asked, suddenly.

My father took a moment. He was used to this routine, and probably hadn't thought about it in a long time. This was regular business; a way of life.

"Most have a lovely time in the last eight to ten months," my father answered, driving through the front gate, "grazing and lazing in the fields." The answer had been simple and accurate; no argument could be found in the words given.

"I don't envy the farmer who comes along to gather those lambs, eating and playing in the grass; looking them in the eye as each is marched into the waiting pen," I countered.

My father said nothing, finally pulling up to the cottage and getting out.

I wasn't really sure how it was going to be, witnessing the slaughter of an animal which had been born and raised on this very farm. They were actually very caring when it came to the animals. Yet, being there, one couldn't help but find the circle of life strange: to raise something living, which was only born to be killed and sold, was a paradox I had never considered before.

Meeting the farm owner, Mr. Reilly, we were shown to the holding pen, where already one lamb had been separated from the group and was pegged in the centre – it was surprisingly calm and peaceful. I felt a little sorry for the creature, and the thought of what was to come made me hesitate in my stride, as I approached with my father, fearing my emotions would disturb its mood. I decided to hang back, wait by the gate and watch.

My father, of course, was old-school, and chose to do his own killing – continuing the tradition as it had been taught to him, and was now being taught to me. He was already carrying out his silent preparation ceremony.

There were certain things which allowed the process to be as humane as possible toward the animal: it had to been done quickly and with little stress, hiding the hammer from the animal and taking up position behind it, to deliver a strong blow to the back of the skull.

My father was calm as he raised the instrument.

Suddenly, this sudden urge came over me, out of nowhere – perhaps brought about by the feel of death creeping up my back. The answer to my question was at hand, yet I was letting it slip away.

I suddenly called out to my father, causing him to pause

in mid-motion, a slightly annoyed expression on his face. The animal now looked around to face me. The eyes bothered me, but nevertheless, I started to walk forward and held out my hand, asking if I could do it.

My father considered for a moment, while the farmer, Mr. Reilly, watched from the gate, smoking from his pipe, curious of what was transpiring; usually such matters were decided beforehand.

Taking the hammer from my father, I took up position, as my father silently gave some direct instructions, showing me the exact place to strike. He took hold of the lamb's body.

I didn't want to draw it out so, without further hesitation, I brought the hammer down with a heavy blow, causing the lamb's legs to immediately buckle. Picking up the knife, my father instructed me swiftly, slicing through the throat. The earth turned dark red and the animal came to rest.

I can't say in all honesty that I wasn't getting some sort of an adrenalin rush, and it was growing more powerful on seeing the blood flow; the pumping of my own blood through my arms felt like a raging river.

We carried the corpse over to the shed, where my father began to teach me the next stage: skinning and gutting – the really messy part! Hanging the lifeless creature up by the back legs, we started removing the skin, from leg to belly first, then moved on to the sternum and the throat. We finished from the shoulders down to the front legs. The only squeamish part was slicing down the carcass, hearing a continuous plopping as the guts dropped onto the floor. Yet, my father maintained a pleasant humour throughout.

Soon, this fine slab would be taken back and put into our walk-in freezer. Come Sunday, a slow-cooked leg would end up on our serving plate.

A whole lamb, depending on the size and particular cut proportions, can provide up to twenty individual meals – just a little insight, for those readers interested.

In the truck, glancing back over my shoulder, I looked at the wrapped meat – once a living creature, which had died by my hand. It was clean and did not smell of death – though I wasn't actually sure that I had smelt anything but blood, throughout the entire process. The sensation had otherwise been all-physical. I did not feel sorrow or guilt anymore; it had been the animal's purpose to feed us, so the circle was now complete.

My father suddenly stopped, as we passed outside the farm gate, and leant over to hug me and kiss the top of my forehead. I wasn't sure if it was an affectionate sign of pride, as he had failed to produce even a smile, before he pulled back and continued driving.

Whether I should talk it over with him, as we drove back

to town, I wasn't sure. There were thoughts going around in my mind, and I had some clearer understanding.

It's quite a thing to hold life in your hand, and be the instrument of death against another living thing – even a lamb bred for slaughter. The animal had died peacefully enough, though, which is more than can be said for some humans.

Most people never expect what is going to happen to them. Or if, in one second, a single decision on their part, good or bad, will decide their future. The animal, of course, had not been given the opportunity to reflect.

It was the same in our profession, with regard to the "targets" – otherwise we wouldn't be very good.

Driving back into town, we saw a large crowd gathering around the main square. Immediately, I noticed the area cordoned off, the police keeping bystanders at bay, along with city-based news crews.

"What went on here?" my father said, turning the truck into our street, and finally parking outside the back of the shop again.

We were in the process of hanging the meat on the hook in the freezer, when my mother came in and told us about the explosion in the town square. It had been Uncle Harry's vehicle, but nobody could actually say what the cause was.

I could see a troubled expression appearing on my father's face. He went straight into his office with my mother, leaving me to finish up, then go up to my room to change out of my clothes.

Like my father, I was also shocked to hear how Uncle Harry had nearly been killed. Only half an hour earlier I had witnessed death by my own hand, to now hear that a close friend of the family had nearly died under unusual circumstances. Vehicles didn't just blow up by themselves, of course. My father and mother were no doubt debating right now just what exactly had happened.

Sprawling on my bed, I took a moment to think back to what I had seen when looking out of the window, as we drove by the incident site. There were a lot of cops, some dressed in white overalls: possibly the forensic team, trying to determine what had caused the explosion.

Only one thought entered my mind: the car had exploded because it had been rigged with explosives.

But then I had to remind myself that, without facts, nothing was ever definite.

Still, it was a cert that my father was thinking the same thing. That's why he and my mother were conversing alone. It was just the way things were done.

I caught Bethany coming out of the bathroom and asked her what she thought. Was Uncle Harry in trouble again?

As was her usual manner, she kept to a simple answer: if we were soon to get a phone call, the answer would be evident. And, like that she left it, walking back downstairs to close up shop, leaving me still thinking, quietly still on the landing.

Moving back into my room, I lay on my bed, considering the whole thing logically. Who would want to do Uncle Harry harm?

I quickly retracted the question, realizing the question – even for someone like me – to be a little naïve: everyone knew about Uncle Harry's past. An old enemy with a score to settle was the most obvious reason.

There were many motivations for wanting to see another person – even a family member – dead. Money was the most powerful and honest of them all.

If it were a bomb, it was the work of somebody with skills. All it took these days was the right contact with the right resources. Our own family business, for example, doesn't exactly have references from clients, and it's not like anyone really walks around with a list of tombstones in their pocket. The world of contract killing is a great mechanical engine, and in every machine there is always one important cog: we refer to ours as "The Handler". These people are the first point of contact; the ones who protect our anonymity.

Uncle Harry was our frontman: meeting the clients, checking that everything was genuine, before assigning if appropriate, depending on the circumstances – but, we'll go into that more later. He was always very thorough, and since we weren't on the market full time, he only ever offered us a contract when he was sure it was suitable for our attention. His commission was around fifteen per cent of what the contract was worth.

In business, it is always best to have a manager – a smokescreen – so that everyone can sleep well at night.

Since we refer to ourselves as specialists, there are certain things we cannot and will not do, if it is not justified beyond the motives of revenge and finance. It is not – and has never been – a decision based on the price of a job, you understand.

I thought back to how my father acted after we left the farm. Was he now telling my mother how easily I had killed the lamb? Of course, it wasn't anything to boast about; it was something which had to be done. I was now maturing into a young woman – an adult. Perhaps that was it: he had suddenly seen I was changing. I was no longer his little girl.

I actually take after my father a lot, in that I occasionally need quiet moments such as this to think things over, before jumping to quick conclusions. At school, I was well known for being very astute and observant, when it came to challenging scenarios and equations, not to mention resolving matters of complexity. Speaking briefly to one of my teachers before I left, he had assured me that the results from my finals were looking very positive.

It felt good to have achieved something at the end of the school year. Hopefully, it wasn't going to be difficult to settle down, now that I had finished with school. The summer would give me time to think about what life had in store next.

I had a summer job, like most kids my age, and it was working from home. Others weren't really looking to commit to anything definite, during the holidays. Stepping into adult life wasn't easy for some – even I had wanted so badly to go to the party that night, but my father's word had been firm. But I knew there would soon come a time, perhaps in the near future, when he would accept that I was old enough to make certain decisions for myself.

Taking a moment to browse the local university website on my laptop, my mind began to fill with so many different possibilities. Even the residential campuses looked appealing. I had the drive to want to go further, but my motivation was also centred on remaining at home and being with my family.

Speaking of which, my mother's voice had just called to

me from downstairs. Descending, my emotional state immediately peaked as I reached the kitchen door, finding that a welcoming sight had been laid out: there was nothing like the smell of Oriental food to put me in a really good mood!

When it came to signature dishes, my mother liked to keep her hand in healthy cuisine, which didn't lack taste when you put it in your mouth.

Sitting at the farthest end, with my mother and sister at the sides and my father sat at the head, we all took each other's hands, bowing our heads, as he gave the usual blessing to the feast:

*"Bless us, Our Lord, for these gifts, and for the hands that made them. Let us give thanks for all you provide and let us never take for granted the simple pleasures that nourish our bodies."*

Listening to my father's words, and feeling the touch of my mother and sister's hands, my mind went back once more to the lamb, and how its body had felt so cold and dead, as we loaded it in the truck. Now sitting with my family, I felt warm and safe around my parents – and even my sister, who wasn't so bad on her good days.

When my father had finally finished, I quickly got stuck in before anyone else.

Tonight, my mother had treated us; the texture of the

meat was smooth and perfectly prepared, and the flavours washed over my tastebuds. I tried to guess which spices she'd used, and could immediately tell she had put a slight organic spin on the sauce. Normally, my sister would have been the first to jump in and take a guess, but she seemed preoccupied.

My father looked across the table to me, clearly about to start a conversation. He wasn't the type to pretend there wasn't something on his mind.

"I phoned the hospital. They say that Uncle Harry is alright; he's stable, a little burnt, but nothing too serious," he reassured.

I was glad to hear this, and sent another *thank-you* prayer up to the Lord.

"Did anyone say what had happened?" I asked casually, though the question was still a little direct and to the point, causing my sister to now awaken and intercede.

"I think we're going to have to wait for the newspapers on that one," she said, eyeing Father cautiously. "No point in jumping to any conclusions."

Bethany liked to play the big sister/older daughter card whenever she could. But, just because I was the youngest, it didn't mean they had to shield certain facts and conversations from me now.

"I wonder how quickly the local police will release the

details regarding the bomb that was used," I said, serving myself some more greens.

All eyes fell on me, recognizing my tone to be more of a statement than a question.

"Who said anything about a bomb?" Bethany quickly shot me a harsh look.

I looked to my parents and shrugged. "For what other reason would a car explode? Either that, or it's one hell of a factory recall!"

The humour was lost on everyone else, clearly, but I wasn't about to drop it; at least now it had been brought out of my father's office.

"We don't know the full facts of what happened," my father said, looking at my mother, to whom I was passing the bowl of vegetables. "If it was something like you're suggesting, I'm sure the whole village will soon know about it."

"Everyone is going to be really shaken up," I continued. "There's going to be a lot of questions, and Uncle Harry has been through quite a lot already." I felt a harsh kick at my ankle, delivered by Bethany.

"Harry is a strong man," my mother quickly jumped in now. "I'm sure everything will work itself out."

"Does that mean arrangements are already underway?" I asked, my foot dodging and pressing down hard on my sister's shoe this time, trapping it in place.

"Arrangements...?" My father's tone was level, but clearly cautioning.

Why we had to go through this routine was beyond me. "Why don't we just come out and say what we're all thinking, especially since it's the same conclusion."

"And just what have you concluded?" My sister sat back, folding her arms in a challenging manner. "Have you had a rummage through the remains with your own little science kit?"

I really hated my sister's patronizing tone, but my father had already decided to try and take control of this conversation, before either of our claws came out.

"This is not an appropriate subject for this time; I think we need to change it to something else." He looked quickly to my mother, as though seeking help to steer us all away from dark waters.

"It's just as well you didn't waste all that energy tonight; it's going to be a big day tomorrow," she offered quickly, bringing up the tournament I was to be competing in the next day.

Bethany charmed in, now: "We should get some extra training in beforehand."

"I have been practicing all week; my strategy is all worked out," I remarked, assertively. "Come tomorrow, I will be bringing back that trophy, and I'll rub Abigail's face into the mat!"

My father shook his head, disapprovingly. "Not a very sportsmanlike attitude. You and her are ranked the same, after all."

"Correction," I quickly countered, a little too forcefully: "I show respect to the art, and she just uses it to get her way all the time. She thinks she's such hot shit!"

My mother's hand came down on the back of mine and she gave me a cautionary look. Father, surprisingly, let it slide and returned to his meal.

I took a moment myself, returning to my own plate. An idea immediately rushed to the front of my mind then, as though it had been propelled by a catapult. "I've been considering various colleges, and the programmes look very interesting," I said, starting a new conversation.

My mother now perked up; "Have you decided what you might major in?"

I shrugged again, pretending to be interested now in my food. "Well, the summer's just started, and I'm going to be working most of it here, so I thought I might hold off on any immediate applications for a while."

My father was surprised to hear this, and took the bait: "It might be tricky to find any openings toward the end of the summer."

I nodded thoughtfully and placed my cutlery down on the plate. "Considering I'm going to be spending so much of my time at home this summer, I thought it would be an excellent opportunity to begin my training."

The statement had left everyone quiet, so I had to go straight in for the kill: "I mean... I have to start learning the family business sometime."

My mother's eyes went slowly from me to my father, who just sat for nearly a full minute in silence.

Bethany, of course, had to be the first to break the silence: "You've just left school!"

"And?" I turned to her now and folded my arms, just as challengingly.

My father's only response was to reach forward and knock back the whole of his glass of wine. I didn't think he would take it this way. Obviously, what I was proposing was a serious matter.

My mother just picked up her napkin and wiped her hands, getting up from the table to excuse herself, leaving her plate half-finished. Father watched her go, but still remained silent.

I was now starting to feel awkward, as my father filled his glass again. My sister was staring daggers, ready to impale me with a vengeance.

We were a family and, as such, I thought an open

discussion about the possibility of my training as a contract killer could be carried out over the dinner table!

Excusing myself, I left the kitchen and found my mother out in the shop, just standing in the dark alone. I could tell she was deeply troubled. My father came out behind me and moved into the shop, placing a hand on my mother's shoulder, which she reached up and touched, acknowledging his presence.

The idea had just popped into my head. I was simply looking for some way in which to feel included; no longer being excluded from this side of our family life, just because everyone thought I was still a child. But, now nobody was talking to me, as if I had just committed the worse crime imaginable.

I guessed no one had anything further to say at this point – at least, not directly to my face. From the landing, I could hear my father and sister talking about me in his office. Clearly, she disapproved of the idea.

Returning to my room, I was once again alone with my thoughts, feeling a little angry that everyone was taking it this way. It was like I was being persecuted for speaking my mind.

It soon became clear that Bethany not only disapproved of what I had put forward that evening, but also felt that I needed to apologize for my lack of respect toward them all.

Though, what exactly I had done wrong, I wasn't sure.

My mother clearly hadn't taken the issue well. It's definitely not a normal situation: telling your parents that all your years of education have led to you making a decision such as this. What parent *would* want their child to follow in their footsteps as a contract killer?

I considered this, thinking again back to the truck: my father's behaviour, slaughtering the lamb – it had almost been a unique rite of passage. Like some cultures, where warriors go out to hunt and tackle fierce predators, wearing their skin home, to show the tribe he has achieved manhood – or womanhood, in my case. I now started to wonder whether I had seen some form of regret in his eyes. Had he perhaps already seen this coming, and feared the worst?

Both of my parents had not immediately objected to my request. But they had not approved, either.

The business I was considering was dangerous; that world meant a life of danger. I knew I would see things and witness horrible acts – mostly committed by myself and my family.

But the question of killing still bothered me. Killing that lamb had not satisfied. Animals and humans are very different things. No human is ever bred to be killed – that is not the circle, or the purpose of life. Human life is sacred.

This was why I needed the question answered so badly. I needed to know why we, as human beings, capable of kindness and compassion, were so readily able to kill.

In my father's earlier life, there were times when he would give people the opportunity to make amends for their actions. And, those who didn't... well, then business had to be completed to the full.

There are different kinds of people and different circumstances – together, they can lead to very different outcomes, either good or bad. But, in the end, somebody has to pay something. Unfortunately, a person's guilt and shame can't make everything right. Just like a sudden bout of conscience cannot stop a bullet, when it's heading your way!

# CHAPTER 4

## Friday 6:09 p.m.
## Ravenfall – the emergency ward.

The atmosphere in hospitals is often thought to be uncomfortable. What makes them so chilling is the obvious association with illness and dying. Nobody likes visiting them – unless of course they are in great pain, or on the brink of death.

It had started as a slow day, until several ambulances turned up at the same time and several patients had to be admitted – though only one had serious injuries.

Sergeant Braccard was standing in the A-&-E hallway, waiting to speak to the head doctor, who was currently overseeing treatment of all the walking wounded from the explosion at Ravenfall Square. They had been the top priority, and made it the busiest day of the week.

It was rare to have seriously injured casualties here; most usually went to The Big City Hospital. Being locals, though, these people had insisted on going to the local clinic.

The atmosphere was starting to get intense, making him

think back to his old days in The Big City, when he used to make these sorts of calls at least two or three times a week. Usually they were gang-related, or a matter of an unpaid debt to a local crime family. Some just had the misfortune to do business with the wrong people.

He had joined the police as a young man, expecting to have a great career in The Big City, only to be branded a "rat", after turning in his own partner for a wrongful shooting.

They'd been called to a local diner, where a drug deal had turned bad and one gang member had taken some customers hostage, just as a patrol car happened to be passing by. Entering through the premises, he and his partner had their weapons drawn, though the young teen member had no more than a knife, held to a waitress's throat. Braccard tried to negotiate with the lad, but his partner had grown impatient, discharging his weapon and wounding the waitress in the shoulder, killing the boy immediately after, with a clear shot to the head.

By the time the ambulance arrived, the pair of them had got into a heated argument about his opening fire, when the shot had been too difficult to judge accurately.

The waitress had lost a lot of blood, but survived, suffering nerve damage. When a claim was made against the City Police Department, he wanted to tell the truth, so that at least the woman would get some form of compensation, having been off work for so long.

The partner had somehow been exonerated of any blame, without any need felt for further investigation. The department covered up the incident and no more was ever heard from the waitress, leaving him only one option: to resign and move away with his family.

Taking up an opening in Ravenfall, he discovered that at least here a man could do some good, without fear of being persecuted, whilst the guilty were allowed to climb the ranks, filling their pockets with dirty money to look the other way. These days, there wasn't much a small-town cop did with his time, except for settle small disputes, and the occasional disruption by the local youths.

When it came to incidents like this, the first two hours had been the usual nightmare. First, there had been a report from eyewitnesses, of a car on fire. By the time the emergency services had turned up, they had not been completely certain what they were dealing with, or how serious the situation was. The panic on people's faces, and the burnt debris all over the street, indicated this was something more significant than a mere collision; more likely an explosion, but resulting from what?

He had himself noticed a strange chemical smell in the air, when first arriving on the scene, indicating that the large explosion – measurable by the level of damage caused – was to be treated suspiciously.   Victims, survivors and eyewitnesses all had their own accounts of what they had seen and heard.

Only one casualty had taken the full force of the blast: the owner of the vehicle.

Everyone had first thought Harry was dead, but by some miracle he had suffered just a few bad burns, and thankfully had come around in the emergency ward, just as he arrived.  The back of his hair had been singed, and he had suffered cuts and bruises to his body from the debris. He was lucky to have moved away when he did, before detonation, as the explosion would have engulfed him.

The entire square had been closed off and shut down. The investigation team would hopefully be coming up with some answers soon, so far being kept sealed behind tight lips.

There hadn't been anything like this in Ravenfall since the war and, just for the record, nobody in our family has ever used a bomb in a contract, no matter what the circumstances.  My grandfather used a grenade once, and that had been a necessity for preservation of himself and my grandmother – but that's another story.

Explosions were very technical, and it took a specialist to make a thorough evaluation.  There was no evidence as yet of foul play, but it had certainly raised suspicions in the community, which would be desperate for answers. Remaining tight-lipped would only hold off the press for so long.

Word was now coming in, over the police radio, that they had checked C.C.T.V. around the main square, and appeared to have found what Sergeant Braccard was expecting. The footage of the vehicle exploding could only be seen from afar, where the camera was positioned across the other side of the street, near the supermarket.

The fact that this had happened to Uncle Harry made Sergeant Braccard uncomfortable; he was aware of Harry's history and connection to violence.

Moving down the corridor, he approached the private room and looked through the small window, just as the doctor was coming out.

"What's the news, Doc? Is he going to pull through?" he said quickly, caught off guard.

Closing the door, the doctor – a man not much older than himself – moved with the sergeant back out into the corridor, filling a paper cup from a cooler and taking a sip. "So far he is stable: only small signs of any serious injuries. He's a lucky man, considering the blast nearly burnt his flesh from his body!" He swallowed the water. "How are things going at your end?"

"We're looking into the matter. So far, all we know is that the vehicle exploded without any cause."

The doctor's eyebrows rose, dramatically. "Oh? Is that official or unofficial?"

Sergeant Braccard knew what he was driving at, but right then he wasn't prepared to commit to any conjecture; no statements could be given on or off the record, without hard facts. So far, all they knew was that nobody had been seen approaching the Range Rover whilst Harry had been in the village, and the ignition key had not been touched before the explosion. Even putting these two sparse pieces together, it was a fair guess that something sinister was behind all this.

It could very well be that the answer was staring them directly in the face. If it were a bomb, it had been aiming for one specific target, and had just missed it by chance.

It was a strong possibility that somebody had tried to kill Harry – and it wasn't the first time, either.

Returning to the village station, he found another news van waiting outside, but he quickly slipped through, ignoring the microphone and camera being directed in front of his face.

Making his way into his office, he sighed, slumping down into his chair. He took a moment to breathe and collect his thoughts in peace.

Immediately, old demons returned once more.

There had been this one time he'd answered a call to a confirmed car bombing in The Big City, where a note had been found: somebody had been pissed off and finally acted on the vendetta. The victim had been a government official; however, no real evidence of any political motivation had been suggested – only that he had hurt someone very badly.

The device had been under the seat, pressure being used to activate it; the bomb was homemade – nothing too sophisticated, which couldn't be found on the web.

The bomber turned out to be the man's only son, who had been abused by his father as a child.

Some answers weren't easy to find. When they were, you questioned whether they really were crimes or acts of justice, given the persons and circumstances involved.

The sergeant had not heard Harry's name in the station since the incident with his son-in-law – and even that case had somehow been resolved without police involvement.

Odd thing, Martin turning up dead, not long after collecting his lottery winnings…?

It was strange how things had ended up. The guy had arrived at the official lottery office, with some business representative they'd been unable to track down, and then the accident had happened: Martin's body had been found at the bottom of some steps, dead from a simple fall.

Of course, Sergeant Braccard was smart enough to suspect there was more to it, but seeing as Harry had made everything alright with the community, even after his own daughter's death, nobody cared to know the reasons. Martin had provided Harry with the funds to pay back what he had stolen – even though you didn't have to be a great detective to figure out this all seemed a little too convenient, the guy suddenly having a change of conscience. And, who was the unidentified business associate?

It had Harry's signature written all over it.

But, like now, no real facts or evidence meant that everything so far going through his mind was mere conjecture. He would just have to wait for Forensics to come up with the goods.

In this line of work, you couldn't catch a culprit or build a case on thin air alone. It was no different from trying to catch a ghost with a net – and they could just as easily slip away.

# CHAPTER 5

### Saturday 7:15 a.m.
### Ravenfall – the secret workshop.

It's not easy to find a ghost who doesn't want to be found.

When it comes to people who make a living outside the law, they quickly learn to adapt a natural talent for being invisible, non-existent and off the grid, so they can't be tracked. Only in the most difficult and complex of jobs might you catch a glimpse of a shadow. But then, just as quickly, the image evaporates into thin air.

His lifestyle was not lavish, though the solitude and darkness were necessities which cost very little…

The figure of the small man was sat on the tall stool, hunched over his workbench, tracing the thin wires with his thumb and index figure – he could find not the slightest imperfection in the coating. His hands were covered in latex, his eyes appearing absurdly huge behind a magnifying headband. Gently threading the exposed flex through a tiny hole drilled into a small Tupperware box, he connected it to a circuit board using a soldering iron.

A radio was quietly playing, just off to his left; the local announcer was currently reporting the explosion which had occurred the day before, in Ravenfall. This caused his hands to pause for a moment, and his head tilted a little toward the broadcast of the reporter's voice, coming live from outside the police station:

*"Both police and emergency services are on high alert due to this, as yet unexplained, attack. Thankfully, only minor injuries were sustained by some local people, and at least one is currently being treated for minor burns, though the victim's identity is currently being withheld. Officials have gone on to say that it was a miracle nobody was killed in the explosion."*

The hand suddenly reached out, turning the radio dial off in a snap and closing tightly into a fist. It was typical of the media to jump to assumptions.

When it came terrorism, it was well known that extremists liked to take credit for their work. This man liked to leave his own calling card, but with a unique trademark.

Carefully, he resumed his work, without the slightest tremor coming from his palms. The lid was placed over the opening, sealing it tight. When finished, he carefully slid it inside a brown paper bag and placed it inside a holdall. Then, he made his way outside, locking the storage doors behind him with a large padlock.

The local scrapyard was an excellent location for him, in

that there were suitably sized storage units for him to carry out his work, undisturbed.

In a brisk stride, he made his way down the gravel road, catching a bus to an industrial estate, where he waited patiently for ten minutes, to be picked up by a white truck.

The driver greeted him pleasantly, but he just sat quietly in the passenger seat. As the guy – a man in his early thirties – tried to make small talk, he kept his eyes focused ahead; he could tell this particular passenger was a very dangerous person, but also very professional in the way he held himself, always looking around and aware of his surroundings. A brief glance at the track marks on the driver's forearms finally ceased the chatter, reminding him that he was being paid to do one job, and some addictions cost a lot of money.

Drugs had never been a vice for the passenger, whose background hailed from a town in the middle of nowhere, where the pinnacle of existence was to raise a family, adding to the population so it felt like more than just a tiny speck on a map. Most of the youths, upon reaching a certain age, had the good sense to move out and start a real life in the bigger world – that was how it had been with his father, according to his mother, who had not been left as much as a goodbye note in his wake.

In such a small community, you had to learn quickly how

to deal with the prejudice you'd receive from your neighbours and family, who were so quick to label her a slut or a tramp. But, rather than abort, she had gone through with the pregnancy and found companionship, once again, with a high school friend, who had not been so quick to judge. He'd been only a year older than her, but he had a good head and a big heart, and took them both in to help her through the worst, finally asking for her hand, in an attempt to almost erase the bad history.

It hadn't taken the child long to learn the truth; he never really accepted his stepfather, or forgave his mother for lying to him for seven years. Some people say that you are never more wise than when you are a child; it's the age at which we see things clearly, because we're untroubled by all the other bullshit.

Before school, he used to sit in front of the television, wearing his smartly pressed uniform, watching the astronauts going up in rockets, into space. It was through this portal that his imagination was allowed to evolve, along with old comic books. It increased his need to excel his intelligence beyond that of a normal child of his years.

He had not been bullied like most children, for his unusual qualities, but actually accepted by peers; he even received a lot of attention from the girls, which just went to show that the girls perhaps weren't always into the muscular, sporty types. He never really had a regular sweetheart, though. Not that he was fickle, or a jerk; he was just more committed to his studies, finding it difficult to stray from his particular personal interests.

The teachers thought he was a good student, so they encouraged his request to join in after-school, extracurricular activities connected with his fascination with rockets and explosives. Watching fireworks ignite in the sky had led him to want to learn more, so he joined the chemistry club, learning how chemicals were used to make explosives and bombs. Over time, he'd become curious about such devices: how they were built; how they were used in different places; the effect of their power around the world. He soon discovered why people from minority groups took such action to get attention; to make people see clearly with a gun or a bomb – it was quite impossible to ignore.

Violence was ugly, but most effective when getting a statement noticed.

Clutching his bag to his chest, he could see that the sun was just rising over the green-topped mountains, to the east of Ravenfall. The night before had been the darkest it had been in a long time – but even these days, the smallest light is able to shine through the blackest mass.

The hard-grafting man was only strong after crawling from his bed in the early hours of the morning, completing his regular sets and repetitions, from one exercise to the next.

Then, it was shower, breakfast and a kiss on the cheek, as he stepped out of his front door, to go to work.

Placing his motorcycle helmet over his head, Laurence kick-started the engine, before roaring down the street and turning left out of town, toward the outskirts of the village.

The construction industry had always played a huge role when it came to the economics of Ravenfall and its community. Constructing buildings meant labourers; running cables meant electricians; all trades were providing jobs, so most of the local youths didn't have to commute to The Big City. Learning a trade through hard work toughened a young man's skin, and taught him the value of earning money with sweat, and the power of his own hands.

Laurence was a strong, well-built young man, who was good with his hands, with or without tools; they were powerful instruments, on their own capable of both building and destroying.

As an amateur boxer, working slowly up the ranks, he worked Harry's crew and as security at a nightclub, to fund his training toward the prize ring. And, he actually had quite a good shot, according to his trainer.

Dismounting his bike, Laurence lifted his visor, to look over the project currently underway, which was putting money in his pocket and helping to pay the rent on his mother's house. The foundation work had begun on the new mall; heavy machinery was digging up and moving the dark soil, building large mounds around the perimeter fence.

The community had at first been disheartened when Uncle Harry told everyone the project would have to be scrapped, due to the sudden loss of funds. But now, thanks to his son-in-law's lottery win and generous donation, everything was going ahead.

And, it was partially thanks to Laurence, too, that it had been made possible. But, you can read about that – if you haven't already – in the other book.

Laurence was smart and usually capable of dealing with most situations, though that morning he was slightly hesitant, as he approached the stern figure in the security uniform, blocking his entrance onto the site. The man may have been round at the waist, but behind the dark-rimmed glasses he had the attention level of a predatory hawk. Laurence smiled and saluted at Jake, the head security guard, who was chewing on his cocktail stick; the look on the old guy's face was like solid stone.

"I may need to check that bag there, to make sure you aren't bringing any contraband onto this here site," he said, holding out his hand.

Laurence took one step back, playfully. "Why would you want to check my lunch? There's only ham rolls and carrot cake."

The guard's lips now parted into a slight grin on one side. "Would that be your mother's special carrot cake?" He looked toward the bag again. "The kind with the extra raisins?"

Reaching behind his back, Laurence produced a small package wrapped in tin foil. "She even made extra. Nice and juicy to the last bite." Laurence held it slightly under Jake's nose. "My mother's recipe is legendary. Never had any complaints, even from the boss."

Jake looked at the offering, then back to Laurence. "Wouldn't be some kind of bribe, would it?"

Laurence withdrew, a wounded expression on his face. "Why would I need to bribe you, of all people?" he asked, in a tone which was almost believable.

"How's about me not reporting you forgetting to sign out last night? I checked the whole site and found it empty, yet your name was still signed in."

Laurence remained silent for a moment, then decided to just come clean. "Oh yeah, well, I was in a bit of a hurry;

had to get to work." He irritably scratched the back of his neck. "The train wouldn't wait for me at the station, see?"

Jake tilted his head sideways, but let the smart remark slide this time.

"Still working that fancy club in The Big City, eh? I don't know why a nice guy like you would choose that sewer over what you've got right here: other *honest* jobs."

Laurence was aware how people felt about him working in one of The Big City's hottest nightspots. It wouldn't have been so bad were it not owned by one of the crime families.

"I'm not exactly qualified to do much else except hard labour and hard knocking." He raised both his fists; "These babies are better than a business card! I took three guys on there, and caught the eye of the head bouncer; he offered me the job right then, for stopping this guy sticking a blade into one of his."

Jake nodded. The kid had a good heart, and he was brave, judging from what Harry had confided. He had shared with Jake Laurence's conduct in helping to get the funds, since the two of them went back a long way. Jake had been thrilled to get this job as a result, and so in turn was inclined to give the lad a little slack.

"And, when is the next title fight going to be, Champ?" he said, taking the offering now from Laurence. "Your mama keeps feeding you so well you won't be able to climb into the ring!"

Laurence took the joke and was about to retort, when he heard the sound of tyres. Jake's gaze shifted behind Laurence, toward an unfamiliar truck now approaching.

Moving forward, Jake straightened and extended his palm out in an official manner, causing the vehicle to stop dead in its tracks. He then proceeded to move slowly round to the driver's window. "What's this?"

There were two occupants, from what he could see; the youngest was at the wheel. Looking in the back, it appeared they were dropping off a delivery; the bags were the usual mix of cement, used on most development projects.

He looked through the paperwork on his clipboard, to check the delivery schedules, whilst Laurence looked at the other figure in the passenger seat, slightly out of view.

The driver quickly stuck his head out of the window. "Hurry up! I ain't got all day!" he called, irritably.

"Hold your horses!" Jake barked back, with complete authority. "Nobody gets past these here gates without authorization." Flipping through the sheets, he took his time, with the attention of a hygienist. "I don't see you down for today."

The driver now slipped his head back inside and took a

more diplomatic approach. "Well, check tomorrow's schedule. You see, this order came in early. The boss wanted me to bring it so it was out of the storeroom; I guess he wanted to free up space."

This would need to be confirmed; Jake didn't like things to be out of the ordinary. He told them to hang on, while he made a call to the head foreman. The driver seemed clearly put out, but Jake was a man who knew his job, and Laurence admired him for that, considering that he didn't recognize either of the men from delivering previously. Almost 30% of thefts from construction sites happened at the front gate. Jake had never had a robbery on his shift, and there was never likely to be – that's what made him the best in the company, and why he had maintained such a perfect record.

He called to one of the work crew, to ask the head foreman to come and verify acceptance, but he was currently high up on the steel structure, so said it was best just to let it through.

Laurence could see Jake's point of view, but came over to talk quietly to him for a moment, advising that it would be unwise to send the delivery away; there was no guarantee that it would come back the next day, if the supplier took offence to them turning their nose up at a favour.

Jake gave it a few seconds of thought, then finally

waved the vehicle on through, directing where the delivery was to go, and registered the time and vehicle on his record sheet.

Laurence had already put his little package on the window ledge of the security hut, and moved inside the compound to start his shift. He watched the truck stop over by the supply shed. Deliveries had been coming in all week, but the inventory was nowhere near what was required to keep the project on schedule, so it was just as well that it had arrived.

Picking up a shovel, he started to work the foundation trench, his muscles slowly warming up until he was in full motion, feeling the burn; he began to breathe more heavily.

A noise suddenly caught his attention, and he saw a figure move from behind the office cabin, who was not one of the regular labour crew. The guy wore no hard hat, but was dressed in overalls with a cap covering his head. He walked back toward the truck which had just come in, climbing into the passenger seat, before the truck headed off of the site. Things would get pretty hairy if Harry found out that safety regulations weren't being followed by the delivery contractors.

But, more importantly, what was the man doing over there?

Laurence would have a quiet word with Jake at

lunchtime. There was something he didn't feel was right about those guys, and his gut was hardly ever wrong.

# CHAPTER 6

## Saturday 8:25 a.m.
## Ravenfall – the butchers' shop.

It is hard to imagine that a family like mine could very well be living next door to people such as yourself.

But then, on the outside, doesn't everyone look normal?

Most days, in fact, we *are* like any everyday family. As soon as the alarm clock goes off, I'm up, in the shower and then down to the kitchen, where Mother has already placed my breakfast on the table, consisting mainly of fine sausages and bacon, while my sister eats her grapefruit. She says she's watching her weight, but I think she is secretly trying to turn vegetarian, like her boyfriend – whom we will come to later on.

Some mornings, Bethany tends to apply extra makeup, to conceal the fact that she hasn't been getting her beauty sleep. But then, night work will do that to a person.

Not that some of our contracts aren't fulfilled during the day. It's just more to our advantage at night; people are more off their guard, and the neighbourhoods where the targets live are quieter.

Dad likes to read the local newspaper while scooping his eggs into his mouth, with Mother looking on approvingly, as he wipes the plate clean with a wink.

So far, nobody had brought up what I said the night before, and this was strange, since my parents weren't the sort to let things just slide by. But now, everyone was back around the table, acting as though last night had never occurred.

Since we're a family-run business, there are no secrets, and when appropriate everything is discussed together, as a family. You see, my parents have never been cold or distant about the other side of the family business.

The sideline of professional contract killing is nothing to be proud of, but it keeps a roof over our heads, and our other business thriving.

I remember this one time at school, my teacher made me stand up in class on "Career Day" and tell everybody what my father did for a living. It was really just a way of getting children to get used to public speaking; everyone knew my family ran the local butchers', and most of my peers' parents were regular clientele. I always used to tell my friends that my father had a very interesting lifestyle for a simple butcher: travelling around the country, making the right contacts to bring in the best possible meat treats, for the simple village folk of Ravenfall.

This, of course, was before I found out about our family legacy.

One time, he'd gone away for the weekend, saying he was doing a special favour for the church. "Sometimes it's good to work for the church now and then; a little insurance for when it comes to Judgement Day," he joked, rubbing my hair and kissing my mother goodbye. There was always a slight concern in her eyes as she watched him drive away.

When my father returned, he always went to put his case straight in the office, then came right back into the kitchen to have a cup of coffee with my mother, talking over how things had been whilst he'd been gone.

One day, I waited in the hallway for my father to come out and leave the office door unlocked, so I could open the door and look inside. It was small, but it suited his needs; the large chair looked quite cosy. I'd never been allowed in there; as he kept all his important documents – i.e.: profit, loss and expenses ledgers, all logged meticulously – on a shelf. I was curious about just how much my father made on his work for the church, and looked up at one ledger which was marked *"Income Records"*. Reaching up, I took it down and opened it to the last page.

The last entry had a lot of figures in the number!

More money than my enemy's father made, in fact.

Surely a butcher didn't earn more than a lawyer?!

I replaced it on the shelf and turned to leave, feeling my foot strike something. Looking down, I saw that my father's case had fallen flat, under his desk. Lifting it up onto the desk, I looked at the combination lock.

You're probably guessing the combination was some memorable date, like a birthday, wedding or significant time in our family's history? Well, I had no idea what it might have been. And, it turned out I didn't have to, because it was not locked. I pushed the spring buttons, the locks gave way and I lifted the lid. Inside, I found the key to my father's safe.

Again, my curiosity got the better of me; those numbers were still playing over in my mind. I had never seen a lot of money before; it was too tempting not to look.

Turning the key, I pulled it open, receiving quite a surprise…

I found no money, but a lot of weapons.

Handguns, small, automatic rifles and large, sharp knives – not like the ones in our shop; these seemed to have another purpose than carving meat.

I didn't know at first what to think.

It wasn't unheard of for people to own weapons – "home protection", I had heard somebody say at school once. But, why the tubular object attached to one of the barrels?

I suddenly remembered seeing something familiar on television, and knew it to be a silencer, to suppress the noise coming out of the barrel when the weapon was fired.

It felt heavy in my hand, but I liked the look of myself holding it, in the upright mirror in the corner of the room. Placing both hands together, raising it carefully, I aimed at my reflection. My finger slowly pressed down on the trigger…

A noise brought my attention back to the doorway. My father was standing there, watching me.

He did not appear angry; he merely raised his index finger toward me, then pointed it toward the floor, calmly instructing me to do the same with the weapon I held. I didn't know what to say in that moment.

"It's time for a family meeting," he said, moving forward and gently taking the gun out of my hand. Then, he guided me by the shoulder, into the living room.

My sister and mother were sitting on the couch watching T.V. when we both entered, the gun still in my father's hand. They were not surprised to see it, as I would have expected them to be.

Sitting us down, my father started to talk. He went back to the beginning of our family, and the work that we have done for a long time: ridding society of bad people. I looked to my mother and sister, who remained silent with a solemn expression, and I knew that my father was telling the truth: my family killed people. We were generations of murderers!

"Assassins" was the more appropriate title, according to my sister, when she came into my room later that day, to talk some more about what our father had told me. She asked me how I felt, now knowing the truth. All I could do was ask why she chose to follow in our family's footsteps.

"Curiosity is like an itch which needs to be scratched. It often leads people down a road they never thought they would ever tread. In the end, it's in the blood," she had finally concluded.

I had heard something similar before, in biology. It was to do with the family genes, passed on from one generation to the next. Did that mean that I, too, was to become a killer? An assassin?

This might surprise you: how open a family could be about a matter such as this. It isn't every day that you find out your parents are dangerous people, but I didn't find myself fearing or hating what they had told me.

That night, I lay in bed thinking it all through, as rationally as I could.

Even a child of twelve recognizes the difference between right and wrong. The Bible says it is wrong to kill – though it doesn't say *who*, or even why.

The next day, I had plucked up the courage to ask my mother if killing people felt right.

She looked at me, earnestly. "The first kill was the hardest emotionally, but only after the fact. I was raised to respect life, and somebody had tried to take mine – so, when I took theirs, I felt it was justified."

I took this in and rationalized it as before. For her, it had been a matter of self-defence. In those circumstances, it was surely right. "Why did you continue? Did you like it?" I pressed further, wanting to understand.

"I still respect life, but there are those who do not, and like hurting people for their own pleasure – those people need to be stopped," she said. I sensed there was something personal to this statement.

What she told me then we'll leave for another time. I should get back to the present.

When my father went away on business, my mother was left to look after the shop, with my sister Bethany and myself, when I wasn't studying in my room. Now that school was over, I had some free time on my hands.

At the weekends, I like to spend time in our back garden, sunning myself, while my mother tends the homegrown vegetables. Since our last discussion on the topic, I've never asked my mother if she misses the life of a contract killer. The old days weren't exactly adventurous, according to her occasional accounts. She had been well trained by my father, but her career had been cut short, as soon as they found out that Bethany was on the way.

Speaking of whom, had now just joined both of us outside. Dressed in her gym clothes, strolling across the grass, I could see her over the top of the book I was reading, coming straight over and putting her hands on her hips.

"Let's get to it, Izzy. I have to get some practice in before this evening," she said, blocking the warmth of the sun on my face.

I wasn't really in the mood but, then again, I wasn't prepared to turn down one of her challenges. So, I put down my book and slid off of the sun lounger. Moving out into the centre of the garden, I took up a defensive position, preparing to go through some sparring drills, as my mother kept a watchful eye from where she was.

"So, you think you're ready to become a killer?" Bethany asked, taking up her own form of defensive stance. "Well, I don't. In fact, I've never thought you had the killer instinct."

We began to circle each other, delivering the occasional controlled punch. One strike toward my head challenged my reflexes, provoking a roundhouse kick to her abdomen, but she shook it off, smiling briefly at my mother, who just shook her head.

"Maybe I can still surprise you," I pressed, taking up my guard again, to continue with the training session.

My sister and I have two completely different fighting styles. I use traditional karate to keep myself in shape, while she uses a unique and modern system known as Keysi (K.F.M.): a modern-evolved street-combat system, founded by Spanish Gypsies. Traditional martial arts such as mine have rules and codes of conduct, whereas winning a street fight is all about dirty tactics; attacking your opponent's vulnerable areas: the eyes, throat and soft tissue points. In her style, the defensive and striking methodologies involved were combined, to work together.

Covering her head with her effective arm shield – known as the "pensador" – she was able to ward off most attacks to the head, as well as the rest of the body, following up with counterstrikes, using the fists and elbows. My punches were good, but her elbows and knees were devastating weapons.

Being a professional killer, you would rarely use your hands – perhaps only as a last resort. These techniques were therefore not about defence, but destruction. That requires a certain mindset to follow all the way through – and my sister never liked to hold back. Throwing me to the ground, she delivered a harsh blow to my ribs, standing over me triumphantly.

Until an arm snaked around her neck, and a foot strike buckled her knee.

My mum may only be a housewife now, but she's still as tough as nails!

"It isn't always about strength of the mind or body," my mother said, as displayed by her perfect example; "it's about taking the enemy by surprise." Though my mother was short in stature, she was nimble and had great internal power, against even the heaviest opponents.

Finally, my sister tapped out, and my mother helped me off of the ground.

"I think it's time we all had some herbal tea, and a little girl-chat in the kitchen."

Heading inside, we sat at the table and spent the next half an hour discussing my potential to be part of the other family business: a contract killer.

Despite my sister's objections, my mother reminded her she wasn't much older than me herself, when she began. It was my life and my decision; if it's what I really wanted, they couldn't say no. Though she did press that I didn't have to jump straight in; there was no reason why I couldn't spend a year at college, then maybe go out into the world to see if anything else appealed.

I now found myself questioning my motivations. I was young and the world had a lot to offer, but there was still the answer to the question that it could not give me: what was it to live the life of an assassin? To take a human life?

I asked my sister if killing ever got to her, at times.

"It's all well and good some officer in the military telling you to suck it up; that comes with the job," she said, sipping her tea, "but most of us are still human, at the end of the day. The worst is becoming withdrawn from people; wearing a sign which says: *'Keep Out. Don't get close.'"*

I could see what she was driving at. In truth, we don't all live alone, like those characters in the movies, or have nobody in our lives; we just keep certain things private, to protect ourselves and those we care about: the ones we love.

Yes, we are capable of love. As you have seen, we can choose to have a family and raise children, who are free to choose their own paths.

The talk with my mother had been brief, but it had put my fears to rest.

When my father had been called into the kitchen from the shop, we all sat down together as a family and talked through everything: how it would begin.

In this sort of work, you end up getting to be a student of human nature, learning a lot about people, but also yourself. There are questions to which we seek answers, but they will not always come so quickly.

"To truly understand this trade, you must completely take in everything you see, from this point on. This will aid you through the process, from amateur to professional."

My father's words did not exactly comfort me – I didn't much like the label "amateur" – but it was accurate nonetheless; I was a beginner, starting out in a career in which few ever got a close inside look, away from the fictional accounts in movies and books.

Right now, reading these words, you must have surmised by this point that this is not about me justifying my family's profession – nor anyone else in this unique trade. I only wish to give as true an account as possible, into the lives of people who are called upon to do what others lack the courage or will to, when needed. It is no different than an official agent from a secret service, carrying out their duties for the good of the country, all of their actions disavowed by the world they serve. At times, the only way to vanquish evil is by destroying it altogether.

And, there is plenty of it out there! Even at this moment, no doubt, some evil force is going about its evil ways.

# CHAPTER 7

**Saturday 6 p.m.**

**Ravenfall – the construction site.**

Have you ever looked at the face of a clock, watching every passing second of the hand turning from one number to the next, wondering if you should be spending your time more productively?

Time is the biggest factor in life. Something you can never stop, until yours is finally up!

It's just a shame, for some people, that their lives are shorter than others.

At the end of the day, when your time does come, you just have to say: *"I did my best with what I had, and with what life had to offer me."*

But, in return, what contribution did you ever make?

It is an arguable fact that nothing memorable found in the history books ever just spontaneously happened; it had to be created and engineered by some power – perhaps a person of vision and will.

Andrea the bomber had enlisted in the military as soon as he left school.

There was nothing to keep him at home. So, with a slap at the front door from his mother, and an order never to return from his stepfather, he had enlisted without their permission.

In his mind now orphaned, he finally got his chance, after succeeding basic training, to undertake a specialist role as an explosives expert, learning more about chemicals and devices from a military perspective.

Travelling the world, he saw reality as it was – and it wasn't at all romantic. Any city or town could be taken hostage by a hostile force, threatening its very way of life. It was truly something to be terrified of – and still is today, in some countries.

He didn't see much combat at the start of his career. And, he only really learnt that sometimes people got killed for no reason, other than being in the wrong place at the wrong time. That was the only psychological defence they managed to drum into his head.

Some say it is the easiest lesson to teach, whereas love can only be learnt from experience.

Hatred, however, is often taught by example, of parents to children, or by leaders to their disciples. The two strongest emotions which conflict in a person can become like a ticking timebomb: the love of life, versus the necessity to believe in an ideal, can leave a bloody wake in its path.

Seeing such horrific sights had conditioned him to want to help. To make a difference.

He had earnt recognition as a top expert for defusing bombs, spending most of his time in dense civilian areas. He was unafraid, and perhaps a bit too cocky for his own good. Every now and then a threat was called in – the locations were usually public or important. Devices were often found in tight places, where the robots were sent in first, before technicians. Once identified, it took a lot of deep, steady breaths and focused attention to disarm a single – and sometimes additionally a secondary – device, usually with just one snip of a wire. There was a moment, just when you were about to cut a wire, that you prayed you'd hear it snip cleanly, straight through – 'cause if you didn't, then you've cut the wrong one!

At times it was quite exciting, despite the trouble going on around him. Defusing one terror threat meant saving a lot of people from getting hurt, and that gave an individual purpose and respect. Putting your life on the line for others made you a hero.

When it came to war and conflict zones, there were so many threats to be faced – bombings, shootings and endless death – day after day. This unique line of work meant that the thought of dying was never far from his thoughts.

After a while, he got used to the chaos, even though the situation was unbearable for the locals, and people were being forced to leave their homes and their land.

On one assignment, his unit had been sent in to clean up and secure a refuge area on the outskirts of a Middle Eastern city; the fight was over, but somebody had to clear up the aftermath. It had been a long, drawn-out war, and many families were in need. Over the months, he had become friendly with a relief aid worker, and they started to date during their time off.

It was coming into summer, and the best part of the year; people were sitting outside cafés, and delightful dinner parties were thrown to raise funds. Life was returning to the city, and the threat appeared to have passed. The year had begun with bloodshed, and now they were celebrating friendship and peace. There were still warnings from intelligence but, foolishly, they were not being properly absorbed.

It appeared that one rebel leader had decided to wage war against oppressors and their allies. Ironically, it had been a refuge truck which had been driven up outside the front of the hotel, where Andrea and his now-fiancée were attending a special convention that evening. The driver, a young man ready to die for his cause, carried out the attack. Sitting in the cab with a detonator in his lab, his actions had been slow and unnoticeable in heavy traffic.

People are only capable of atrocities if they believe they can get away with it. A knife, a bullet and even a bomb can miss its target; the human will, however, is the deadliest of weapons.

Andrea saw a huge, white light stream in from outside, followed immediately by a loud bang, sending them all hurtling back onto the floor. The structure collapsed on top of them.

Death and destruction littered the whole building – what was left standing of it, anyway.

The explosion shook Andrea's eyeballs from side to side and blew out his eardrums. He tried to sit up, but his body was still in shock. Looking out through the haze, he saw a large pool of blood; many of the unmoving bodies were smoking or on fire. The air went bad in no time, causing him to gag, as he could see and smell what remained of his friends and colleagues.

Suddenly, panic set in and he started to look for his fiancée. He found that the explosion had thrown her clear to the other side of the room. Shrapnel was embedded over her entire body. All he could do was hold her in his arms, fighting back the smell of burnt hair and skin, until finally the medics arrived and attended to the scene.

But she was gone, along with all the others; there was nothing anybody could do.

By some miracle, he had sustained only minor injuries. Six of his colleagues and friends were dead, along with the love of his life; he had been spared, while everyone he loved and cared for had just been taken away.

It was heartbreaking how the good spirit of that day had been destroyed in an instant, when so many good, innocent people were viciously murdered.

Things were never the same from that day onward.

The impact it had on the country caused troops to once again return, and with heavier artillery than before. Overnight, martial law had been declared, and the whole city locked down. There was no proof the rebels had been behind the attack, and they were not claiming responsibility – no doubt knowing that the military would go in and make them pay. It seemed that the old world of reason was dead and gone.

Andrea could find no honour in being a victim, or being bested by the enemy. The fact that he alone had survived left him the burden of honouring the others.

The pain kept him awake, and over time spread inside him, until he eventually found himself growing numb. Apathy soon became his best friend, setting him free from the misery. It started to show in his work, and he was soon no longer considered reliable to conduct his duties.

They offered him early retirement, but what good was the modest pension, for services to his country which had cost him everything he had held dear to his heart?

The body is a machine. It can feel pain in so many ways. It has so many feelings which can motivate a person's actions, to do good and bad.

We can't pretend this isn't part of the world. Terrorists' tactics do bring change, even at the cost of lives, but it is God's will which brings change for the better, for all mankind. When we choose to take up the fight at his side, and fight for the world, our actions are then surely just and patriotic.

A switch suddenly flipped in his mind. Out of nowhere, a need to find the enemy and destroy them, once and for all, became his new mission.

With the assistance of other rogue soldiers, who had been sitting around just itching to settle the score for their own fallen comrades, they set out on their own mission.

It wasn't easy finding the rebels' hidden base; a refuge was a place of safety and security.

But, safe refuge never lasts for long. Nor false identity. Like a snake, you have to be sure to shed them regularly. This had been the enemy's only mistake.

With the help of intelligence, they captured the rebel

leader and made him swallow a special gift Andrea had put together. They detonated it in front of his men, before executing them all on the spot.

But this action had caused more terrible demons to come and shake him from his cot. A squad of M.P.s placed him in shackles and delivered him before a military court, charged with war crimes: the rebel base they burned down had been occupied with civilians, whom they had executed along with the soldiers. There had also been allegations made of rape and torture. The other soldiers had already gone AWOL, leaving him to face the trial alone.

Though his defence managed to plead guilty by reason of insanity, he was stripped of rank and locked away in a military prison, in a tiny room with only a bed and a toilet.

He had been a patriot, willing to serve and fight for his country, and this was his reward.

They locked him away for five years, with nothing to do but play everything out, over and over again in his mind, and talk it over and over with the medical specialists. But, he wasn't treated and pampered, like some headcases; they had just wanted someone to blame and punish, for the sake of politics.

Upon his release, his personal belongings – which didn't amount to much – were returned, and he walked out a free man with a tarnished service record; getting a decent job would be difficult.  At the gate, he threw away his dog tags; no longer would he serve any other institution but himself.  He would use the skills they had given him to buy the life they had stolen.

And, this was how it had been for the last seven years: travelling the world and applying his trade, for those who needed old scores and vendettas resolved.

Normally, he didn't lower his standards and take on small jobs such as this one, but times were tight and he needed money.  Besides, with this particular job, he could actually relate to his client, since they had both been wronged.

Losing family – a loved one – is the greatest tragedy, and the need to seek justice is no crime.  Sometimes innocent lives are lost in the pursuit of this, but there always comes a price.

Ascending the ladder to the top of the water tower, Andrea removed a medium-sized pair of binoculars from a leather case and looked out to the horizon, taking it all in.  Soon, everything before him was about to change.

Bringing both lenses up to his eyes, he adjusted the focus until the whole construction site was in full view.  The site seemed completely deserted, all except for one figure: the security guard carrying out his rounds.

There are so many ways to take a life, but only one to create it.  Yet, even birth involves a certain amount of pain and destruction.

Likewise, not all genius has a beautiful side to it, or benefits the good of mankind.  The world cannot always agree on much, except the need for bloodshed, from time to time.  Mankind… nations… we all harbour grudges, which we are unable to develop the ability to resolve, so instead allow vendettas to build up, to the point where there is only one course of action to be executed.

In our line of work, there is always good money to be found in hate.  Old scores needing to be settled.

Sometimes, the wrong people just get caught in the crossfire.

There came a sudden flash, and a massive fireball erupted from the foundations, smothering the metal structures, as it reached up high into the sky.  Exploding metal drums shot up into the air like cannonballs.

The tips of his fingers gripped hard at the lens tubes, feeling the explosion's shockwave begin to travel his way, finally impacting and washing over his body like a powerful surge.

The incredible roar and fury which struck into him did

not scare in the slightest; it actually charged every cell of his body, making him more alive – just as it did every time.

Dark smoke spread into the street, obscuring everything from view.  Taking in the smell of the air, his mind raced with possibilities, to his next creation.

The adrenalin buzz now wore off, and he seemed to return to normal.

Since the target had been missed on the first attempt, there was the need to make the next more dramatic and stealthier, since now they would most likely be on their guard.  He had been warned that his prey would no doubt enlist the services of people like himself, and was not to be underestimated.  But, this had only made the contract more exciting!  If all was otherwise so easy – the fox entering the hen hut without the opposing farmer and his gun – what fun was there in the kill?

We are all potentially lethal predators – it just comes more naturally to some than others.  Most of us don't want to accept that killing is in the human D.N.A.

But, there comes a point when you kill too many, and then you'll never be able to stop.  Soon, you start to see blood everywhere: on yourself and on other people.

It stains so deeply, you can never wipe clean your soul.

# CHAPTER 8

### Saturday 7 p.m.
### Ravenfall – the high-school gym.

You don't always have to be at your best.  Just *try* your best.

Every child wants to hear this and make their parents proud.

There are always going to be moments when you think your best isn't good enough, and all you're going to do is disappoint.  You got to always push forward.  Never be satisfied with second best, never give up, and you will achieve things you never dreamed possible.

Sounds good, doesn't it?

There aren't many chances awarded to us in life, and those who do not grasp them with both hands always end up regretting those missed opportunities.  You have to keep trying and fighting, and never give up.

Though, sometimes in life, you don't have to fight so hard; you can look for a better way.

That is, unless you are competing in the local school Kumite Championship Tournament.

Most people don't understand that learning karate, or any martial art, is just another way of learning new life skills. It's not about just kicking and punching; it goes much deeper: you learn about choices, consequences, giving it your all and challenging yourself. Real strength is only possible through discipline and hard work; nobody achieves it by doing nothing with their lives.

When it came to my education, I was well-liked by my teachers, and surprisingly accepted by my peers, which must sound strange compared to all those other badass characters in the movies. I think you know the ones I mean: those often presented as isolated and alone. Well, not in my case. There really is no reason for my deviance, considering we live in such a small community, which looks after its own.

Of course, there are always a few exceptions; in every town you will find families who consider themselves a cut above everyone else – usually because they have money or status. These people are always looking to deliberately stand out, viciously competing against any rival brave enough to try matching their intellect, which they often feel is superior.

Abigail was the perfect example of this. She was beautiful, blonde and tanned, but to anyone who opposed her, or considered themselves equal, she was like old meat in the fridge: bad for your guts! A spinning back-kick had just sent her current opponent to the mat, writhing in agony.

Keeping myself warm, I was carrying out press-ups on my knuckles, whilst facing the competition match in which my toughest rival had just won her last point. I had been excited from the start, trained for months and my family was there to support me. The atmosphere was high in the school gymnasium, which was full of people applauding and cheering.

Our school spirit was always strong when it came to competitive tournaments; it gave children the opportunity to discover new talents outside their academic interests. Of course, like any school we had the usual sports teams, and I myself was a true sportsman – a competitor, with a style of fair play my sister never seemed able to adopt in a fight.

My mother had encouraged me to always show confidence and respect for others – even when it came to boys who, by their youthful nature, forgot their manners at times.

I'd only been sent to the principal's office once, for twisting a boy's wrist because he put his hand on my knee, causing me to react instinctively. That I might have broken it would not have been a crime in my eyes, and I'd made this clear – though, in fact I had only strained it a little, just to get the point across, that a gentleman should be careful where he places his hands. Else he might lose the use of them.

Our family was respectful, and since the lad's arm wasn't badly hurt, I'd been let off with a caution – and so had the boy, who was lucky to have only been shown up in the cafeteria.

My best friend thought it was kind of cool, and from then on I had built myself a reputation as a badass, which I kind of liked, since it was always boys who were only seen as tough.

The announcer gave a nice little speech, introducing me now onto the mat. Every parent and peer member on the benches clapped and cheered. My father bellowed loudly, whilst my mother whistled a high pitch; my sister Beth kept her own composure and just clapped half-heartedly.

Taking up my position opposite Abigail, we immediately faced off with each other.

But head games and tactical manoeuvres were all child's play; the hardest lesson was conquering your own fears. Awakening the internal warrior gives you strength, and makes you the one to be feared, or else the enemy will always prey on your weakness.

Right from the start of the first round we circled each other, delivering the faintest punches, to try and psych each other out.

You should never be afraid of hitting somebody, because they won't feel the same about you. Every punch has a purpose: to strike or cause a distraction from true intentions. Strike and move, step in and out, circle and remain focused.

If your head wasn't fully in the game, it was liable to get knocked off – which mine almost was by Abigail's quick backfist, costing me the first point.

As an act of war, it demanded an immediate response.

Keeping on the move, I kept my guard up high, not leaving her the slightest open target. Abigail delivered a round kick, but I blocked with both arms and countered with my own backfist, then a reverse punch. It was pretty textbook, but effective in awarding me a point.

The score was now tied, but not for long. Dropping to the floor I swept the legs out from under her and delivered a punch. It was now 2 to 1. Abigail was well trained, but her choice of moves was predictable, and arrogant to the point of carelessness.

The next entrance strategy seemed simple enough, though just because you get older every day, doesn't mean you get everything figured out all at once. In Kumite, there are no warnings – just as it is in life. She had a hot temper and, like a volcano, she erupted.

The best type of punch is one with the power following through, after the fist has made contact. But this girl had only one philosophy: the only reason you strike is to inflict pain.

A shot to the ribs temporarily dropped me to one knee. With everyone I knew watching the both of us, I had to suck up the pain and get back to my feet. I had to do whatever it took to win the next point, and I wasn't about to let her get away with that last shot. My side ached terribly and made me feel a little off-balance, but even when you think you're beat, you have to keep fighting to stay alive.

I suddenly remembered my mother's words: *"Take your enemy by surprise."*

Waiting at the edge of the mats, I started to limp slightly and let my front shoulder sag down, leaving myself open.

As predicted, the girl was considering taking the bait.

Looking into her eyes, I could see the fire inside her was raging more and more, her fist clenched so tightly that I knew the next blow would do more than just sting.

Externally, I gave the impression that I was weak, while inside I allowed the strength to build, just like Abigail. Only, I wasn't using my anger; I remained in control and focused. Like the old saying goes: *Not everything is as it seems.*

Which is what Abigail soon discovered, just as she delivered a high roundhouse to my head, which I avoided suddenly, now back on the offensive. The poor, spoilt bitch never knew what hit her: a well-delivered combination of edge hands and a spinning kick to the back of the head! Collapsing forward, she was dazed, unable to even hear the ref award the last point to me!

The biggest bully in school had just got her bell rung, badly. Though not *too* badly; this was a sport, after all.

It was sad that there could only be one winner, but at least the best man won. Still, as long as you fight with honour, it doesn't matter who wins or loses.

I bowed in respect to the referee, and was about to do the same with my opponent when, without so much as a handshake or congratulations, Abigail, now fully recovered, had turned and walked straight off the mats, disappearing into the crowd.

There is nothing I hate more than people with poor manners, and those who display constant stupidity toward other people's feelings. Common courtesy seemed beyond most, while others were just incapable, due to a lack of respect toward their fellow man.

"Just because her father has money, she thinks she has the right of entitlement," I said angrily, getting changed with my mother helping me. "I won fair and square. The least she could have done was display good sportsmanship."

For one terrible moment, I caught myself wishing I had

delivered a more severe blow. But the mercy you grant an opponent leads to one of two roads: friendship or vendetta. Not that she would be my first choice to make friends with.

I winced as my mother looked at the bruise on my side, although it wasn't bad and no real damage had been done.

"It's not good to have bad blood between two families in a small town," my mother said, helping me on with my coat. "I think her parents should be proud she got so far, but only one can be victorious. There should always be some solace in the fact that you tried your best, no matter the outcome."

My mother had a great way with words, but it appeared that not all shared her philosophy. Coming out into the car park, it looked as if Abigail's father was being hard on her, just because she had tried to play the game her way, and I'd still got the upper hand. I guessed that some parents just couldn't stand to see their child lose at anything.

My own, however, celebrated my first place. With trophy in hand, my father hugged me close as we walked over to the car, holding back a moment to talk to me alone.

"You did us all proud today, and I hope you feel the same way about yourself." He kissed me on the forehead. "I think your mother and I did a good job raising you to be so strong."

I wasn't sure if this was the time or place, but now

seemed as good a time as any: "I just hope I don't disappoint you, when it comes to following through with my promise. I want so much to carry on our family legacy; it means so much to you, I'm sure."

Concern now entered his eyes. Had I said something bad? Had I made it sound as if I was doing this out of some form of obligation?

"I remember the day I saw you holding my gun. I felt this terrible horror grip at my heart. A good man – a good father – should expect the worst; anticipate the tough times to come."

My parents had never tried to predetermine how my life would turn out. Many try, as they feel it might make things easier for their child in the future.

"When were you planning on telling me? We have no secrets in our house," I stated, with slight humour.

My father looked over to the car, where my sister and mother were talking quietly, allowing us our own space.

"Your mother and I had a difficult time, deciding when first to break the news to your sister. Like you, she didn't know what to think at first. But, one day, she did exactly the same as you: told us she wanted to join the family business. It turned out that she was a natural."

So, it had been her choice, too? Had she been just as spontaneous? I was tempted to ask. In the end, I guessed they had done like any parent: just allowed their child to choose.

"What troubles me the most is whether or not taking a human life will come so easily." The question had finally been put forward, and I waited patiently for the answer.

"I always hoped you would never ask that question. It is something you will come to face, a long way down the line, and only then will you get your answer."

With that, he put his arm around my shoulders and led me over to the car. But, with each step, I could not shake the disturbing sensation I was feeling at that very moment. My father's choice of words had been a little cryptic. Did he not think I was capable, like my sister Bethany? Was my training ahead going to be more difficult, or even a waste of time?

*No.* I stopped myself and cleared my mind, allowing such thoughts to fade away; all they were doing was letting my emotions rule my logic capability.

It was then that it had hit me, that I had not been paying attention to what my father had told me before: *"To truly understand, you must take in completely everything you see and do, from this point on. This will aid you through the process..."*

There was nothing complex in these words; the philosophy was no different than my training in karate, or learning subjects at school. Each day of my life had been a learning process. From this point on it would be no different, except that I would have tougher lessons, and perhaps the consequences would be more severe. Now that I was coming of age, I would be responsible— no, that was incorrect; I *was* responsible for my choices.

Anyone can be shown how to kill, just like at the farm, when I'd taken the hammer from my father's hand. It had been my choice, due to my own curiosity. Did that make me strange?

The answer to this was simple: everyone is curious from time to time, and at my stage in life, it was only natural to explore new sensations. The fact that I had got a small chemical thrill out of it was just a small part of being human; how our bodies were designed to react. Maybe someone else would have vomited, but it was not in my own personal make-up – that is just the building blocks we call "genes", found in each and every one of us.

The fact that killing an animal didn't sicken me doesn't make me weird; I was just able to justify my actions: I was slaughtering an animal which was born to feed and nourish us humans.

Of course, not everyone saw it that way, but that was again their own make-up, and they were entitled to their opinion, as was anybody. But, the death of the animal had been inevitable, no matter whose hand had struck the fatal blow – even had it lived on and later died of old age.

Standing in my bedroom, I realized that life wasn't always about puzzles; it was, at times, a matter of perspective. *"It is something you will come to face, a long way down the line, and only then will you get your answer."*

I finally understood. Like anything in life, the experience and the different sensations were the true teachings – the truest and purest way a person learnt about their nature. It provided the necessary knowledge; the answer to life's hardest questions.

I took a moment and sat down on my bed, forcing myself to be completely truthful. Why was I choosing to carry on in my father's and ancestors' footsteps? It was another question, but more relevant than my first, since it was something I hadn't considered before, and could well be the missing part of the puzzle.

My reason for wanting to remain at Ravenfall had been my family. That was the perspective I should have been focusing on: the root of our family legacy.

Looking through a storage box I kept above my wardrobe, I found an old scrapbook I had put together in my younger years, about the history of Ravenfall, and how our family had thrived since moving here from The Big City. Yes, my great grandfather had been a city dweller, and only moved here with my great grandmother when he started up the butcher shop, to raise my grandfather during WWII. It was in that war that my grandfather had found his calling, despite his own reservations toward killing, from what my grandmother had once told me.

With every turn of the page, I looked upon the faces of every generation of my family, and considered how difficult it must have been for them. But, still they had continued our legacy. How could I be the one to break it?

Even though reading this you may have difficulty understanding, legacy... is legacy. Everything one generation builds and leaves behind is sacred. It is not an obligation to continue a legacy; it is a responsibility. Every legacy has to be protected.

So, I had much to learn and fast. And the only way to accomplish this would be through experience. But, just how much would my parents allow?

Looking out of the window, I gazed to the distant bright lights of The Big City.

I may have seemed young to everyone, but that night, inside, I felt as if my very impulses were guiding me, challenging me even to go against my parents' guidance at times.

I wasn't going to learn anything about the world by allowing myself to be locked up in my bedroom, reading books and theorizing the facts of life. In order to learn, you had to live.

And a life without danger was no real life!

# CHAPTER 9

## Saturday 8 p.m.
## Ravenfall – the emergency ward.

There isn't always a reason why certain things happen, and why to certain people.

It was unbelievable, just unbelievable; it just couldn't be. Uncle Harry was suddenly having a moment of tunnel vision, and the whole reality of what he was being told was overwhelming.

When it comes to security, there was no way to take every precaution; anybody could be got to, with the right time, planning and the willingness to sacrifice innocent lives.

He could imagine the security guard Jake, sitting in his hut, drinking his coffee, when suddenly all the walls and windows had burst in on him. That was the last thing he ever saw.

The two men had known each other for a long time, and Uncle Harry had trusted his professional judgement for years, with the care and in the best interests of his business. The fact that he had been killed in the same manner as Uncle Harry nearly had, the previous day, made him question whether some form of punishment – by somebody he had perhaps wronged in his younger years – was now coming back on him and the people he knew. He had paid for his crimes before, and it had cost him dearly. Twice, in fact.

And, what of the twins? Were they to suffer the same fate?

Ever since bringing them home, he had never been this far or this long away from them before, and he was now insisting on leaving the hospital, so that they could be protected. Thankfully, the housekeeper Mrs. Sykes had reactively covered the both of them in the car explosion, and all had been found unharmed when she and the twins were brought in with the other casualties. But that bomb had nearly killed all of them, nonetheless.

An attack on himself was one thing, but nearly killing his grandchildren... two innocent babies...? Who could hate Harry that much?

Well, he would find out – and someone was going to pay.

Sergeant Braccard was now trying to calm Uncle Harry down, saying that the police were doing everything possible. But, without knowing the motive for the bombs, there was nowhere to start. They couldn't catch someone who was clearly trying to make a point, by means of immense destruction, without some form of a lead, or some relevant connection.

It suddenly occurred to Harry that it might have been an ex-employee; all construction workers at his site could gain access to the explosives.

Sergeant Braccard agreed that this could be a possibility, since the bomber had working knowledge of structural engineering, demolition and more than likely basic electronics. They could look at Harry's employee records and the types of explosive his company used. The question now was of building a list of suspects.

"Anyone threaten you recently, or that you feel would be capable of this sort of attack?" Braccard asked, tactfully. "How has your relationship been with... the 'City Officials', of late?"

Harry knew what he was suggesting, and it wasn't original. "I've had a truce with those people for years. They've had plenty of chances to do away with me in the past, but I've left them alone, and they've left us alone." Harry coughed hoarsely now.

The nurse came over and tried to put the oxygen mask over his face, asking the sergeant to leave, as this wasn't the right time to be conducting this interview. But Braccard needed to ask questions; without any leads, they would get nowhere fast.

He hadn't meant to get Harry so worked up. Since he was so good for the town, Braccard knew it was best to keep on the right side of him. Those who hadn't in the past came to a bad end. It was a sure bet that those sins might now be catching up with him.

Tactfully, Sergeant Braccard began to go over what they had discovered at the first scene. A great deal of effort had gone into looking for parts of the bomb: anything which could possibly indicate what type of device was used, if any, and who could have made it. Short of a nuclear bomb, anything which explodes always leaves traces behind. Often, these could be collected and reassembled, to give some idea of the device used.

Forensic tests had proven it to be a bomb: a sophisticated, custom-made kind, for which you couldn't just get blueprints from the internet. Pieces of a receiver had been found in the remains; it appeared that they had used simple cellphone technology to arm the device and set it off.

Somebody, somewhere, was always thinking up something new! This was, after all, the age of technology!

They had actually found the evidence quite quickly; no attempt had even been made to conceal the fact that a device had been the culprit.

The device could have been attached to the car the night before, or earlier that morning, yet they had waited until Harry went into town to detonate it. Why? Was the objective some sort of public execution, witnessed by the townspeople? Fortunately for him, somebody had hit the button early, before Harry had even got into the car. The bomber wouldn't have been far away, and probably watched the whole thing from their own vehicle. The guy didn't just want to blow Harry up; he wanted to do it in a very personal manner, and hang around to see the damage done.

Sergeant Braccard had a rough idea of the weight and size of explosives, to result in the damage caused; the heavier it was, the more of a vacuum it created.

Whoever made this one really wanted it to go off spectacularly, whilst taking Harry's life!

Leaving Harry to rest, Sergeant Braccard went back out into the hallway and looked out of the window, down into the car park. Outside the hospital a news crew had set up camp, waiting for the opportunity to talk to any officials regarding the incident yesterday.

Media-driven investigations were the worst kind. What had once been a 24-hour news cycle had now become a 10-second news cycle, and every media station wanted to be the first to break the top story – often only verifying with what little information they had. The speed at which they could get this out to the public seemed to be the only consideration. It was very frustrating and distracting, taking up unnecessary time, getting people worked up without any real hard facts. It put the investigation itself in a compromising position.

There was talk of a terrorist cell operating on the outskirts of The Big City, prompting a major concern that there were perhaps extremists looking to do harm to somebody – maybe a notable resident of Ravenfall.

Given the village's reputation for providing sanctuary for people with shadowy, dark pasts, fingers were starting to point toward those who had military or criminal history. Harry was a man with a dark past, and though that was ancient history, there may still be somebody who held a grudge.

But, so far, they had nothing to go on. It could be any number of suspects; the bomber was a contractor, for sure.

And, since they'd missed Harry once, they'd be looking to try again. Steps would need to be taken, to ensure there weren't other surprises waiting.

The guy could have been hiding any number of traps at Harry's house, or around town – and a professional could be very creative about where to place them. A bomb was only a machine, and the best way to get around one was to usually follow logic – but that was not necessarily the right way. A good explosives technician is like a magician: he wants you to think what he shows you.

They were looking for someone with a particular knowledge of bombs, and something about this work suggested military tactics. The man knew exactly where to put the bombs, to cause the most damage.

The local police were not equipped to deal with this, which meant working with the City Bomb Disposal Department. That was something they didn't want to do here: to bring in outsiders; Ravenfall preferred to look after its own problems, and leave the city with theirs. That was the common understanding of how things worked these days. But, sometimes it was a matter of swallowing your pride to ensure public safety. They had no choice but to call in for help. If they even attempted to find and disarm another device themselves, there was the likelihood of the bomber activating it by remote again.

Was revenge against Harry the reason? If so, why not just put a bullet in him; why choose this method?

The real terrorist threat, their greatest weapon, was making a statement – a car bomb was often the method of choice for this.

Explosive devices were not a typical form of assassination, but more common when the target couldn't be gotten close to by the assassin. Any target, whether a president, a government official or a representative of some superpower, could be killed with a car bomb. It was a crude but unstoppable device, because there weren't many ways to protect against it, whatever the protection level.

The devices used here, however, were too sophisticated to suggest it was a group of this nature. A random serial bomber was also unlikely; Harry definitely seemed to be the main target.

The police needed help. It wasn't a question of manpower, but rather time, before the bomber would strike again. They had to put an end to this, before more innocent people got hurt. Time was very much of the essence; they had to find him and stop him. There was going to be a great deal of pressure from the community. It was to be a tenacious labour, looking through video footage and waiting on further forensics results.

Harry, of course, had his own resources.

Asking the nurse to get him a telephone, he could feel a familiar pull, drawing him back into his old ways. Despite his promises in the past, he wanted the bastard who had put him in that bed, and come after what was now left of his family.

At dangerous and uncertain times, you cannot always

rely on the law to understand the mindset of a devious bomber or terrorist. The cops of Ravenfall were not paid to understand the mindset of such people, but simply to manage the odd occurrence when it happened. Extreme situations called for extreme measures – and the services of certain people, who had the necessary skills and drive to take down any threat to the community.

Mutual interests such as this would bring our family's attention and service once more to Harry's calling.

# CHAPTER 10

## Saturday 9 p.m.
## On the train to The Big City.

When it comes to family values, you don't exactly put everything down on paper and frame it over the fireplace.

Bringing something into this world does not necessarily give you the power to decide how it should be used, or how it is meant to exist. I figured that my parents gave me life, so they gave me free will over how I was to live it. And, they've always done their very best to support me in every independent decision I made, about my education and lifestyle choices.

That night, I decided to take a little trip into The Big City.

As a normal seventeen-year-old, I pretty much do what other kids do; high school had come to a close and, at this point in any young person's life, it was good to go out and celebrate. I decided that night I was going to live it up, since I had missed yesterday's senior party. Winning the karate tournament, I deserved a little fun, and a taste of the world.

My mother liked to look in on me at night, opening the

door and peeking in through the crack, to see me curled up in my bed.  A couple of pillows usually did the trick, though could not fool well-trained eyes.  The best prop to use, if you wanted to give the right effect, was a mannequin with matching hair, presenting the right illusion to unwanted visitors when carrying out night-time operations.

Picking out a suitable outfit, I stood in front of the mirror, admiring my own shapely form.  Thankfully, I don't bruise easily, so there was no need to apply any excessive makeup.

I figured that, when I got older, I didn't want to be one of those kids who say: *"I missed out; I should have been going out instead of being cooped up all night."*  Going out to the same pub, seeing the same people on a day-to-day basis, was just too monotonous for the young people of Ravenfall.  These days, if you wanted to sample the good life, and no longer wanted to play by society's rules, you went to The Big City.

A change in scenery was always refreshing, and a short ride on the railway got me a thirst-quenching taste of The Big City atmosphere.

Some people say the biggest problem with the younger generation is that we're always looking for shortcuts, and those who find them end up heading for a big fall.

The same could be said for queue jumpers; the joker

leaping in the puddle before me sent a small wave, only just missing my best shoes.

The Pelican was the hottest place in town, which accounted for the long line outside. Everyone was dressed in their best – including one guy who was, strangely, wearing sunglasses. The only people who wear sunglasses at night are usually blind or famous – or perhaps want to appear the latter; this guy certainly had full use of his eyes, as he looked me over with desire.

Because I was only seventeen and could not pass so easily, I had managed to make contact with somebody at school, who had fixed me up with a false identity card – a good quality one, too. It was good enough to get me past the bouncers and through the doors.

Immediately, I felt like I had entered a different dimension.

In places like this, all labels were left at the door; even weird-looking morons could mix with models, it seemed. You could leave whatever the outside world troubled you with, until the sun rose once again. The beat of the music had everybody in a good mood. People were stretching over the balcony to look down on the huge waves of arms across the dancefloor.

All the security team wore dark blazers with gold lining, and most were heavily built, looking like they juiced and hit the weights almost every day.

Through the strobe light, the different shades of lipstick made me feel kind of plain. The high-class society took up the V.I.P. area, wearing stylish clothes and drinking the house's finest champagne. My own choice of attire was acceptable, since I didn't carry that much upstairs to fit in a low-cut frock.

Of course, there were the usual good time girls showing a lot of skin, but with one rule: you could only touch when you were invited. Couples who wanted to lose themselves kept to the dark corners, pressed against the walls.

This was better than what had been planned last night, since alcohol was being served. I managed to grab a half-empty glass, but put it back down again immediately after the first taste. It must have been the cheapest, grossest beer they were selling. Yet, people were laughing and knocking back the liquor, emptying their wallets and charging to their credit cards.

You had to have days where you stopped stressing about life and just live it. There were people here who dealt with their problems any way they could. These days, everything was ecstasy, cocaine, or some just settled for a simple J. I don't do drugs, and try not to judge others.

From the sounds coming from the next stall in the ladies' toilets, it appeared somebody was indulging in another exotic form of pleasure. Why people choose toilets I have no idea; I guess it was the only real privacy one could get here.

That night, I wasn't looking for company, so I sat alone at a table, until a familiar figure spotted me from the crowd.

I almost hadn't recognized Abigail, as her hair was all moppy and her choice of attire was less luxurious than usual. She had clearly been drowning her sorrows heavily. It appeared that the whole *"everyone loves me because my family is so rich, and I'm so pretty"* act had done a complete 180.

Moving through the crowd, she shoved people aside, just to get to where I was now starting to rise out of my chair, ready to move quickly if necessary.

"If it isn't the champ!" Her words were slightly slurred. "Since when did they start letting minors in?"

She was one to talk; we had both been in the same year at school!

"You think you're really hot shit, don't you?!" she hissed, squaring up close in front of me. The saliva spat from her mouth onto my face, tempting me to make the first move – to give her one shove and let gravity do the rest – but we were now starting to draw attention.

It's bad to be paranoid and think that the whole world is watching you but, considering this is the age of C.C.T.V., it was likely all eyes were probably totally focused on the both of us right then.

"It was a good fight. I gave as good as I got," I said, placing my feet stealthily in place. I could catch her off-guard easily, but then again, in her condition, so could anyone else.

"And humiliated me in front of the whole school! Those flashy moves! Second place is no place in my family; unacceptable to my father, who can't stand to see me a loser!"

There were always issues within a family which could be delicate, particularly evident when they came with phrases such as: *"Second place is no place..."*

"Whatever issues you've got are between the two of you. I just came out to have a good night." I looked to the next table and noticed an unattended glass. "Why don't you go find some rich guy to cry over? Bare your soul... and whatever else? Maybe he'll help you forget your troubles."

The suggestion struck home hard. It doesn't matter how directly or indirectly you suggest somebody to be a cheap slut, even in a wasted condition they so easily pick up the innuendo. Reaching up, she made a grab for my hair.

But I was still in control of my reflexes; easily parrying the outstretched limb, I snatched up the glass and threw the contents in her face, delivering a front pressing kick, to send her back into the crowd.

Gravity pulled her down on her ass, at the many feet of the crowd, who just looked down and laughed at the wet little girl, with dark eye-shadow running down her face.

As predicted, she pulled herself up and came straight at me again, with both arms out. She grabbed for my top, painfully digging her nails into my breasts. Sometimes girls could be real bitches, getting so angry they lose all composure, leaving only wild rage and kitten claws, pulling and tearing like a ferocious lioness.

Many people don't realize that anger is the primary emotional motivation which leads to rash actions, which in turn leads to mistakes – which then gives you the upper hand.

There are two types of opponent: street fighters with no technique and the warrior, who can give as good as they take – to quote my sister: *"Not always by fair means."*

Abigail's footwork looked a little unstable, so I used this to get the best of her, like before. But, this time, I used her own momentum to throw her sideways, into the bar.

You can't always avoid a fight, but you can choose when it needs to end. In any fight, there are always consequences, and things need to stop before they get too far out of hand – especially when you're about to be on the bad end of a bottle!

Abigail had snatched it up from the counter and, with a murderous look in her eyes, I knew that things had now gotten serious.

*Are you fucking kidding me?*

The loud, bloodthirsty scream was enough to confirm that she wasn't.  As such, she left me with very little options for survival.

There are three rules in a street fight involving weapons:

(i)   Never get hit, if you can help it;

(ii)  Never hit unless there is an opening available;

(iii) When the opening presents itself, never hold back.

She was taller than me, but size is only a factor if you have no knowledge of the human body.  No matter how big a person, you'll always find one spot which is their most vulnerable, and that you need to exploit by any means, fair or unfair – it doesn't matter when it comes to defending your life!

But, winning isn't always enough; sometimes you have to make a point.  Sometimes you have to break a person, or end up getting broken.

As she lunged forward, I raised my arm using an outside parry, deflecting hers, and delivered a spear-hand strike to the eye, with a powerful upward knee strike to the crotch. The areas of vulnerability are no different on a woman than a man; when you do strike at a particular target, it will have the same desired effect.

Letting the bottle fall from her hand, I gave a downward elbow to her back, causing her knees to buckle, bringing her down onto them, before finally finishing with a harsh round kick.  Her nose exploded on impact, sending her back once more onto the floor, bleeding badly.

Snatching the bottle up, I shattered it against the bar and bent down over Abigail, her face now covered in blood, and nose slightly bent out of shape.

Thankfully, I suddenly found my hand wanting to let go of the bottle.  The fight was over, and there was no need to go any further than I had already.  That wasn't who I was, despite the fact that she could have killed me, and perhaps deserved it.

A hand caught me by the shoulder, from behind.

Looking around, I saw one of the bouncers towering down over me.  The figure was somebody I recognized immediately as Laurence, one of Uncle Harry's employees. He had caught me at a bad moment: I was underage, with a false identity card and a broken bottle now at my feet.

As more security started to burst through the crowd, he practically picked me up in one arm, off the ground, and carried me to the back, toward one of the emergency exits. Kicking it open, he dropped me outside and told me to make myself scarce. Then he closed the door.

I found myself standing alone in the alley, breathing heavily. The same adrenalin rush I felt before at the farm was coursing through my body. My hands trembled slightly and I took a moment, closing my eyes to try calming myself.

But, instead, I was presented with a new revelation, found deep down in my soul.

Sometimes it's difficult to look inside, to confront the ugliest demons our minds create.

I had fought bravely, faced a life danger and acted in self-defence. But, if any cause means acting hastily, even when protecting your own life, was that wrong?

I know it's an old line: *I was just defending myself!* But I hadn't started the fight – just ended it, hard.

Walking along the dark streets, I put some distance between myself and the nightclub, wondering if Abigail was alright, and what her father would say in the morning.

Finding an all-night diner on the corner, I sat on a stool at the counter and ordered a soft drink. The place was quiet and practically empty, which gave me peace and more time to think.

Whether or not the cops would be looking for me, I

wasn't sure. So far, they would be getting only one side of the story. Then again, I was underage and had been on licenced premises.

Then, there was the damage I had done to Abigail's face. It was a guarantee she wouldn't be doing any photoshoots for a while.

I wasn't entirely convinced that she had been fully incapacitated, and that she wasn't coming after me again that night. The suggestion kept me looking over my shoulder every now and then, expecting the door to burst open, or the sound of a car pulling up outside and the rush of footsteps.

I was starting to go over the fight in my head, and was curious about how my body had reacted. The release of adrenalin was very normal in a life-threatening situation, causing the fight or flight response, though my instinctive reaction with that bottle had come out of leftfield. Would I really have gone through with it?

My watch alarm was going off: I had about half an hour before the last train left The Big City, to take me back home to Ravenfall.

I decided to be cautious; it was late and I had ended up in an area which was unfamiliar and looked pretty rough, the streets a perfect urban environment for surprise ambushes.

Keeping to the edge of the pavement, away from open alleyways, I made my way back to the train station, constantly looking up and down the street.

I got to wondering again if it was our genes that truly determine our destiny?  And, if so, just how deep was the imprint nature buried?

It is a typical defence for a child to adopt: blaming the parents or their upbringing on why they become the way they do.  But families and people are not perfect, no matter where you come from, or how you are raised; the darkest pieces, which form the ugliest side of a personality, is the hand fate deals us.

This sort of life was one big gamble and, win or lose, we all play the same game, from one day to the next.

# CHAPTER 11

### Sunday 12:10 a.m.
### The Big City train station.

I had managed to reached the departing platform to Ravenfall with five minutes to spare, my thoughts still concerned over what I would say to my parents tomorrow.

I should have taken this into consideration, before doing what I did. At least I hadn't lost my sanity, and kept control of my senses.

Speaking of which, I suddenly felt another presence at my side. I was shocked to see Laurence, now dressed casually, standing on the platform.

"I'm glad to see you're still in one piece. This city can be pretty rough, you know," he said, with a slight irony.

The train was now approaching, and I stood quietly for a moment, until it came to a standstill.

"Don't you normally ride a bike?" I queried finally, watching some people get off, not paying us any mind. A guard stood at the open door, waiting.

"I had a small accident," he said gesturing for us to board. "Had a little trouble on the way home: this damn truck, with a lunatic driver, pulled out right in front of me. Could have sent me flying over my own handlebars if I hadn't swerved in time. Ended up in a ditch."

We took a seat opposite each other, in an almost empty carriage. The other occupants were an old couple, partially drifting off, arm in arm, as the train started up. We left The Big City, its lights slowly fading out behind us.

"*You're* lucky to be in one piece!" I stated, sitting back comfortably. "Good thing you wear a helmet!"

He nodded, looking down at my slightly wrinkled attire – or was he checking out my boobs?

"Unlike that girl you pulverized. The manager wasn't too happy you disappeared like that," he said, unwrapping a stick of gum. "But, you'll be glad to hear that no official charges have been made; she insisted on the matter being kept quiet."

The words were a little comfort. Strangely, inside I found the situation truly laughable, now. Poor Abigail, not wanting anyone to hear how she got beaten twice in one day – and by the same person!

"I should thank you for pushing me out of the door. But why did you do it? Shouldn't you have detained me, or something?" I asked, removing my ticket as the guard came down the aisle.

"Technically you're underage, so it was best you made

yourself scarce." He handed his ticket over to the guard. "My boss wouldn't be happy knowing we'd let a minor into the club."

I raised one eyebrow playfully, as though it were an observant thought. It never occurred to me that way. I guessed I was in the clear, which put me in a good mood. "So, does that mean I can rely on your discretion?" I asked.

"Absolutely, without question. I work for Harry, and your family is pretty tight with him, so let's just call the matter closed," he said, raising his hand dramatically.

The statement had brought a different topic to the table now: "Have you heard anything about Harry?"

Laurence's expression became soft. "They say he's alright. That damn explosion nearly killed him, and those two infants."

This was a shock to me: nobody had mentioned the babies being there.

"That new housekeeper he's hired, she saw the whole thing; saved their lives," he went on to explain. "Harry owes that woman a debt of thanks. Acting the way she did, she must have maternal instincts. Self-sacrifice is something to be admired."

The last statement now brought a smile to my lips. "Like when you saved my sister, Bethany?"

Laurence took the reference and shifted slightly in his

seat. A lot of people would find it disturbing, talking to someone whose family are contract killers. I mean, the term "boundaries" isn't even close to accurate.

"Well, I just acted on instinct; no medals needed," he said, trying not to sound too cavalier.

The train rocked slightly as it turned a bend.

"Your sister say anything about how grateful she might be, say, if I were to bring her flowers?"

I shrugged, thoughtfully. "She's a bit fickle when it comes to guys. Thought she had something serious..." I stopped talking, not wishing to give away any more family secrets.

If you choose to keep secrets from people, you better have a good reason. In my case – my family's – secrets are what kept us out of the law's reach.

"Guess it must be difficult. A lot of guys might find what she does a little intimidating," he said, trying his best to be tactful.

I laughed, just nodding. It wasn't every day you dated an assassin.

"I don't know how somebody could ever kill another random person?" he said flatly, out of nowhere. The words had come out so directly, I was shocked – as well as relieved that nobody was close enough to hear this sudden change in the conversation. Was this guy seriously even trying to talk about this with me? The reason most people talk so much is that they hate to think in silence.

"You can't really think of it as random – otherwise, there's no value," I said, matter of fact.

"I'm sure you give good value for money. Do repeat customers get a discount?" He was pressing a little, making me somewhat curious. I could see that he really wasn't going to drop this. Funnily enough, I wasn't a bit bothered by this new invasion into our private family business – even though we didn't know each other that well; family business wasn't something I was prepared to betray.

But, honestly, the way I was feeling right then, I found myself wanting to offload on this guy.

It really mattered to me, to talk it over with somebody outside my family, and didn't require me to book myself in for analysis.

"I really need to get some things off my chest. And, seeing as you're here, and I can rely on your discretion... would you be willing...?"

He merely nodded, resting back in his seat and folding one leg over the other to get comfortable, looking me directly in the eyes.

"We believe what we do is a service to humanity," I said, noting a crack appear at the side of his mouth. "We aren't the first to rid this world of bad people. Sometimes it's the only answer."

"You sound like a vigilante, yet you charge people for killing those who they don't like," he said, with only a small hint of sarcasm. "How is that a service to humanity?"

Normally, this skeptical tone would have irritated me, but since he had done me a good turn that night, I let it slip by and continued: "We don't think of it as personal. Vendettas are the result of an emotional response, fuelled by revenge. We have rules; certain contracts that are not based on revenge, but resolution."

Laurence took my words seriously now, and considered for a moment. "Isn't that why man created laws?"

"Technically, God gave laws to man, who either chose to follow or go against His word," I countered, feeling as though this were turning into a sort of debate.

Or, maybe even the start of some game?

He interlocked his fingers together, trying to keep himself composed now. "What about *'Though shalt not kill'*? That is, I would think, the worst of the commandments to be broken. How does one justifying killing, to free the world of the evil of one person?"

I now took a moment and decided on my next move. It was, in fact, becoming a bit of a chess game, and I hoped he was a worthy opponent. "How can you justify a corrupt system, run by people whose actions seek not justice for other people's wrongs, but a chance to fill their pockets with silver or gold?"

He remained silent now. Perhaps anticipating his next move?

"God's law came before man," I added, further, "and man chose to corrupt His teachings for his own benefit, rather than for the good of his brother and neighbour."

Laurence just sat quietly, not saying anything or moving. My efforts to try and make our intentions seem just appeared to be having an impact. Tapping his bottom lip with his finger, he came back on the offensive. "What price do you ask your neighbours for services given, that our system fails to provide?" he countered, finally.

It was a good move. The topic of money always attached the largest stigma to every contract. The idea of killing another person for money clearly didn't go over too well with Laurence – as it doesn't with a lot of people.

"We don't gain any kind of pleasure in what we do. If others aren't prepared or able to take the actions themselves, they should be willing to pay, like any other service," I came back with – a simple answer.

Laurence now gave me a curious glance, as the train rocked once more. I was growing increasingly interested in where this debate was leading us.

"You think it doesn't feel good, watching an evil man die for his sins?" he challenged. "Being there, how can you not feel anything?"

Now I found myself in an awkward position; the game had suddenly fallen into check!

"I don't know about people," I decided to be upfront and truthful; "I've only ever killed a lamb."

Laurence now raised his eyebrow, quizzically. "How did it make you feel?"

The sensation was not something I could explain to him right then, and that gave me the motivation toward another tactful manoeuvre. "How did it make you feel, seeing my sister kill all those men?" I challenged now.

He thought for a moment, perhaps having the same trouble.

"How does it make you feel when you're pounding on those opponents?" I followed up, looking at his giant hands. "It doesn't always take a bullet, after all."

He opened them and leant forward to display them more clearly, making them into fists. They were a destructive sight, to say the least; very powerful and strong enough to break even the hardest skull.

"I've never killed anything bigger than an ant, except maybe a fly. But size doesn't matter – only the reason. And I will concede that sometimes death is a necessary punishment," he said, sitting back once more, waiting for my next move.

But, there wasn't really any more to come from me at the moment; I was just thinking about his last statement. The word "punishment" was the most accurate way to describe our actions.

"So, what are your plans after the summer? Going away to college?" he asked, as if changing the topic now.

This slightly disappointed me; the game was getting interesting, and I wasn't about to surrender my own king just yet. "Do you enjoy the sport or the violence?" I asked, reaching forward to touch his hands, gently.

Surprisingly, I found his eyes now wandering over me with complete precision. But I didn't mind, finding my own doing no less than the same. "You train in just as lethal a profession; a lot of fighters have died in the ring!"

"I've never killed anyone, or anything bigger than a fly," he repeated, and came back again to counter, "or a poor, helpless lamb, or a stuck-up bitch, for that matter!"

The motion of the carriage stirred us both again. Was he starting to enjoy this little debate we were having? Hard to imagine, I know, yet there we were, around other people, just sitting and talking about the subject as discreetly as possible – no differently to as if we were two young people on a first date.

"You have this reputation for being a nice guy, but how does it feel when you have all that power over those losing opponents, each falling down, one after the other?" I noticed a little twinkle in his eye, as I cupped his knuckles.

He remained silent, his eyes merely staring at me, as though once again visualizing what had gone down in the club – not that it had been the first time he'd seen two chicks go at it.

"Would you ever kill somebody? I mean, you don't seem the type, but you have the right tools." I looked at his hands; they were as hard as stone.

The question was invasive beyond any other, but he felt like being truthful now.

"When Harry's son, Martin, stole my grandmother's jewellery from our house, I felt like burying these into his face, over and over," he said, clenching his fists tighter. "If I had caught him first, I would have beaten that man to death with these fists!"

The look in his eyes told me he was earnest, but I wasn't taken aback; such an emotional response was only natural. But, then he withdrew slightly, perhaps feeling that he'd let me in a little too quickly.

This kind of ritual was something I would have attributed to my sister and her past boyfriends; she was always pulling away whenever they got too close. My mother, on the other hand, had once said: *"A person doesn't come in pieces and parts, so you can put them together from scratch; you have to begin from the inside outwards."*

This could go both ways, good or bad, but I had to respect him for his honesty, just as he had with me.

"There nothing wrong with that, Laurence," I said, softly. "We are all guided by our impulses, and though they may conflict with other people's opinions, we can never betray them, as we just end up betraying our own nature."

He looked back at me now, as though something new had broken through, before his eyes.

Often, all we see is the outer shell, but if you look hard enough you will see the most attractive qualities a person truly possesses on the inside; the truth. You hear it for what it is and you can't deny what it stands for. I think we both found this to be refreshing: to just sit and talk, without fear of any prejudice.

Though, the look in his eyes was starting to captivate me now.

I didn't want things to go too quickly for the both of us, so I quickly changed tactic again, asking if he would ever leave Ravenfall, to perhaps move to The Big City. Again, Laurence shied a little; it was clearly a sensitive subject, which his own mother had brought up quite recently, and things had got a little heated.

The crazy thing was that, every now and then, even Laurence thought about moving there. It was rough and run by a crime outfit, but the job at the club was well paid, and there was more to be found for a guy with his potential. What he could earn would be enough to set him up good and proper, to become a professional contender. But he didn't want to leave his mother, who was unable to support herself; he could not just walk out on his family responsibilities. His mother had always supported him growing up, and now he felt obligated to do the same, being the man of the house. The money he was getting from Harry wasn't brilliant, but it was regular, and he was getting plenty of exercise into the bargain.

I looked him over again: it was certainly working to his favour. I thought that he liked what he saw, too, but I could tell there was some fear still keeping him slightly at bay.

"Well, I'm sure a lot of people would miss you. A lot of the girls would probably be disappointed to see you go: not a lot of prospects in the village, after all!"

He took my innuendo with interest. Perhaps the wall had finally fallen now. There are a number of ways to suggest to a guy that you are interested. But, right then and there, I was sure the most obvious was appropriate.

"I have to go to the powder room; we can continue this... when I return," I said, walking away.

I went to the end carriage and stopped at the door, waiting for a moment, despite the toilet cabin being unoccupied.

In a very short time, I could feel his presence behind me, reaching under my arm and opening the door. We guided each other inside.

They say that sex and violence have a close relationship, when put together in close proximity. Well, we couldn't have gotten any closer than in a train lavatory!

When you dig deep enough, all the protective barriers break away, and you find the distance between two people begins to narrow, particularly in such an enclosed space.

The feel of his mouth on mine, of his fingers over my body...

I'm going to stop there; the rest is far too personal, and it's not that sort of book.

As first times go, I will admit that it wasn't what I had planned, but it was certainly memorable, and gave me a clearer insight into sexual liaisons in public conveniences!

Exiting the carriage when the train finally reached Ravenfall, we walked from the station in silence for a while, before he asked whether I would ever go professional with my karate.

Everyone in Ravenfall respected Laurence as something of an amateur contender and, as one competing athlete to another, he complimented me on my finals win at the school. It hadn't even occurred to me that he attended the tournament fights.

Boxing was seen as an old-school sport, when it came to fighting with your hands, whereas martial arts required the ability to use the whole body as a weapon.

"If it came down to you and me in a fight," I said, giving him a playful tap in the ribs, "I'd give you a run for your title!"

He laughed suddenly, bringing his arm around my head and locking it to his body. "You see? I know a few tricks myself!" He gave me a little squeeze, then let me go. We were, after all, two civilized people.

Any previous anxiety had disappeared, which surprisingly started to trouble me, after we parted company outside his house.

The world is full of challenges. No matter what you decide to do with your life, there are always going to be risks, whether in a job or a relationship.

There was only one place where you knew you were truly safe, to think over your troubles.

Slipping back into my room, I crept into the bathroom and stripped down, to look myself over. I found there was no serious bruising from the fight – or any other marks from the train!

Washing my slightly torn and bloodied top in the basin, I looked back at myself in the mirror, I hadn't changed much physically in a year, but there was something different now. My face was untouched, but somehow I found a different image staring back at me. Strangely, it startled me for a second, and it didn't seem to want to vanish.

I can only say that if you don't know to what I am referring, then you must yourself still be a virgin.

But there was also something else, looking deeper into my own eyes; perhaps I had found an open doorway leading down into my soul, which was crying out for me to listen?

I just stared and allowed the visions to come back before me, playing over everything from the bar. I had actually come close to killing somebody!

Each of us reacts differently in heightened emotional situations, and I had to credit my training somewhat; even in contact sports, control sort of came with the territory. There was nothing wrong with liking the thrill and danger which came with fighting, but if, however, you made it a full part of your life, it affected more than the flesh. That is to say, something deeper than the bruises; now something within the human soul had changed. Had I perhaps become less domesticated, and something more primal was beginning to evolve?

This had been an important night for me. The experience in the nightclub had not been a game, or a matter of honour; it had been an act of survival.

Inflicting physical pain on another human being, you can so easily become conditioned to the possibility that executing death is within the capability of anyone. But now I felt as if some deep and powerful spirit had been woken in me.

I now found myself challenging my act of mercy. True, I had been right this time, but was mercy something I could afford in the future?

The realization of almost taking another person's life was far greater than you could ever imagine; no person could ever be prepared for the overwhelming power which came from holding another person's life in their hands.

If Laurence had not stopped me, my whole life, my family's life, would have changed. I now had to find a way to channel this power productively, so I could maintain control as needed.

Descending the stairs quietly, I made my way out back and opened the walk-in freezer, stepping inside. I moved over to the lamb we had hung yesterday morning. It looked very different now, in this cold setting. The temperature started to make me shiver, ever so slightly.

When you push yourself too heavily into a corner, you

either feel trapped and helpless, or you give yourself the opportunity to define who you really are, and what you truly believe underneath.  Limitations are the burdens we place on our own shoulders; fear keeps us from wanting to explore further than what we already know.  Everyone has their limits, but if we are able to overcome, we are able to see beyond.

Unbelievable as it may sound, I tried to put myself in the lamb's place.  I was not an animal bred for slaughter – although humans could perhaps be seen this way in some cultures!  Point of fact, I was the opposite; I was to become the touch of death, and the lamb had seen me coming.  But, had it sensed my intentions as I walked over, and before I had taken its life?

Standing there as I was, feeling my body weaken and begin to die, I reached deep inside myself and gripped hold tightly to all that kept me alive, and gave me strength.

Perhaps that was the animal's reasoning: knowing its time had come, like the other animals at that farm, it just accepted its fate.

The willpower to endure pain and suffering, and accept the end of life, is a technique almost anyone can adopt; a lesson to help see beyond the frailties and find true internal courage in the human will.

Like life, with age our innocence fades, and what we

thought impossible is so easily within our grasp, if only we were to find the courage to achieve beyond the limitations we shackle ourselves with. The human race, throughout history, has shown this many times, generations evolving and redefining what came before and what is to come next.

What was there in store for me, and what did the future hold?

# CHAPTER 12

**Sunday 8:45 a.m.**

**Ravenfall – local police station.**

Is it difficult to keep two worlds separate from each other? Having to lie and occasionally keep the truth from certain people?

When a life, or way of life, depends on it, then I suppose it isn't too much to ask. Whether you like it or not, some secrets have to be kept; it isn't always a matter of choice.

Everyone has different sides to their personality, which is useful when making tough decisions, and it's your job to act in the best interest of those you swore to protect.

On good days and bad, we show these sides as a smokescreen, protecting loved ones. To try and explain otherwise is to invite people into the darkest parts of human nature.

You know, of course, of what I speak; we all have them, and they are the hardest conflicts to struggle with throughout our lives. Not all have the strength to bear this terror.

Sergeant Braccard was having a particularly difficult

morning, trying to assure the community and his own family that the public school was safe from bombs.

Then, making a call to Edner, the wife of the security guard who had been killed in the explosion at Uncle Harry's construction site, he had tried to comfort her as best he could. He had been trained in the ways victims' families coped with life-changing tragedies, but sometimes going by the manual just wasn't enough.

Coming through the station entrance, he was met by a very unpleasant sight: dressed from head to toe in black, a tactical officer was waiting for him at the reception desk.

A thin smile appeared on his lips, as his former partner addressed him, coldly: "I was told by the City Police Department to expect one of their best men. I guess he had something more important to do."

The man kept his face under control, as he took Braccard's statement in a professional manner. "Actually I do, but certain political figures don't like the idea of bombs going off so close to home; looks bad in the voters' eyes," the man said, following into the office.

Sergeant Braccard wanted to get this over with quickly; he was already running late for the council meeting.

Lieutenant Holloway was an ex-military type, the kind you had to be cautious with: they weren't the sort to miss a trick, and could conjure up their own out of nowhere.

The fact that the man had actually made Lieutenant, the ribbons on his chest looking brand new, made Sergeant Braccard grateful that he was no longer a member of the B.C.P.D. It actually surprised Braccard that Holloway would take this particular assignment; he'd have been more at home in his own office with the secret files and listening at keyholes, for the next little bit of gossip which would prove useful. It was impossible to keep anything secret inside the City Police Department for long. It was only a matter of who had the most dirt, and who didn't mind getting their hands messy.

Lt. Holloway knew just how fast word could get around when it came to these sort of cases. The names of the people charged with overseeing them, considered dependable and capable, would surely be up for a quick commendation, depending on how fast it could be wrapped up, before the start of an election. This was as political as it got – there was no sense in hiding the fact. Everyone was looking to be on the front page, to take credit for putting a name to paper and passing it on to anyone else who mattered – or who could perhaps make things happen to a career.

"This businessman – the local contract developer, who nearly got blown up and had his construction site barbecued last night – what do you know about him?"

Sergeant Braccard sat in his chair, leisurely going through his daily reports, and didn't seem to be paying much attention to this particular question. He was actually taking more interest in a certain report which had come in last night, with regard to one of its youngster residents, who had been beaten and mugged over in The Big City. The father would no doubt be on his case sometime that day, asking for quick results, as any caring parent would.

"Do you currently have any suspects who want to see him put in a box?" Lt. Holloway practically bellowed in the office.

Sergeant Braccard now looked up, as though somebody had let off a bad smell in the room. "If we did, we wouldn't have needed to call you boys in; I'd have the guy sitting in the cell, ready to go to court and answer for what he's done. But, you know, when you've got crime and criminals, it takes a certain meticulous brain to hopefully make a match."

Holloway just stood saying nothing, a clear, cool expression still on his face.

"So far, we haven't come up with anything: no motive and nobody taking credit, so we're just going to have to leave it to the old-fashioned investigative powers of policework." Sergeant Braccard placed the report in his desk drawer and leant forward on his forearms.

"Hopefully, you won't get too close and stain that uniform," Braccard said in a reassuring tone. "If we find the bomber, and he decides not to be taken alive, that is."

Holloway was now regretting having taken this assignment, but he wasn't about to just tuck his tail between his legs and drive back to his department with egg on his face. Since he was there, he had to lay down the ground rules of how things were going to be run.

"I'm going to need an office and an outside line to the city, so we can get some more men down here to control this situation," Holloway said, looking down at Braccard's name plaque: the title of *"Sergeant"* reminded both of them who the ranking officer was in that moment.

Holloway had his own men from the city bomb squad on standby, sitting around on their asses, when they were ready to hit the bricks and the streets. Sergeant Braccard didn't like what he was proposing. He'd wanted to avoid this altogether and keep everyone – especially the locals – calm, without outsiders coming in, stirring shit up. The idea of a team of goons coming into his village and doing bag searches would cause uproar in the community.

The fact that this man was standing in his office, making such demands, made him even sicker. If he'd been given a real cop – which is to say not a coward, who'll run at the first sign of trouble, or pass the blame if the battle ended in dark red – he'd have gladly given up his own office. Unfortunately, the most he had to offer was the storage room, though it was well air-conditioned.

"You never got The Big City, Braccard," Holloway growled, in his newly appointed office. "That's why you weren't good enough to remain in the department. You weren't prepared to be a team player; to follow the code of backing up your fellow officers."

Sergeant Braccard stood by a shelf containing evidence bags, not denying what Holloway said was the complete truth. "And here you are now, standing in my storage room at my station," Braccard countered, placing his hands on his hips. "A guest in my village, helping us poor folks out, instead of being over there, on your knees under the mayor's desk!"

Holloway's face was starting to grow red, and steaming under the collar.

"It's funny what officials are willing to pay well for. Must have to stock up heavily on the lip-balm though, eh? Keep from getting a chapped mouth."

The guy had taken the bait, and a wide swing, which missed Braccard's head by a mile. A web-hand strike to his Adam's apple put him down on his knees – which was ironic, really.

"At least here we don't need to worry about such

accessories!" Braccard bellowed back as he walked out, leaving Lt. Holloway to catch his breath.

In his car, Sergeant Braccard could still feel the pulsing of the impact on his hand against the steering wheel. Very effective – he just hoped he hadn't hit too hard and knocked something loose; it would be a shame if Holloway's voice was no longer as pretty as his looks.

What doesn't kill you just makes you very sore!

Some things were hard to forget and forgive.

If you were ever to discover a time machine, which could change the course of your life, what destination would you choose? That one significant moment which could have made your life, rather than break it into pieces?

But we can't go back; the decisions we've made are irreversible.

We wouldn't necessarily change anything anyway, except to try harder to get a more accurate, fair outcome – at least then we might be able to live with our failed efforts.

Sergeant Braccard was still a good cop; he just had a chip on his shoulder which would never fall off. Being proactive was his single psychological motivation when it came to policing a small country village. Contacting outside agencies had been a desperate act, but it had been the only sensible decision, as they were outmanned and ill-equipped to deal with a maniac bomber. Bringing in outsiders didn't get him off the hook; it just made his job more complex.

As he lived here, and had got to know the people, they knew him and liked his attitude. As a young officer, he learned there were things done a certain way, but this village was at least incorruptible, along with its appointed officials.

The Mayor of Ravenfall, Mr. Robertson, was seated in the centre chair at the village council meeting, along with the other four members, all deeply troubled by the recent events. This was serious, and they had to have something soon to tell their people.

"Has the City representative arrived yet?" Robertson asked, as Sergeant Braccard took his seat. Clearly, the council were eager to know just what sort of person they had been assigned.

"Matter of fact, we had our meeting before I came here. I think we made a real connection!" Sergeant Braccard said, reassuringly.

The village council liked to look after its own, and they knew Braccard wasn't happy about calling in city help, but they had backed him because it was the smart move. Someone was declaring war on a citizen of Ravenfall, so they were bringing out heavy artillery and taking no prisoners.

"How's Edner doing?  We sent over a goodwill basket and card.  The whole community is there for her, whatever she needs," Robertson prompted, looking around at his affirming members.

Sergeant Braccard took out his notebook and began orating his recent report: "We got a call this morning from one of the construction workers.  He may have seen something yesterday which could be of help.  I'm going round after this to get his statement."

The council now piqued at this news.  Perhaps things were looking up already.

"Does our liaison know about this?" Robertson asked, carefully.

"Well, like I said, we reached an understanding," Braccard said, getting up from his chair.  "Hopefully, we can solve this matter quickly, then he and his boys can get the fuck out of this village, and back to that sewer they call a city!"

He turned and left them all looking after him.  Nobody said a word.

# CHAPTER 13

### Sunday 9:10 a.m.
### Ravenfall – the butchers' shop.

Is it normal to choose a career in death?

The best person to ask would be the undertaker – although, they never meet the client while still alive. The undertaker welcomes all, dead or alive!

A poor joke, maybe, but a profitable business nonetheless. That is one industry which will always thrive; death is always good business.

Working in a butchers' shop, you get used to the sight of corpses. Not to mention the aroma of blood. What comes out of an animal's carcass is not as bad as you might think; it's all edible when properly prepared, so there isn't much that goes to waste.

The handling of animal guts would gross some young girls out, and maybe it did at the start for me, too, but after a while I just got used to how God made His creatures.

We humans are really not that different – not that I have ever cut up a human body!

My sister Bethany, on the other hand, is very skilful with

a knife, and has a high level of knowledge when it comes to the human anatomy. Part of the training to become a good assassin is to learn anatomical knowledge; it gives you the confidence to carry out a quick kill with complete efficiency.

At school, you get to cover the major organs of the human body, but more attention for us is to focus on certain blood vessels (arteries) closest to the surface of the flesh. Underneath the skin there are the muscles and tendons which, if damaged severely, can disable a person, leaving them weak and vulnerable.

Working hard, knife in hand, I was currently slicing large portions of steak on a cutting board, ready to be put on display in the front window.

The wonderful colour of red meat may be sickening to some people, but it really is the best source of protein to ensure good health. Everyone has at some point looked through the window of their local butchers', and seen those large cuts of meat hanging up on hooks: the legs and ribcages of a cow, for example. It's actually surprising how much nice roasting meat you can get out of a rear leg (the round). The best parts are known as "oyster steaks": the tastiest and juiciest cuts, which we secretly keep back for ourselves – well, most butchers do.

The severing of the tendons around the femur bone can

be quite tough, unless you have a really sharp blade, so you can get to the other muscles: "unbundling", as we call it.  We don't just throw the bones away; they're actually quite good for making stock – all that is required is to remove any excess fat from the bones and add an assortment of vegetables.

My mother was a dab hand in the kitchen, always looking up new and interesting recipes.  Now washing her hands clean at the sink, she had put a dish into the fridge and come through to the preparation area, asking me to get ready, as we were going to Sunday Service.

Riding with the whole family down to the village square, I could already hear the church bells ringing, calling all residents to attend.

I don't know if you believe in God or not, but I'm not going to be shy about this matter.  Devoting your life to a faith is not a waste, if you truly believe in it with all your heart.  I think it's important to believe in something, even if it conflicts with other people.  So many question God's existence, particularly when they ask or need something and He chooses not to answer.  But, just because you don't hear, see or receive, doesn't mean He does not exist.

Walking down the aisle, I glanced around, as many knelt at their pews and crossed themselves, before taking their seats next to family and neighbours.  Here is where a community truly comes together.

Looking to the front pews, I could see Abigail and her parents talking to our priest. Her nose was taped up and her eye bandaged; she was looking a little pale.

Nothing had been mentioned of her that morning – no phone calls threatening legal action – so my parents had been in their usual jolly mood. My sister Bethany had heard some of the gossip passing along one of the pews, regarding Abigail's unfortunate attack in The Big City; apparently her watch and wallet had been stolen.

I took a moment to cross myself for what I was currently thinking, and hoped that God would forgive me.

Sitting beside me now, Bethany had put on her best dress and tied her hair back, looking very attractive, and a wonderful sight for most of the young lads who looked our way. But her attention was drawn somewhere else, her mind not really focused on anything external.

Like everyone else, you didn't need to be audible in the house of God to be heard. People come to church to speak to God, but really you can converse anytime, anyplace, no institution required – He is, after all, ever-seeing and ever-knowing.

Some people think that church is a place to go when you've got nothing better to do. But, while school prepares you to deal with life, it never addresses its end – and that is where church plays the biggest part in your life, preparing for the inevitable transition from this world into the next. The Church always has its own power, in any community. It can so easily bring about change, in the way people think and act.

The town may have been full of sinners, at one time or another, but they were all proud enough to come here each Sunday: to sit together as good neighbours, in their best clothes, their hearts open to the words of God, hoping that their sins might be washed away. Sometimes, five minutes in confession could separate a person from these burdens – if only for a short time.

When you spend your time in the house of Our Lord, you are permitted a lot of time to think and, if needed, to tell your thoughts to somebody who is caring and understanding.

Our priest once stated: *"It is not about what we say to others, but what we choose to say to ourselves, and how we judge our own actions – especially those which conflict with God's law."*

You might well be wondering how we, as a family of sinners, find the nerve to come into the house of the Lord, sit before Him with blood on our hands and dare to ask forgiveness. Well, ask those we kill: how do they cause suffering to others, and not ask His forgiveness?

This was in fact the topic our priest Father Brannon wished to address today, with us all.

"We are all sinful, as the Bible tells of Adam and Eve. Temptations are around us all the time, and not all have the strength to resist. Do we find ourselves fearing the judgements of our family and neighbours, or more so the Lord Himself?"

This statement caused a slight stinging in my own heart, and I tried my best to clear my mind of the night before. Such thoughts in such a place should have shamed me, but it is moments like this when young minds begin to wander.

When it comes to taking up with the Church, not all people are so open-minded. There are religious beliefs versus personal ethics – often in families, when children get caught in the middle – particularly if it isn't your sort of thing. The generations of today get lost at times, but don't necessarily look to the Lord for guidance; most are quite content to turn to booze and sex.

"Judged rightly by one, and not so by another, it makes no difference; you alone live with the actions, with the guilt that builds like a bad poison, slowly destroying your soul," Father Brannon continued, receiving some nods from those who had already opened their hearts and minds.

I took the words in, but questioned silently if a man or

woman could truly know whether their soul is damned by their actions, and can be saved on the day of their judgement.

I looked at Father Brannon, continuing his speech. It must have been a mighty hard job, to be a man of the cloth – especially these days. Having people turn up on your doorstep downhearted, needing your sermons and church music to warm their hearts and bring comfort, that there is some meaning to life.

So patient we can be, waiting for the Lord to reward us for our good deeds. A person takes up a position of the cloth to share God's love, and to provide guidance to those who lost their way; in return, they get a free pass into Heaven.

When I was younger, Father Brannon visited our school, and I asked why God allows people to do the bad things they do, shortly after finding out about my family's legacy. I think I was looking for the answers my parents and sister had failed to give me. He had answered with what seemed a simple quotation from the Bible: *"Free will. We all choose our own paths, though sometimes we can be pulled in certain directions, resulting from particular cruelties and injustices!"* He had spoken this to the whole class.

This was something my own mother mentioned to me

once. She had been brought to this country against her will, and received much cruelty. My father had saved her and offered her a new life with him.

But, that is another story for another time!

The point is, in life we are all offered choices and temptations. It is our decision whether or not we choose to walk down certain paths. We alone are responsible for going against certain laws God has set down.

When it comes to nearing our own end, we are so quick to make an act of contrition, hoping our sins will be forgiven. It's funny how open a person's heart can be toward God, when they fear the end of their life.

But it surely can't be as simple as to just say, *"I'm sorry,"* and not truly mean it in your heart. God can look into your soul, after all.

"It is difficult for some to control the darkness in their hearts; they are not always capable, or remorseful enough to be compelled to change their ways," Father Brannon continued. "If you don't really repent for your sins, then you can't expect to be truly forgiven. And, those who show deep, genuine regret will find God's healing hand removing heavy pains."

Looking around, I saw a sudden peace come over so many faces as the words continued, giving fresh hope to their lives. This was the peace of faith; how strongly and powerfully it brought comfort. People could rely on faith alone, even with so little proof that something truly exists.

Throughout history, man has fought wars in the name of faith, even slaughtering his own brother, staining himself in their blood. Here, God is not the only one who decides who lives and who dies. And, again God does not object to this. So, man has free will to choose another person's death.

We all have bad thoughts against God's teachings, including intentionally causing or wishing harm to other people. Can you honestly look back on however long your life is now, and say that you have never wished harm to another person? Some weigh up whether certain people deserve to die more than others. In many ways, this is how we choose our contracts. If you are being truthful, you cannot live your whole life and not admit there was at least one time you wished ill will toward another human being, for who they were, or what they may have done to you. Look deep down in your heart, and you'll realize it's just part of being human.

"There is darkness in all of us – whether they are mere thoughts, or wishes to call on the end of a life by God's hand, or another's," he continued again, as though he were reading my mind. "Often, when God does not hear these thoughts or prayers, it is by the hand of another that the wrath is brought down on the heads of those who do evil. But, still there is a price to be paid."

But, unlike God, we do not feel obligated to answer all requests.

Sometimes, the death of an evil man can be justice – particularly those whom the laws of man cannot touch. None of the lives we take are innocent.

"Those who serve God will strike down with a righteous fury he who attempts to poison his brother, take what is his and destroy all he owns." Father Brannon's voice rose now: "God does not take kindly to those who go against His word!"

I found some comfort myself in these words, and wondered how the rest of the family was feeling at that moment.

Those who kill with God on their side are not murderers, so they do not go against His word. Only the wicked sought revenge, and God always punished the wicked, without sparing or showing pity or mercy to those who go against His law. Those who question His will are punished, severely – just like the word Laurence had used the night before, on the train. People only choose to be good because they fear consequences; if there are no consequences, we give in to the chaos. The people who build lives on the foundations of others' suffering are aware of their actions, but they choose not to care.

So often we accept the terrible parts of life because they're so common, and they never really touch us, but so often they do the ones we know or love.

Does God have a plan for the world, or for each of us who live in it?

Sometimes life is a leap of faith, but so few are able to put their trust in a safety net they cannot see, and are fearful of a condemning plunge. I remember my mother saying to me: *"What we see in our lives drives us to either run or embrace it. Motivations lead down paths where our strength of faith can be tested."*

As I looked around at my friends and neighbours, I knew, truthfully, that there was at least one time they too had sinned, and on this day wished to amend. So easy it is to abruptly change our beliefs; to turn to the Lord and ask Him to save us from our situation.

My great grandfather was the same. I found one of his memoirs one day, in which he had written: *"God forgives sinners who open their hearts and ask Him to reveal Himself."*

The revelation, the form that He chooses – so divine and unique to each – must surely be a true miracle, so how can you not accept it?

I myself do believe in God: a higher power; a creator; an

architect.    I also believe in purpose; in each person choosing to face their destiny.

Now my time had come.    Maybe *I* was soon to be tested.

Despite my previous anxieties, I was strong, and chose with my own free will to walk the same path as my ancestors.  I trusted that faith in God would guide me on my way.

By the end of the sermon, I looked to my parents and smiled.  It seemed I was not the only one who had found comfort.

As usual, Father Brannon stood by the large church doors leading outside, shaking everyone's hand and thanking them all for coming as they left – plus a good word to the family members who were unable to attend.

Opening the small gate into the car park area, we were suddenly approached by a familiar figure: Uncle Harry's right-hand man, Victor.

The newsflash about the bombing at the construction site had taken us all aback that morning.  Hearing of the death of Jake, the security guard, had us all on edge.  But, my father had remained calm; he told us we needed to just be patient and carry on.

Now that Victor had come to see my father, I knew that Uncle Harry was calling us in for assistance.  What luck:

my chance to get some real, first-hand experience!

Returning quickly home, my father had gone into his office and taken his pistol from the lockbox, slipping it into his jacket pocket. He gave a cautionary nod to my mother, who would make preparations around the house while we were out, then we were off to pay a visit to Uncle Harry at the hospital.

I couldn't help but wonder just what preparations mother was making.

# CHAPTER 14

### Sunday 11:00 p.m.
### Ravenfall – the emergency ward.

Always keep your eyes open and your ear to the ground, because you never know when trouble is on the horizon. Some of us look harder than others; most just wait for it to happen.

Who can truly say when the next bad thing is going to happen, from one moment to the next? Even those who claim to be psychic are not above the occasional bit of bad luck! The only future that I would choose to see – if any – would be the good coming my way. No worries about spoiling the surprise; it would just make the anticipation that much more exciting.

Unexpected trouble was a rarity in Ravenfall, and when it did stir its head, Uncle Harry was usually able to handle most matters.

Approaching Uncle Harry's private room, another man dressed like Victor was seated outside the door; my father recognized him to be Hector, Victor's brother and only remaining family. He wasn't as broad as Victor, but he looked just as tough. He nodded as we walked past.

Entering the room, we saw there was a guy dressed in a smart suit, talking to Uncle Harry by his bed: it was Harry's Lawyer, who also happened to be Abigail's father, Mr. Terrence. He had represented Harry for the past five years now. Occasionally, Harry used him to collect and put together files, with certain names and details... I don't really need to say anymore, so I won't! He wouldn't have been my father's choice, or mine, for reasons already explained. He and Uncle Harry were currently talking over the police investigation into the explosion at the construction site.

"Somebody called the cops, statements have been taken from passers-by, they've probably viewed the C.C.T.V., yet apparently nobody has seen anything!" He took a moment to wipe his glasses. "In my opinion, this is down to extortionists."

This was old territory for Harry. The city police had already requestioned him, but he hadn't been able or chosen not to give any reasons why he might be coming under attack. There were only a few names on a list of people he trusted, and we had just arrived.

Excusing himself, Terrence picked up his briefcase and brushed quickly past my father, leaving us to carry on our own business. There were some things he didn't know and others he didn't want to, even if he was already an accessory by law.

Uncle Harry smiled when he saw me, and invited me over to give him a hug. "You're getting to be a big girl. How does it feel to be liberated?" he asked.

"I've only left school, not jail," I laughed.

Looking at him at that moment, in his private hospital room, all bandaged up around the head, I ashamedly couldn't help but count my own lucky stars.

"When I was your age, my father sent me to boarding school, and those walls made me feel like a prisoner; the teachers were my wardens. I wasn't sorry to say goodbye to any of it."

"I thought that was because you were expelled?" I countered, quickly.

My father broke in now, quickly moving the conversation to the reason we were there.

"I need to know how much you told the local and city police, and what you've chosen to hold back," he said, taking up the role of a complete professional.

Uncle Harry looked back at me again, somewhat puzzled. "Is it alright... to talk...?"

"Izzy is starting her training, as of today," my sister Bethany said, standing by the door, looking out for any potential interruptions from the hospital staff.

Uncle Harry minded my father with curiosity, who just went straight back to business.

The possibility of a crazed bomber coming after Uncle Harry troubled my father, who had guessed something serious was starting to stir around town. Now confirmed, he immediately set to asking the necessary questions, no different to the ones the cops had already asked – only now Uncle Harry was more willing to co-operate fully.

"I honestly don't know who would break the peace this way; I haven't had any harsh dealings with anybody recently," he said, taking a sip of water. "The police think it might be a personal grudge, but if this attack was made by a professional, then whoever hired him is making no effort to hide the fact someone is gunning for me."

My father clearly recognized concern in his voice. "Then we have to find them – the bomber and his employer – before they succeed." As my father said it, he was addressing my sister, who nodded, still keeping watch outside.

It was reassuring to hear my father's voice take such a firm and assertive approach, to the threat which was now facing our home and our community. However, to overcome certain enemies took more than courage and steel; you also had to rely on intelligence – your greatest weapon.

The cops would no doubt be doing their best at that moment, but they were not privy to the resources available to people in our profession. All they knew was what the evidence was telling them: that both bombs were made by the same person; the fragments recovered were identical in both cases.

The odds of the bomber being a specialist – probably military trained – were also high, so they would be looking over the usual suspects, with certain past records of this sort of history.

But, even if they did find this guy, then what? It wouldn't be advisable to have regular officers of the law from Ravenfall or The Big City to move in on someone like this; he could be carrying explosives and have suicidal tendencies.

Still, my father figured this man was not so out of control as that, due to the sophistication of his work.

Without any style, there is no glory, just catastrophe.

My father believed it more likely to be the work of an outsider, even from The Big City; the technology was too advanced to be used by anyone associated with The Organization.

This seemed to be something of an obsession: first going after Harry then going after his business, and not caring who else got hurt in the process. It didn't sound like the people who ran The Big City; it wasn't really their style. What was the sense in making innocent people suffer or die? It wasn't good for business in these modern times.

"If there weren't any deaths, they would not get as much attention," my sister quickly cut in, indicating they wanted attention pointing toward Harry. He had nearly been the first victim, but they had failed, so now he was to be labelled the cause.

So far, the attacks had been on Harry and his business, but nobody had brought up the subject of extortion, as Terrence had suggested; no demands of that kind had been made.

Though, it did turn out that Harry had received a strange letter that morning, in a brown envelope. On an A4 sheet were a group of numbers, cut out from what looked to be magazines, in different sizes and style types: *"25"*, *"11"*, *"30"* and *"5"*. Part of a cypher, perhaps? The killer was taunting; trying to make a game of all this. The numbers had no clear significance to Harry, and they weren't much use to us at that moment, so my sister just slipped the note into her jacket; she would set to work on them later.

Right now, we needed a place to begin: preferably, a person with the answers to help us with our investigation into this assassination plot. Without any motive; the possibility of finding the person who wanted to do Uncle

Harry harm was going to be very difficult.

There aren't many defences against aggressive human nature. True, they were still human, flesh and blood, but we couldn't kill what we couldn't see, and this guy was a professional, able to destroy then disappear without trace!

I could not deny all of this was very exciting, and sent another buzz of adrenalin through my body, forcing me to place my hands in my pocket, so nobody would see my hands shake. I had to remind myself that innocent people were also now at risk, with one casualty already, and that was a code even our family didn't like to break. Our family never used bombs to complete a contract; the wrong people usually got hurt. Collateral damage was something we never allowed.

One target, one bullet, no fuckups!

In some ways this was now personal, even to us, as it was starting to affect the community, and our family had a history with this village; we would do anything to protect it. The question of what we'd actually do when we found the people responsible was simple to answer: get what we needed, then bury the problem in a deep hole with their brains blown out.

But, we still needed somewhere to begin.

Thankfully, it turned out that there was a witness: Sergeant Braccard had come by to tell Uncle Harry that

Laurence had seen somebody acting suspiciously on the construction site, the morning before the explosion. Harry had made a call prior to our meeting, asking him to drop in and explain.

Now seeing us all present, in conference, he was a little taken aback – especially by seeing me again so soon. But, he gave nothing away. We knew, of course, that he was trustworthy.

Going into detail about the delivery that had been made the morning of, and the fact that a strange figure had been seen by him, walking around the site, there was a good chance that we'd got our first break.

The delivery truck had come from a regular supplier, and now we had somewhere to begin; the driver was our best shot at finding the bomber, or at least getting a better physical description.

No doubt the cops would also be looking into it, but we had our own methods.

It was usually against our family's reputation to turn to these sorts of tactics; heavy-handed persuasion we preferred to leave to others.

"We could always bring in my... associate," my sister suggested, tentatively.

All eyes now fell on her; my father warily regarded her suspiciously. "Mr. X..." The way he said the name sounded like a bad taste in the mouth.

"Can we control him?" Uncle Harry asked, cautiously.

My sister let a slight smile slip at the corners of her mouth. "Well, to a degree."

Our father, however, didn't seem convinced.

"Maybe a wild card would come in handy on this job," Harry jumped in, quickly, "considering the opposition. The man has knowledge of technology and the people who dabble in it."

My father relented, though clearly unhappy about bringing in another party on this – particularly a wild card from outside the family.

You see, when it comes to clients, we deliver only efficiency. Our tradecraft is second to none; old-school rules still apply. Why? Because there's a fine line between a contract killer and a psychopathic serial killer!

In real life, we try to leave as little carnage behind as possible. If you want to make it look like a serial killer, go hire somebody else. Brutal and butchering is not our style; despite the fact that we're in the business of cutting up meat, we don't enjoy making people suffer, or leaving our targets in pieces. We're not here to set examples, just to perform a necessary service.

Of course, there are those who do take great pleasure in their work.

# CHAPTER 15

**Sunday 1:45 p.m.**
**The Big City slums.**

There are only two types of contract fulfilment in this business: making something look like what it is, or making it look like something else – the latter is not always easy.

Everything has to be planned down to the last detail; there's no room for mistakes when you're a contract killer. It is best to get in, do what has to be done, then leave just as fast.

When it comes to a business transaction of an illegitimate nature, there is always the vendor and his escort. And then there is the buyer… who should always have the manners to be on time.

The only time you ever really want to be late is the moment you are going to die.

At times, life can be very scary. You never really know who's who in this world. Some people are just cruel by nature, while some are able to show mercy and compassion. Then there are those who can be seduced into choosing to live in both worlds!

There is nothing worse than having to do your work in a dirty basement. Not exactly the most ideal of spots: a confined space with no other exit points.

When an order came in over the phone, a time and place was set and all parties were required to attend in a prompt manner. The vendor, a small, fat man by the name of Mellark, was currently building quite a nice reputation, running angles all over the city, as though Christmas had come early. Cashing in on all the top buyers, who sent more business his way.

He was a bad man, into guns and drugs, selling them one apiece or as large stock. If you had the money, he had the best prices in the whole city.

So far, his day couldn't have gone any better. The large gym bag in his hand contained around five kilos of heroin, ready for sale.

Fortunately, everything great in life is only temporary – much like his product.

Hearing the door open at the top of the stairs, the sound of footsteps slowly descending invoked in him a businesslike attitude, as he straightened his tie and pulled his trousers up at the belt. As the tall figure of a dark-skinned man came into view now, he caught his breath.

The light-blue Hawaiian shirt amused Mr. X, who was dressed smartly in a dark, long coat.

Mellark seemed sober and cautious enough now to hold a serious conversation, which was rare for people who peddled drugs.

Only, Mr. X was a first-time customer, about whom he hadn't heard anything bad or anything good. Without a reliable referral, it made him something of a risk, and it wasn't good to mix drugs and high stakes. Hence the reason for the ape at his side – a grim-looking character.

Mr. X lowered his eyes to the gym bag, while Mellark focused on the briefcase that Mr. X was carrying down the stairs and across the floor, stopping not more than ten feet away.

The only thing an assassin should be cautious of is another killer. Vigilance is the key to survival, as trust and honour are seldom commodities within the criminal world. Mr. X looked over the large man, noting the misshapen left hip, where the gun was hidden from view under his sports top. These guys were just hired muscle, with very little discipline. One minute everything can seem to be going smoothly, then the eyes start to shift around and the body language can appear shaken and nervous; then comes the smell of fear in the air. Before you know it, a weapon is discharged and everything goes dark.

"The price we set was five large, and that's better than the market value. You won't find this type of quality product anywhere else for that," Mellark assured, with his best sales line.

There was a routine to how exchanges were conducted: first came the merchandise inspection, before any cash was brought to the table.

"You ever try it?" Mr. X asked, but received no quick answer. "So, how do you know it's such great quality?"

Mellark was already starting to regret accepting the meeting with this smartmouth yuppie. "What do you want? I'm not selling washing machines!"

Mr. X now cracked a tiny smile for the first time. "Well, if you were I wouldn't be here; my clients don't like the flavour of lemon detergent."

Mellark had a humourless disposition and very little patience. "We're not going to have a problem, are we?" he pressed a little. "It isn't polite to walk into a man's place and question the quality of his product; my feelings get hurt easily..."

"As could your face," Mr. X threatened, unprovoked by the big guy's hand twitching at his waist.

Usually at these moments an apology would be given, seeing the large ape rubbing the top band of his trousers, anticipating the remedy to this dilemma. There's always a man standing behind another, but that particular man is not necessarily stronger than the other's philosophy.

The ability to foresee the future is every gambler's dream; better than an ace up the sleeve. Every man has seen good luck and bad luck, and recognizes the difference between the two when one or the other comes calling. Some guys are like high rollers; they like to put everything down on the table, gambling their life, as though there was no tomorrow. Walking into a room with another shooter, you had to have ice water flowing through your veins; not the slightest drop of sweat in sight. The only advantage over everyone else is your ability to think, throughout the entire situation.

And, when a gun is drawn, you had to have every intention of pulling that trigger, because the other guy isn't going to wait.

You might say it's like the Wild West: a duel of nerves.

Most don't even bother to aim; they just point and shoot from the hip, hoping to hit the target.

But, stress will always kill you faster than a bullet.

Mr. X wasn't looking to commit suicide – just homicide.

Dropping the briefcase to the ground by his foot, he raised and extended his arm; a tiny automatic appeared like magic from his sleeve.

A cold clear mind puts the other guy in a box, while you reap the rewards. The ape's body and gun hit the floor right by Mellark's feet.

Of course they always run, because they know better than to even think of reaching for that gun. Making for the stairs, Mellark hadn't even got halfway before the bullet struck him in the back of the thigh, making him drop forward in a cry of pain.

The feel of the stranger's grip, and of being flipped over to gaze into a barrel which still had one round left, made him growl through gritted teeth: "Do you have any idea who you're fucking with?"

"My employer regrets it had to come to this, but there was an understanding that you weren't supposed to be operating on this side of the city." Mr. X came slowly over to the stairs. "They understand a man has to make money, but only smart business keeps you in money."

In this line of work, there are excuses for all kinds of bad behaviour. Some people say that the old-school days are gone. Nobody of the new generation knows how to conduct good business anymore. Back then, there was a certain charisma and style necessary, if you wanted to make friends and avoid enemies.

"They've decided to let you walk away this time," Mr. X said, retracting the gun underneath his sleeve. "Think yourself fortunate that you didn't end up like your friend over there; it would be a shame to ruin that shirt!"

Mellark had made the mistake of underestimating this

man who, as a hired hood, clearly had a degree in the science of violence and pain.

"It might be wise to lie low for a while; let that leg have some time to heal," he said, in a civilized tone. "Do we have a clear understanding?"

Mellard winced and nodded, as Mr. X ascended back upstairs, with the empty briefcase still in his hand. It was a gift from his father, so it held too much sentimentality to part with.

No man lives forever, but he can live longer than the next. So far, Mr. X had a good head start. How a man carries himself tells you all you need to know – though, on the inside, the fear always remains present. It's the wise gambler who knows when to cash in their chips and call it a day.

This isn't the sort of business you get out of so easily, especially if you're considered to be a valuable asset. You can try and get out, to start a new life, but where would you even begin? The past always stays with you – it just affects different people in different ways.


Everyone has their own coping mechanisms – not all are good for their health.

Mr. X liked to have a little drink after doing his business.

Seeing a contract through made one appreciate his fine class of whisky even more.

Sitting in one of the finest bars in The Big City, taking the end stool at the counter, he smiled pleasantly to the woman in the low-cut frock, as she refilled his glass. Taking a small sip, he allowed the sensation to wash over him.

He picked up a familiar scent, now creeping in over his right shoulder, after the door behind him had closed. Seeing it was a friend, he remained composed, allowing my sister and I to approach. We noticed not the slightest shift in body language.

Holding the glass as though it were a baby's hand, he looked up at the mirror on the back wall, taking Bethany fully in his sight.

"You look like you haven't slept much," he charmed. "Missing me already?"

I smirked at the question, but quickly wiped it from my face as though it were a bad stain. My sister indicated for me to take a seat in a booth, where she could still see me. Since I was there to take my sister's lead, I left the two of them alone, as they clearly had some catching up to do.

"What's with the young blood?" he asked as she sidled up, keeping her distance slightly. My sister always came strapped, whenever visiting the city.

Though I had been here the night before, now the atmosphere on the streets seemed quite different, looking out of the front window. The woman behind the bar was looking toward me with a questioning gaze. I had forgotten to bring my I.D. with me this time.

"My sister Izzy is on a ride-along, starting her new career in the family business," she said plainly, watching his every move.

Mr. X now made a gesture which immediately removed the hostility from the bartender's face, calling over to ask me if I wanted anything: a glass of milk, perhaps? I scowled, bending one of the table's cardboard coasters between my hands.

"She got a short fuse on her, that one," he quipped, noting Bethany was keeping her hand close to her waist. "Glad to see you've become more restrained. Care to partake of lunch with me?"

My sister had the reflexes of a coiled snake. If anything were to go down, she'd be responsible for me, so she decided to play it a little cooler.

"I haven't heard from you in a while, so forgive my cautious manner," she said, sitting down on the stool next to his. "I know we parted on good terms last time, but you never know when a change of heart might change the status of a relationship."

Using people for sex – disposable pleasures rather than meaningful relationships – was a common social norm in our particular circle. It wasn't a good idea to let people too close, or under the skin.

With Mr. X, thinking about oneself came very easy; he had never really trusted or truly relied on anyone, throughout his entire career. My sister and I, on the other hand, had been raised with the understanding that family were the only ones you should rely on. Sharing an assignment with another contractor is extremely rare and risky.

Even if it's your own sister's boyfriend!

In this business, dealing with people means one of two things. Money is a popular topic in our society. It comes in one hand and goes out the other.

My sister ordered me a deluxe cheeseburger and fries, while she and Mr. X chose a light salad without any dressing.

Uncle Harry's predicament was, of course, the main topic of discussion, and even Mr. X was surprised to hear about what had been occurring over in Ravenfall.

It is wise not to underestimate a bomber; they are usually smart. This one had already rigged two bombs, and left no trace that led directly to a name or cause. My sister already knew that we weren't dealing with some enthusiastic amateur; a man didn't embark on an enterprise such as this if he was not completely confident in his own expertise. This had already been demonstrated by his first bomb, which Harry had only just survived, thanks to sheer luck.

Mr. X offered to make a few enquiries through the network. My sister knew hardly anything about who he worked for, or where he received his contracts. He had "friends" or, to be more accurate, *contacts* in a lot of places, who had ears and might come in very handy if you wanted to find out why someone had a price on their head. And, most importantly, who had picked up the contract.

There weren't too many local talents who nowadays used car bombs, so it had to be an outsider. This made things easy; you couldn't just turn up out of nowhere these days, without somebody noticing you on a screen. Even the Big City Organization had people who worked at airports and railway stations on the payroll, to report any unusual sightings which flagged up.

Mr. X was a legend in our circle. A freelancer, who wasn't the type to get cooped up in an office – or in a binding relationship, for that matter. He took a great deal of pride in his work, and never allowed anything to jeopardize his reputation.

Though "pride" was considered to be a deadly sin, the

fraternity recognized the importance of self-esteem, especially in regard to one's own work ethic. The only downside was that it could make a person arrogant, if not controlled.

He was completely ruthless when he had to be, and his father was no different, though his mother was a little disappointed with his life choices. He was charming, highly intelligent and capable of making lots of money spilling human blood – so, generally a good provider to bring home to your parents! But he wasn't completely cold-blooded; he did have this strange, unexpected honour at times.

But, working for years with detached emotion eventually takes its toll, even on the toughest.

It had actually been a chance meeting which brought him and my sister together, and they had chosen to keep in contact, beginning a sort of monogamous relationship, but maintaining certain boundaries. This seemed to be continuing, despite the little predicament with his nephew. Of course, they still had to be discreet about their relationship; they didn't want our unique community to know they were dating the competition. Not that there are any rules; it's just not wise to allow your weaknesses to become exposed.

I think it even frightened my sister at times, just how close the two of them had become.

Watching the two of them, all the hardness seemed to melt away like ice when they reached a mutual connection, looking into each other's eyes. I started to suck a little too loudly on my straw, causing that connection to break.

He immediately took his leave for a moment, to make the necessary enquiries.

Love can be so complex at times: from day to day there are obstacles you have to navigate, to keep a relationship as you want it to be – especially when you cross a line that involves family. Of course, in the case of Bethany it had only been business… and self-defence.

They clearly hadn't spoken of it since, and I didn't like to pry; it was between the two of them. We had to stay focused on finding the bomber.

Any reservations which existed before, about bringing in Mr. X to help, had now been resolved, as far as my sister was concerned. I knew my father was still going to be a little skeptical, but that was just his protective nature, like any parent. It wasn't like they were going to disappear together and retire – that only happens in the movies. Honestly, the topic of marriage is something which never came up.

However, since we have a bloodline to maintain, it was a subject which was bound to be brought up sooner or later – though, in this case, it would be much later.

# CHAPTER 16

**Sunday 3:00 p.m.**

**The Big City slums.**

Half of this job is about waiting, and the time between the start and the end – the kill – is fucking boring; you end up anticipating the moment when it finally arrives.

It's not an aphrodisiac; it's nothing to get too excited about, because taking a human life is nothing like stepping on ants with your foot. There was no question, no doubt in my mind, that when my time came to do it, I would feel something. I wasn't quite sure how I'd handle it.

Sitting in the back seat of Mr. X's car, I looked out of the window while the radio played a pleasant classical tune, helping my sister and Mr. X to remain composed and focused.

Some people are afraid of silence, but it can give a person time to think. A certain part of your mind travels into your own soul.

It was, of course, important not to drift off too far – that made you sloppy. The paramount thing was to think about what had to be done.

The waiting, however, can really do a person's head in. Sitting around quietly in a car, smoking yourself to death – or chewing gum in my sister's case, since she decided to give up. This was amusing to Mr. X, seeing as they normally couldn't get through one date without having her ask to bum one of his, and she never paid him back. At that moment, she was trying to exercise self-control, despite the wafts of smoke coming across from his side of the car.

"Did you want me to open a window?" he asked, but she ignored the bait. Turning the music up, he smiled pleasantly, taking a big drag.

He'd never really worked a job near Ravenfall before; the only time that had come close had been a personal matter – which had even been to Uncle Harry's benefit.

Executing the man who had been responsible for the death of his nephew had put an old vendetta to rest for Harry, as well as getting rid of the competition, to buy up the land to build his mall.

Sitting quietly for a few moments more, my sister looked down the narrow street, toward the store where our target usually did his shopping. Mr. X had gotten the name of the truck driver from the supply company, which was under contract with Harry, not to mention some of his other acquaintances. It was quite fortunate they were willing to play ball, giving us the address.

Arriving twenty minutes earlier, we were now waiting for the driver – a man named Franklin – to leave his apartment, pick up his evening supplies and make the same way back again. People were so predictable when it came to following routines. Since he lived alone, there would be no interruptions or complications.

When it came to getting answers, Mr. X had a flair for persuasion, and he was very gifted. A man with his reputation was something to be admired. He had been in the business a long time, and had managed to survive purely on his instincts, which came in handy when telling the truth from a lie – and he wasn't a fan of liars.

It was going to be an interesting afternoon – not that I enjoy watching people in pain. If the guy was smart, he would co-operate to avoid any extreme unpleasantness.

Another fifteen minutes passed and played out exactly the way we had anticipated; Franklin came out of his building and walked past our car, making for the store.

"Okay, get ready," Mr. X said, in an authoritative voice. "We make this fast and silent."

I caught a disapproving glare in my sister's eyes; clearly parameters had not been laid out as to who was actually running this operation. I was just there to observe two professionals at work.

Walking back up the street, with groceries in hand, Franklin hadn't even seen us coming.

Mr. X and my sister cornered him at his front door, and a swift punch from my sister to the jaw sent him to the ground, unconscious.

"Maybe we should have waited until he got to his room," I called, from behind them.

Mr. X addressed my sister quizzically, as well: "Now we have to carry him up!" I followed up with a tiny smile.

Mr. X reached down and picked up the key. "You and your sis definitely have your hands full!" With that, he disappeared inside, leaving me and my slightly red-faced sister to carry the load.


By the time Franklin had come round, we had taped him to a chair in his kitchen, with both his arms bound at the front.

My sister was sitting at the table, while Mr. X was making himself a cup of fresh coffee.

Slightly dazed, Franklin's eyes looked at the both of them, then slightly paused on me with curiosity – I don't know why it is I have such an effect on people.

"If it's money you're looking for—" he began, but my sister quickly silenced him. The best way to keep someone quiet? Stick a sharp blade in their mouth!

"All we're looking for are some simple answers to straightforward questions," she said, direct and to the point – as she liked things to be.

Taking a sip from his mug, Mr. X took one of the chairs and placed it in front of Franklin, sitting down in a cool and composed manner. Slowly, my sister removed the blade from his mouth and leant back in her own chair once more, not breaking eye contact. You see, everything you want to know about a person is in the eyes. Fear is the easiest thing to spot, meaning the truth is sure to follow.

"Well, is someone going to ask, or am I supposed to guess?" Franklin said, looking from her to Mr. X, who was still drinking, leisurely.

There's a difference between sarcasm and a dose of skepticism. At this time, he was just acting as though he wasn't afraid – but then, they all do in the beginning. Sometimes it is just a matter of waiting for the fear to set in. When they see no escape, there is no use in holding out.

"Yesterday you made a delivery to a certain construction site, but the delivery was not scheduled for that day. You had someone with you... someone we're interested in finding," my sister said, bluntly.

There was a long pause; the man's expression did not change. "I'm only a driver; my boss tells me where to go and what to—" he began, but was silenced by the feel of hot coffee splashing his face, as Mr. X threw the contents of his mug straight at him, with a disapproving snarl.

"You should change to a different brand," he said, placing the now empty mug on the table. "The kind of coffee a man chooses to drink says a lot about him – just like his appearance and attitude. The lady asked you a question."

Franklin took a moment to recover from the slight burning sensation on his face, spitting and blowing throw his nose. "Kiss my ass!"

I allowed myself a little smirk; the guy wasn't smart after all.

Some people talk a little too tough; it gives the wrong impression. Everyone appears tough at first, but nobody wants to pay the price that comes with it.

We had no truth serum to hand, so the only option was torture.

But, you didn't always have to break the body first.

Looking back to the table, Mr. X spied a deck of cards, then looked back at Franklin.

"You a gambling man, Franklin?" he asked, picking them up and shuffling them in his hands. "I myself like to play the occasional hand, from time to time."

He reached down and took Franklin's left-hand index finger. "My personal favourite game is 'snap' – I don't use cards, though." Mr. X started to squeeze.

When it came to Mr. X, he was not afraid of inflicting pain on anybody. And, a master when it came to pushing the right buttons. It wasn't the regular, dime-store psychological bullshit, either; it was as though he had the ability to look right into your soul, and cling to your desperation not to feel pain. All it took then was the right amount of pressure…

Franklin started to wince and now looked my way.

It was in moments like this that it was important to stay unemotional, even when the bone finally broke and the cries and moans blurted from his mouth.

In truth, I really didn't like seeing this. I looked at my sister, whose own composure hadn't changed.

"There are nine more little piggies," Mr. X said, reaching down for the next.

"Stop! Stop! Stop!" Franklin pleaded, looking up, teary-eyed. "I only drove the guy; I had no idea what he had in mind."

I was glad the man was quickly seeing reason; I'm not sure I could have stood there and watched his other fingers ending up the same way: bent out of shape and swollen.

"What did he pay you?" Mr. X asked.

"Five… five hundred and…" Franklin stopped and looked briefly up to the cabinet.

My curiosity got the better of me, so I took down the biscuit tin on top of it, opening it. I was a little taken aback to find at least half a kilo of white powder in a cellophane bag, inside, along with a wad of cash in small denominations. The guy was clearly dealing, as well as indulging in smack – which, personally, I really had a problem with. A girl from my school had seriously overdosed one time on junk.

"That's worth a lot of money," Franklin said, "so why don't we make a deal?"

The guy offering us the drugs as a bribe made me even sicker. "Do we fucking look like drug dealers?!" I protested, tearing the bag open and moving over, to pour the contents over his head.

It was people like this who made the world an ugly place. Such people are toxins in our society; their poison pollutes and spoils. I despise everything they do and stand for, and it makes me angry when people think we all live by their standards.

Sitting there now, covered from head to toe in white powder, Franklin continuously coughed and choked. Grabbing his jaw, I felt like tipping the rest down his throat.

Mr. X quickly stepped in and pulled me away. "Easy, little sister. You've already made him a snowman; let's not make him melt away just yet."

Taking some more gum out of her pocket, my sister unwrapped and rolled it up in her finger, before slipping it into her mouth. "You'll have to forgive our companion; she's new to this."

I couldn't believe she was apologizing for my actions! Not to mention downsizing me in front of this man. She wouldn't have done that to Mr. X.

"The guy is just a small fish," Mr. X whispered in my ear, pulling me back again. "If you haven't understood the brief, we're supposed to be going after the prize catch."

I took a moment and realized that he was right; we had to keep emotion out of this.

Besides, looking around this room, there were some interesting accessories standing out. Some of the goods looked new and expensive, yet didn't fit with this man – especially the feminine beauty treatment packs.

So, the guy was into petty theft as well?

Probably stole from his own neighbours, like Harry's son-in-law Martin – and we all know what happened to him for his crime.

"Maybe we should try a different tack," I said, picking up a bottle and moving over to the kitchen sink, uncapping it.

"Don't... Listen..." Franklin again begged, "my daughter's birthday's coming up. I just wanted to be able to get her something special!"

There was a picture on the wall of a family portrait. He looked a little cleaner and healthier in it than he did right now, but drugs do that to a person.

It turned out the guy only saw his daughter once a week, on weekends, since his separation. Maybe he was a druggie, but he still loved his daughter. I know everyone has a story – a reason for doing what they do – but that was no excuse for crime; for dealing poison which took the lives of young people like his daughter.

"Well, if you still want to make it to her party," my sister jumped in now, "I suggest you tell us what we want to know."

And, of course, he did.

The offer had come from "The Salesman", a person both my sister and Mr. X knew very well, so we had the lead we needed.

Cutting Franklin free, we cautioned him to keep his head down for the next couple of days, and not to get in contact with anyone. Now that we knew who he was, and his family, we had enough leverage to leave him still breathing, and his daughter still with a father.

Whether that was a good thing, I wasn't sure, to be perfectly honest.

"What happened in there?" Mr. X said, as we came out of the building, returning to his car. "I thought you were in training, here to watch and learn?"

My sister quickly stepped in: "She's a little new. Just give her time."

"I can speak for myself; I don't need you justifying my actions like you did in there," I said harshly, though she didn't show any sign of regret.

Mr. X took a moment, then looked at me seriously. "Would you really have done it... taken that man's life?"

"No more than you—" I stopped myself, not wishing to push any further.

"How would we then have got the information we needed?"

My sister came up and put her hand on my shoulder. "You've got to remember the old motto: *'This is nothing personal'*."

"I know that, but that doesn't mean I was out of control!" I protested, shrugging her off. "I got him to talk, without using any heavy-handed tactics."

Mr, X clapped his hands in a patronizing manner, which even annoyed my sister. I was about to say something, but my sister gave my shoulder a little squeeze. The caution in her eyes made me apply a vice. But the trouble with biting one's tongue: you end up with a bad taste of blood in your mouth.

Getting back in the car, we drove back home, where I

was told to call it a day. They went off to follow up on the next lead, which probably meant a little risk was involved.

And, it was that very risk that my mother had been seeing to while we'd been out.

Father was working in the shop, and Mother asked me to follow her into his office. There, I found a selection of new guns on my father's desk.

"So, *these* are the preparations!" I said, feeling a tingling build in the palm of my hand. "Where do they come from? The Big City?"

She nodded, picking up an automatic. "We always restock; never use the same weapon on another job. Bullets can be traced – but not without a gun."

I thought she was exaggerating at first; my sister Bethany always carried her own Sig Sauer pistol. But then I realized that one pistol looked the same as its brother.

My father preferred the Colt, which is the one my mother was currently handling: removing the magazine from the handle and pulling back on the slide, to clear the chamber.

"Izzy, you are a clever girl. What I'm about to say now, I don't want you to feel as though I'm treating you like a child," she said, carefully. Something told me she was about to get serious, and I always found these moments difficult, because most of the time they didn't really fit her nature; it was like she was adopting an alter ego.

"These are instruments of death. When you pick one up, you are doing so to take a life," she said.

I nodded simply, remembering my father telling me something similar before. "I'm no stranger to firearms; I've been hunting—"

"Izzy!" she cut me off, quickly.

The mood suddenly became heavy between us, as she reloaded the gun and handed it to me, with the barrel facing toward her – very improper, considering the safety was off. When she let go, I began to move it away.

She ordered me to keep it in place. "I want you to point that at me, Izzy, and place your finger carefully on the trigger."

I shook my head immediately. Had she lost her mind?

But, she grabbed it and aimed it toward her chest again, just over her heart, and let go, keeping eye contact with me. I wanted to put it down, but I had to obey my mother; it was the deal we had made.

"How do you feel, Izzy?" she asked. Through her eyes, inside, I could see only emptiness.

My hand began to tremble, and my eyes started to fill with tears. Why was this happening?

If she asked, I would not do it; I could not pull the

trigger! I actually begged, silently: *God, please don't let those words come out of her mouth!*

But, instead she quickly took it back from me, and came around to give me a tight embrace. I, too, held her to me just as tightly. I couldn't stop the tears, as my hands came up to my face. We now withdrew from each other, and were eye-to-eye once more.

"I never want you to ever aim a gun at anybody again," she said, slowly, "unless you intend to pull that trigger and accept the consequences."

The words – her voice – seemed cold. But I nodded, not arguing or saying anything.

She then sent me to my room, and again I cried, closing the door behind me. What had just happened?

Slowly, I slid down the door, sitting and resting my head on my knees, trying to forget what had just happened in my father's office. Then I stopped, and began to remember my mother's words: *"Accept the consequences."* It had been a lesson; my mother had been teaching me. My training had begun.

And here I was, sitting on the floor and crying like a baby.

Picking myself up, I wasn't sure if I was supposed to go downstairs, to tell my mother everything was alright or not, but I honestly couldn't face her at that moment.

Did that mean that I had failed?

I began to feel so frustrated that I suddenly dropped to the floor, face down, and started out in a set of push-ups and crunches. I found a new question repeating itself, over and over in my head: *At what point do you stop having to prove yourself?*

It bothered me that my mother had acted the way she had, and that my own sister didn't think I belonged on this side of the family business. It was perhaps true that my inexperience was dangerous, and if I was not careful could slow them down – or worse, get somebody killed! Maybe bowing out gracefully was the right thing to do?

But I still wanted to be included. Hopefully, when something useful turned up, I would be let back in play again.

I hit my knuckles into the floor. Had I not learnt anything?! This wasn't a game; it was life and death, and at the end someone was going to die. At that moment, I found myself not wanting to pull the trigger more than ever. It didn't even matter that our family had a job to do.

Having Mr. X along as an invited guest was starting to make things interesting. Now that he and my sister were working alone together, I had no doubt they would find some time to do some personal catching up – something I wouldn't be sorry to miss being around!

What draws a woman to a man of such darkness and violence?

The answer in this case was simple: deep down, they shared the same passion. Each was not afraid to give in to their darkest desires; they chose not to deny themselves what they really want. Right then, I imagined that was the rough feel of hands and wild, hungry lips.

It made me think back to my own time with Laurence on the train, and I wondered how he compared to Mr. X. But then, I'm really not prepared to share those thoughts. As much as I do want to be open and accurate, you have to appreciate that certain aspects of personal life are not meant for public knowledge!

The fact that my sister and I have chosen to write our adventures for the world to know is already a slight breach of professionalism, and is only tolerable as long as we mask it as mere fiction – that, I will leave for you to decide.

Collapsing backward and breathing heavily, I looked up at the ceiling and allowed my mind to finally clear. All this anxiety was doing me no good.

I suddenly heard my father's voice, calling me from downstairs. We were supposed to be going out together, to get some more training in for the day.

I was hesitant, perhaps not wishing for the lessons to continue. But I had made a commitment, and was determined to see this through.

Changing quickly, I looked to my reflection. Again, I could see a slight change in my features. It was not just the red eyes, but as though something was starting to reach outward.

Could it be that from this day forward I was slowly transforming into someone else?

So far, my inexperience and emotions were the biggest hurdles to overcome. If I was going to do this for real, I would have to work harder to detach myself. It's easier when you feel nothing at all – which is why Mr. X was so good at what he did, feeling neither good nor bad about the actions of his hands or weapons, which was important. Mother had only just taught that to me.

But, how exactly do you begin to separate the good from the bad inside yourself?

Each of us has a little of Heaven and Hell in us. Temptation versus morals compels us to do either good or evil.

You might not think that the concept of right and wrong is a priority to a killer, and for some this is so, but to my family it is important to care about something in life – I hope you have at least learnt that from reading this book so far. If you follow me still, you may even find that you have learnt something significant in these pages.

There are times in life that we are all faced with difficult questions, and the journey of discovery is not always so straightforward sometimes as others. When you don't have a moral compass to guide you, it's so easy to lose your way.

# CHAPTER 17

## Sunday 4:25 p.m.
## Ravenfall – the emergency ward.

Everyone has suffered a traumatic experience at one time in their life.

The scare – the fear for one's own life – makes a person see everything from a completely new perspective. Living and dying are concepts that even we as humans choose not to explore in depth, until our own mortality is threatened. Some choose therapy, while others just try and deal with their demons in their own way.

But shutting up, sucking it up and trying to get through by yourself isn't always productive.

Uncle Harry was a prisoner to his thoughts, as his body lay bandaged.

Most burn and blast-related injuries are usually complicated, and looking down at himself, Harry already had so many scars, created from a life of violence. The shrapnel had cut his back up pretty badly, and cried out every now and then; despite the medication he was being given.

But apart from the pain, he was going stark mad from just lying around in bed all day, having others attending to his affairs in the meantime. Whomever had set the bombs was still out there, and just sitting there helpless every day, the frustration kept getting worse. Powerless and helpless, it was unnerving for Harry, no longer feeling in control. Even now, he could still smell the burning hair on the back of his own neck. Soon, the paranoia would suffocate him worse than a hangman's noose.

He had come to realize that the bomb had not just affected him physically, but mentally... no, emotionally. Everything was catching up to him now. Looking back on his life – his achievements, his family, all he'd been blessed with and taken for granted – it continuously played over in his mind; it shackled him underneath the bedclothes, from where there was no escape.

It was crazy just how close he had been to death – now and on so many other occasions. As a younger man, he'd always been a risk-taker, who liked to live life on the edge. *"No questions asked"* had been the motto on his first stepping-stone to life, since the beginning of his school years.

Whenever a dispute could not be settled diplomatically, or people misbehaved and needed to be put straight, he and his old associate knew how to settle things, the old-school way. When it came to doing someone over proper, they were meticulous to detail, starting from the head down to the socks.

And as they got older, things got heavier and rougher, until by the time it was over, someone would be in traction, and they'd be inside for the next three months – which gave a person plenty of time to think.

Still, thinking positively and optimistically doesn't always lead a person back down the straight and narrow, to repentance and following in his father's footsteps.

Harry hadn't done the things he did to rebel against his father, for being a good and honest man of business; he had been there for Harry, providing and indulging, which wasn't often asked. His father had taken care of him – perhaps even spoilt him a little too much – as he believed it was important to take care of the things we love the most.

But, sooner or later, every child had to grow up. And part of growing up was making choices, and being accountable for those choices.

A parent can only protect their child so far, so he had arranged for the lawyer to cut a deal. Though it had been hard seeing his son go to prison, it had taught him the one lesson in life he had failed to teach Harry: *Everyone is accountable for their actions.*

Upon his release, there had been no hard feeling

between the two of them. Harry wanted to become the man his father thought he could, and over the next two years he had done so. Working side by side, under his father's supervision, he learnt much about the construction industry, and made great efforts to ensure his father could rely on him when it came to making difficult decisions, particularly toward the staff. Thanks to Harry's investigation, the exposure and dismissal of their appointed foreman – a mole, feeding information to the competition – had proven Harry's loyalty to the company. It had earnt him trust and respect, not only with his father, but with everyone in the community, whom he swore he would never let down again.

It turned out, however, that he couldn't completely change, when the Big City Syndicate had moved in on the town, threatening and taking from his friends and neighbours. Though he had tried not to get involved, once again his own dark nature had got the better of him; a man is what he is, and must do what needs to be done. So, he had waged war against the criminals, on their own turf, hurting their people until it became too much; soon, innocent lives were getting caught in the crossfire.

When you went to war, you had to expect some casualties.

But, if you took on organized crime, those who had

more men and more bullets, it was only going to end in more bloodshed. He had been very lucky to come out of the endeavours still in one piece.

There always seemed to be this lucky angel following him around.

The name of his angel had been Helena, and she hadn't been just another skinny girl, like all the rest. When he held her in his arms, and felt the touch of her lips on his own, nothing else seemed to matter, because he had found true love; there was nothing more he needed than that. When things started to get serious, and they discovered she was having his child, he started to care enough to call a truce with the Syndicate. Terms had been reached and he had tried to go legit.

But then, his best friend turned on him, killed all of his friends... and the mother of his child.

Now, too, his little girl was gone. All he had left were his two grandchildren – the last of his bloodline, and his one last chance at redemption.

People try making every effort to redeem themselves for their sins. Unfortunately, there are some that can never be forgiven – by others or themselves. Just saying sorry is not enough, if the sincerity doesn't come from the heart.

Feeling the tears welling up in his eyes, he bowed his head and asked in prayer, finally, for God to grant him forgiveness – not for his sake, but for the two infants he'd sworn to protect. Now he was old and had lost his edge, what good was he to them?

He could feel his body turning numb, and the pain started to vanish.

Perhaps this was his time? As quickly and senselessly death comes calling on all of us, you cannot ignore the sound of the tapping of his scythe.

It is not weak to admit fear when you are about to meet your creator. It is surprising how true humanity breaks through even the hardest of faces.

Crying unashamedly into his hands, he felt a light touch on his shoulder. Withdrawing, he looked up into the face of Mrs. Sykes. Held in her hands, she had brought him some fresh flowers and a bag of grapes.

"I did knock, but you must not have heard me," she said, with a kind smile.

Normally, in these moments, he would not have cared for company. But that was the old Harry. Now, after he had finally let go and asked God for a saviour, an actual angel had appeared!

He invited her to sit beside him, in the chair. He wanted to know how the twins were; he hadn't seen them for days. Were they here, he asked.

"They're out in the reception area, sleeping; your man

Victor is looking after them." She glanced around, rather uncomfortably, at her surroundings. "I didn't want to disturb them. I could bring them in again tomorrow?"

Harry never thought her to be the squeamish type in such places, but he was so glad she had paid him a visit.

"How are things back at the house? Are you and the children being taken care of?" Harry asked, obviously still concerned for their wellbeing.

"Everything is fine, though I'm not used to having a bodyguard. Not that I don't appreciate his efficiency; he could perhaps just be a little more discreet at times." She leant in to whisper now: "The poor postman nearly had a heart attack when Victor burst through the front door this morning, ordering him to put all deliveries on the ground and step slowly away!"

Harry went on to explain that, since receiving the letter from the suspected bomber, his men were on high alert to be wary of all envelopes and packages.

A second letter had been left for Harry at the hospital reception desk: another sheet of paper with three more numbers cut out of magazines, as before: "8", "45" and "50". Harry had passed this information on to my family, but the seven numbers didn't really add up to any specific code. Perhaps a bank account number, if they were asking for money?

"It's a funny thing, him sending me those numbers. I don't know what he's trying to tell me with them. Maybe a date from the past, or a time in the future when he intends to strike next?"

Now Mrs. Sykes became a little uneasy, shifting in her seat. "Why is this all happening to you?"

The question was not unexpected, and justified, considering she had nearly been killed too in that bomb attack. Dagger-to-the-heart subjects were not his most favoured of discussions with others; everyone had their reasons for keeping their past hidden, locked away in a box. But, Harry believed this woman deserved the truth. So, for the first time in his life, he opened up his heart, holding nothing back: everything about his past life of crime, and what had really happened with his son-in-law Martin. By the time he was finished, Harry felt as if the weight of the world had been lifted from his chest.

Mrs. Sykes now seemed even more troubled.

Of course, that was only to be expected; he couldn't blame her if she resigned right then and walked out of his room, leaving the twins in Victor's hands.

"So, it's blood money? Everything you built, and what you were going to build...?" She now struggled to conceal the shock of what he had told her.

Harry could see no point in defending his actions,

though he wanted her to understand his motives. "It was all for the good of the community. That mall would be of great value; it would have provided new jobs and income. The people of this village have only thrived because we look after our own – we always have done."

"They were certainly happy enough to take the money."

"It was owed to them. Everything that was precious had been taken away, and even I couldn't get it back as I promised." That really did eat at Uncle Harry. Money couldn't replace family heirlooms and precious keepsakes, but sometimes it was all a person could rely on, to comfort them in harsh times.

Unfortunately, now Harry had encountered another problem, which was causing the community further distress: work had ceased at the site, and a lot of people were out of work.

It was terrible for Harry to admit such a thing, but if he had died in that car explosion, maybe the bomber would have ended it there, and a good man wouldn't have been killed by the second bomb.

"You'd prefer that? Really?" she asked now, with some tenderness returning to her voice. "You'd really give everything, to see nobody else hurt? But, what of those two boys? You are all that remains of their family. I'm not one to judge whether what you did in the past was right or wrong, but now they need you more than ever; it is your duty to raise them, and see that they don't end up like you."

Those last few words shook Harry a little, but he could see from her eyes that they were ones of sincerity – and they could not have been more true: his past was behind him, and they were his future.

The family he'd always had should have come first, and that was the one thing he had to change right away. It would mean a fresh start, but he was willing to sacrifice everything.

Warmly, she held his hand, and together they became lost in each other's eyes.

I guess the signs are always there, if you look deep enough into your own heart.

How funny it always seems, to the people who think they have everything, to actually reach a turning point and realize that true good fortune is found in the company of kindred spirit. No matter how twisted an individual can become – dining day-to-day on the misery of their victims, and the dead who haunt them, day and night, in the shadows of their minds – one can find solace in forgiveness, both from God and others, who are willing to forget the past and help guide us to the future.

My grandmother once told me: *"You can love someone enough to die for them, but the real commitment is to come back to the living, and make your peace with the dead."*

In the end, we can all find peace if we allow love into our hearts.

# CHAPTER 18

## Sunday 5:15 p.m.
## Ravenfall – the woodlands.

The most preferred method of execution or control is the use of a firearm. A rifle or handgun is always a good incentive; people aren't going to do as you say with the point of a finger.

As I discovered, when my father caught me sharply by the wrist and redirected my index – which was meant to be the barrel – away from himself, and kicked the legs out from under me. As I crashed to the ground, he bent my wrist so that my own finger was now redirected back at me.

"At this point, you decide what action to take!" My father's voice was stern.

I hadn't done much weapons defence training in my karate lessons; the basic knife scenarios were different to the ones my father had been taking me through, before moving on to this level.

Whenever training in these scenarios, it is best to begin with and empty hand, so as to first master the motor mechanics. Then, as your skill improves, move on with a training aid.

As a side note: real guns and knives should never be used, even at a professional level!

"You should never point a gun at another person unless you intend to use it," he said, pulling me back up to my feet.

Again, my thoughts returned to my mother in the office, which led me to follow up my father's statement with: "Because, when you squeeze the trigger, you are changing someone's life. When you kill somebody, your life is forever changed."

My father looked at me for a short moment, then nodded in concurrence. "You're a quick learner. That's good, Izzy. It's not like a game; you can't expect them to come back to life. You have to know what you're doing in the moment and accept the consequences."

I sighed heavily. "I get it. Are all lessons going to be like this?"

My father looked harshly at me, not caring for my choice of tone. "What we're teaching you is nothing like school! They prepare you to go out in the world and live a normal life; we are teaching you the trade craft of death!" he said, strongly.

The word itself – "death" – is usually a difficult subject to escape. It bombards us on a day-to-day basis, particularly in the media. People try not to think about it, or refuse to accept it, but nobody is immortal.

"I still want this. I'm just..." I couldn't bring myself to say it; I thought I was shaming the family by doing so. How were my ancestors looking down on me now?

My father came over to me and put his hand on my shoulder. "I'm proud of you, and so is your mother. No matter what you choose to do in your life, we'll always be there to support you."

These were the words I had been waiting for, and the look of pride in his eyes told me that he meant every one of them.

He pointed his index finger at me, suddenly.

Deflecting and controlling, I brought my foot around and knocked him to the ground.

He smiled, looking up, his finger now pointing at his face. A smile appeared on my own. "So, where do we go from here?"

The temperature outside was mild, so the conditions were ideal for my father and I to do a little shooting practice now, while everything was quiet.

You might think the term "apprenticeship" out of place for what I was about to undergo, but any trade – whether a butcher or a professional killer – required learning through firsthand experience. It's not every day you get schooled in the dark art of killing, but there is a whole history to be found in books and on the internet.

My first lesson with a semi-automatic pistol began with the drawing of the weapon from a holster; depending on the type of holster you chose, it was an exercise which needed a lot of continuous work.

I had only been hunting with my father using rifles, though the principles were the same, except the weapon was much lighter and very compact.

Loading and cocking a weapon, then reloading, were the next stages. You had to become very familiar with the workings of the weapon, making it your best friend. It was a special relationship.

Training was similar between the police and military, as well as people in our profession, who had not had previous training in either service!

When it came to aiming, it was best to start with a two-handed grip: raise forward and aim down the barrel; only squeeze the trigger when the target is perfectly in your sights. We started off in a standing position, then moved vigorously through to kneeling and even lying down, repeating them over and over, until I was panting very hard.

It may have just been a training drill, but only training hard prepared you for the real thing!

I was trying to imagine what it would actually be like to pull the trigger on a person, and not a target! A gun is said to give peace of mind, but it won't provide courage. It's the fear that heightens the senses, and brings everything into focus.

Life has many lessons. Some are easy and others take a lot of practice – it is no different when it comes to learning this kind of trade. The theory and practice of assassination takes as much time as it does to live your whole life; to be truly efficient, you should always be studying and evolving the art of killing. You need to know more than just how to pull a trigger; you have to know about people, and what certain people do in this world. You have to be able to solve problems, at times under pressure; quick thinking will make the difference.

Ending the session for the day, we made our way back to the truck, listening to the birds calling out, high up in the trees. My father had taught me a lot about these forests. They had a lot of history, dating back to the war, and particular relevance to our family.

Times had been so different back then, and Ravenfall had gone under a different name. When the soldiers had invaded, times had been hard for many families in the village; some were taken away to work camps as prisoners, just because of their religious beliefs.

Even today, you could find some spot on the globe where this was still happening, and there are always those willing to fight for such tyrants who engineer it.

As a younger child, my father would take me and my sister out to the little hut, high up on the bluff; you could see the whole village and the land beyond. It had been built as a command post for a militia, of which my grandparents were a part, living out here, free in the wilderness.

I did ask my grandfather, seeing as he'd been reluctant to join, why he had stayed and not run away – gone back to live in the village, away from the danger. He told me that, in war, some men follow orders without question, and some men follow only what they feel is right in their own hearts. There are times you need to clearly understand something, and there are moments when you just have to listen very carefully and obey. I was now trying my best to be a good student, and make sense of what he had told me.

Driving back into town, we were met at the entrance by a police barrier, though the officers were not local. All were dressed in black tactical wear. They asked if we were residents and checked my father's identification – something which I found to be offensive, but my father was calm and accommodating.

Once we were allowed through, we could see more going about town, some questioning residents and some with dogs, carrying out searches.

Everybody now knew what was going on in Ravenfall.

People use bombs because they think they can scare people, and make them do what they say. But, with a community like Ravenfall, which over the years has seen its share of terror and tyranny, it just makes us angry, and brings us all together. You can't shake these people until they wobble like jelly; we're made of much stronger stuff.

It was the war which made our people strong, and we've never forgotten why we choose to live here, away from the corruption and the evil shit that goes on out there!

To outsiders, Ravenfall might be considered the village that time forgot. Those who live in The Big City forget that there is nothing wrong with life in a small town. At least here people know their neighbours, and all want a simple, carefree life. There was nothing cruel or unusual to be found on these streets.

Of course, behind closed doors each had their own life. And every life had a past. But each man's past was his own business.

Walking around the local supermarket, the aisles were full of whispers and chatter. My father would give the occasional nod, while the locals continued talking about the village coming under some form of martial law.

*"Those men with guns! It's like the war all over again!!"*

At the checkout, my father ran into Sergeant Braccard, who was currently being quizzed by the store manager, over how long these "Big City people" were going to remain. He knew, of course, that they were making everyone nervous, but they were there for the village's safety. When the town had been completely cleared of danger, they would be leaving.

Passing by the community centre, I looked at the old memorial, in the shape of a raven carved out of stone, spreading its wings high in the air. It had been made in memory of those who gave their lives during the war.

Times change, but there were still those who felt it was vital to remember where life began, and how those who came here first built this safe haven with their own hands. So it was engraved:

*"There are days of remembrance, and there are days of tribute.*
*It is with love and passion that we keep these memories alive.*
*Keeping them deeply ingrained in our hearts."*

There are people who sit around and moan about

what's going on in the world. And there are those who do not wait for it to sort itself out.

When people are forced to live by certain rules, or pretend this is how things need to be in the world, and it becomes too strict, society becomes its own avenging force, tearing down the walls imprisoning and shackling its freedom. Life is about making choices, and being accountable for actions and consequences.

Human circumstances often lead to some form of conflict, resulting in the deaths of hundreds or even thousands of lives. What are people prepared to do when their very way of life is threatened?

This was a question my grandmother had put to my grandfather, when she asked him to join and fight in the militia, and this is what he had tried to explain to me, though I never really got until that moment.

It was a bloody war, and many tyrants were put under the knife. People had taken back their freedom and liberty, rising up against their oppressors.

The human spirit was an unstoppable force, greater than any army – as long as you believed passionately in what you were fighting for, your homes and your family.

*What they destroy, we can rebuild!*

That had been Ravenfall's motto ever since.

Though it had been hell, years of endless turmoil, the

conflict had eventually ended. From the rubble, they rebuilt homes and tended to the lands. The crops came every season, and their lives were their own once more.

Ravenfall was the kind of town where you could get along, as long as you kept certain skeletons in the closet and left old bones buried.

How do people trust each other in a town like this, when so many of its foundations were built on soil stained with so much blood?

Now and then, some of the older locals were still haunted by their own pasts; you'd be lying if you could say you'd completely got rid of all your demons. These people had seen so many horrible things; they just stay in your head forever.

Though the local people know intimately the atrocities which took place during the war, and the evils which never really vanished from the land, generations still thrive to this day.

It was very difficult to watch the uncomfortable terror starting to appear in our neighbours' eyes. Nobody had taken responsibility for the bombings, and nobody had been arrested, so it was clear this wasn't over. What was next for Ravenfall?

We still had to watch out for our own safety. There was still a bomber out there, and he'd already taken one innocent life.

# CHAPTER 19

### Sunday 7:25 p.m.
### The Big City outskirts.

Sometimes, the only way to make an impact on the world is to blow a hole in it.

But, to make a work of art of the highest quality, you had to have patience and the right amount of time; impatience was not a factor when handling explosives.

Hours, days, weeks… it all depended on the size and the technical specifications. The work of a perfectionist was slow and would not be hurried, no matter who or how much.

It was not always practical to have every component to hand. There was a large market for purchasing the necessary materials; it was just a case of finding the right vendor.

A good place for my sister and Mr. X to start was with the trafficking of certain explosives in and out of The Big City. True, it was only a guess that the guy might shop locally for the few bare essentials, but if so The Salesman was more than likely the wholesaler he'd go to, as discretion was always assured.

Unfortunately, The Salesman was not easy to find, as he kept moving his operation so he couldn't be tracked.

It had taken some persuasion on Mr. X's part to get one of his regular buyers to talk, and finally a recent address was given.

Pulling his car up outside the large warehouse, Mr. X checked his weapon and caught my sister's arm, just as she was about to step out of the car. "I need you to stay out here," he said, with a stern voice.

My sister Bethany had seen this coming; men always liked to take point. But, asking my sister to wait in the car, while he went to take care of business, brought about her real dark side – and if you had seen it before, you really wouldn't want to see it when she was armed.

"Why don't *you* wait in the car, and *I'll* bring back the souvenir?" she said, removing the blade from under her jacket. My sister was not the sort to fall in line with anybody except our parents.

"This is not me being macho; somebody needs to be back—"

"And the first choice is the girl? Out of harm's way, while you stroll in, guns blazing? Nothing macho in that at all!" my sister said, twirling the knife in her hand.

"When have you ever known me to be sexist?" he

asked, in an almost uncharacteristic hurt tone.

"I'd say about thirty-five seconds ago," she countered, quickly.

Moments like this – two professional killers sitting together in a car, tension starting to build and neither wishing to back down – could be unpredictable. But they just sat for a moment.

When it comes to partnerships, communication is everything. That way, you lessen the possibility of mistakes and misunderstandings. You have to trust them as much as they trust you. But, that's not always easy when you're in rival company.

Just because you've been intimate – even more than a few times – doesn't mean that you have committed your heart. The term "heartbreak" was more than a figurative one to us. The ones we fall for aren't always the people they say they are, and that is no different when it comes to ourselves. Being honest in a dishonest, backstabbing world, is a one-way ticket to the morgue – especially if your lover is the type to carry a gun.

A relationship is no different to a partnership; trust must be established and all cards need to be laid out on the table, so any previous concerns can be reconciled, no matter how small. Avoiding awkward topics wasn't an option for the two of them – not if they wanted to keep seeing each other, which by now even you will have gathered is a likely step forward… as long as they didn't have to keep watching their own backs.

"I don't normally do partners; I'm still trying to get used to this," he said, finally.

My sister began to run the tip of her finger along the blade. "What exactly is *this*?" she said, firmly. "Is this a partnership, or is it just temporary?"

"I thought that was the deal," he said, slightly taken aback. "What do you think will happen when this does all come to an end, regardless of the outcome?"

She turned away and looked out through the windscreen. "I suppose you're just going to disappear out of my life again."

He knew this was going to come up sooner or later, but right at that moment it really wasn't appropriate. They were working, and could not afford for their emotions to take over.

The only thing I think an assassin is frightened of is exposing their true feelings: the fact that we are capable of love and appreciating family values. It must have hurt even Mr. X to hold back certain details regarding his nephew's death.

"I thought it was best to give us some space. What happened was incidental and, honestly, I don't blame you for that. I got what I needed for myself and my family, end of story."

She merely nodded, flipping the knife over in her hand, and resting the tip on her thigh. "So, I was no longer a consideration? Obviously I wasn't expecting you to invite me to the funeral, to pay my respects," she said, going slowly, "but just how much did you tell them?"

Mr. X took another moment; he really wanted to get on with the business at hand. "When all is said and done, it comes with the craft. We all play our roles," he said, taking out his own gun. "Now, we have two choices here: old business or new business?"

She returned the knife to its sheath. "How about you let me take the lead, as it's my family who owns the contract, and you watch my back?"

He thought for a moment, then leant in to whisper: "If you trust me that much not to put a bullet in it, then by all means lead the way."

People as a whole can be nasty, selfish and self-centred at times; the darker side of human nature comes out when we feel the need to push away those who get too close.

Entering the warehouse, she took the lead, while he remained back, as requested.

It all seemed quiet and calm inside, but this only heightened Mr. X's senses. His perception of things around him was greater than most people – this was his greatest asset, which he based solely on his decisions. It was the reason why he'd been able to do this work up until now.

He was unable to remember the last time he'd had to rely on another person – a colleague. Having to consult a partner in decisions made him uncomfortable – not that he doubted my sister's capabilities; he just liked to be in control.

Thrusting a hand out abruptly, he suddenly caught her by the shoulder and pulled her back, just as a hail of gunfire came their way. The bullets sprayed the wall, missing them by miles.

Looking up, they saw the figure of a man dressed in a grey, pressed suit, standing at the top of the stairs leading to the office. The guy was using an M-16 assault rifle; he obviously wasn't a very good shot.

Mr. X and my sister, however, were accurate, and both scored perfects hits: one in the shoulder and one in the thigh, throwing The Salesman off balance. The gun he'd been holding fell from his hands and he collapsed to the floor, groaning in pain.

His visitors approached, cautiously.

Gruffly dragging him to his own office chair, Mr. X took a bottle of Scotch from the desk and took a sip, not offering any to my sister, knowing well that she didn't care for the stuff.

"We need to make this quick; time is ticking away!" He placed his foot over the open wound on The Salesman's leg, invoking a cry of immense pain. "We're looking for a pro, likes to use sophisticated devices. Anyone like that frequented your shop lately?"

The trouble with dealing with the "middleman" is that they always act so stupid: always just delivering information or goods from one anonymous party to another. The only one who isn't anonymous is the middleman – and they know only too well who both parties are, otherwise they would be fucking stupid!

"I have a business! A reputation to uphold!" he said, through gritted teeth.

My sister now took the barrel of her gun and pressed it hard into the open wound on his shoulder. "I'm going to burn you and this whole place, unless you start giving us something useful."

The strongarm tactics might seem extreme, but you can't always trust what people tell you, especially if it doesn't benefit them financially. But, of course, they weren't about to pay this guy – not after the welcome they'd received.

"You and I know a lot about each other, so let's not play

games," Mr. X stepped in again. "Nobody needs to know we are having this conversation. All we want is whoever you sold explosives to in the past week."

"It's not my business to ask names," The Salesman cringed.

"But you do ask for references; a man in your line of work has to be cautious when doing business with strangers," my sister countered, taking the liquor out of Mr. X's hand. She poured the rest of its contents over The Salesman.

Removing the lighter from her pocket she moved forward, but did not strike the flame.

"All referrals are made via email," The Salesman said, quickly finding his tongue again. "I don't ask who or why, just the amount!"

"So, how much was it this time?" Mr. X enquired.

They let him sit up to get comfortable for the moment, but my sister did not withdraw the lighter. "How much did they pay you, and how was the transaction made?"

"The usual: wire transfer from a secure network; half upfront, half on delivery."

"Who collected it? Man or woman?"

"It was a man. Not local. He looked as though he knew his stuff."

Mr. X gave my sister an approving look. "We would like

to make his acquaintance."

The Salesman reached into his pocket, but hesitated as my sister flinched.

"Go slow."

"I have a number in my book; he is awaiting a delivery. That's as much as I can give you."

My sister finally withdrew and threw the empty bottle in the waste basket. "That's a start. Time you made that call."

"But I've not taken delivery yet," The Salesman protested.

"That's not a problem; he won't be requiring this consignment after all," she said. Grabbing him by the jacket, she pulled him out of the chair.

He hobbled over to his desk to pick up the receiver and dial the number. Before he could tap the second number, he and the desk both exploded.

Falling back onto the floor, both my sister and Mr. X remained still, unmoving in broken glass and dust. Neither tried to speak. Only the sound of ringing could be heard in their ears.

*Snap!* The world suddenly came back, as though the volume had been restored.

Quickly, my sister began to take inventory of herself, finding that she had not sustained any serious injuries, as was the same with Mr. X. Returning to their feet, they quickly made their way outside.

Collapsing back against the wall, my sister took deep breaths, while Mr. X removed his flask from his inside pocket, now offering her a sip. Taking a large gulp, she coughed and found all of her senses returning.

The bomber had cleaned his tracks, planting the bomb in case someone came asking questions.

They couldn't remain there much longer, but it was clear that neither was in any condition to drive at that moment. But the nausea was slowly beginning to fade. It was becoming replaced by anger.

Kicking at the debris with her foot, she now felt even more determined to do everything she could to find and kill this bomber.

She wasn't sure if Mr. X felt the same, as he donned his shades and made his way back over to the car, climbing back into the driver's seat.

Slipping slowly inside next to him, she tried to focus her mind on the current objective. Their lead had been blown to pieces, and they were no closer to finding out who was behind all this. There was a very important conversation to follow.

Starting the engine, they slowly drove off site and returned to Mr. X's apartment, where they showered, changed clothes and then reconvened.

"We're going to get this son of a bitch!" were the first words to come out of Mr. X's mouth.

My sister just nodded, wanting to go over everything they already knew. They had to respect the fact that they were hunting the most deadly of adversaries. Who it was and why he was doing this was a mystery which needed to be solved.

Why was Harry the target, and why now? True, he had rubbed shoulders with some bad characters, and made enemies with certain members of organized crime, but it had been years since the peace had been broken. It needed to be resolved now, before more bombs started to go off. The responsible individual, or group, was going to feel the full weight of swift justice.

So far, the intel collection process was meagre, but sometimes even the smallest details were the most valuable: possible suspects, motives and opportunities.

For example: who had sent the letter with those strange numbers? They had to mean something to somebody. Why were seven numbers of such great importance?

Suddenly, my sister grabbed her phone and opened up the Lotto app, selecting the draw history date, where she looked up Martin's winning Euro Lottery ticket.

*"5, 25, 30, 45, 50 (8 & 11)."*

They all matched exactly!

She slammed her fist down hard. Why hadn't she thought of it before?

So, the bomber, or his employer, was referring to the lottery winnings; the money which had belonged to Martin and was now going to be held in trust, under Harry's care, for his children.

Someone was looking to make sure that wasn't going to happen, perhaps by removing Harry and stepping in out of the blue to try contesting the claim? Or perhaps some other legal way; the will, maybe?

Who would be able to do that, and was it even possible?

They needed to make a call to a certain legal firm.

# CHAPTER 20

## Monday 9:26 a.m.
## The Big City courthouse.

If you were to ask a reason for wanting another person dead, revenge is the most common motivation, followed closely by greed. One way or another, there always appears to be some form of benefit in a person's death.

Even when it comes to family, the concepts of loyalty and love weigh very little on a scale tipped by gold.

There are people who are lucky to be born with everything it takes – money and power – to do whatever they wish with their lives but, for some reason, find it's still not enough.

A parent teaching their child intelligence without the virtue of honesty can lead to extraordinary circumstances.

For example, family business disagreements can cause the most fatal of what appears to be a robbery gone badly, though on some occasions there is enough reason by the investigating detective to suspect foul play within the company itself.

Joe Hartley sat behind the defendant's desk before the

judge, as the prosecution laid out the evidence before the twelve jurors, who had so far looked upon him with great distaste.

It appeared clear enough that Joe had been responsible for his boss's death, but the implication of another party had also been put forward. The business and finances had now been placed in the first son's hands, so David had become a wealthy man following his father's death. Of course, the cops had been unable to prove the connection between Joe and David, no matter how hard they'd tried to lean on Joe. Suspicion of guilt was not enough in a court of law.

True, the two men had been "very close friends" for some time, despite David's father's disapproval of his son's choice of lifestyle, threatening to cut him off without a penny.

One evening, David's father's body had been discovered in his office, sitting behind his desk, with a bullet wound in his chest which had come from a revolver. Joe had been the only other person, according to the security guard, to have been working late that night, and nobody else had been seen entering or leaving. The gun had not been found, but a cufflink belonging to Joe had been discovered in front of the dead man's desk.

It could have been planted there, but why try and frame

Joe?

It was all up to his lawyer now, to try and bring this question to light, leaving the jury with enough reasonable doubt to acquit his client of murder.

Mr. Terrence sat quietly behind his desk, listening to the prosecutor's words over and over, damaging his defence case – like a wrecking ball knocking walls into rubble.

You often read about men who spend their lives and careers making money off of the rich and powerful, manipulating facts and poisoning a jury's mind, to sway it toward their thinking.

In a court of law, when the moment seems to be turning out of your favour, and you've supposedly done everything humanly possible, but everything looks set to shatter with the strike of a tiny wooden hammer, the only way to ease the pressure from your throat is to cough a request for a short recess.

Slowly slipping from his chair, Terrence moved out into the hallway and made for the gents' toilet. Standing at the sink, he took a breath and removed his glasses, closing his eyes just to listen to the sound of the running water.

Behind him, the door opened and David, the dead man's son, came in to stand only a few feet behind him, just looking at the lawyer's reflection. The eyes didn't open to his presence.

"They say the hardest thing in this business isn't asking the client to make a choice, but having to make your own on their behalf," David said calmly, over the sound of the water.

Still Terrence remained still, not wishing to open his eyes or shift out of his tranquil state of mind.

"But at the end of the day, you just have to remember, at any cost, you have to win," David said, walking back out, leaving Terrence alone with his thoughts, if not his conscience. The only way to win in a case such as this was to leave that shut tightly in your briefcase.

Your future in the profession sometimes depended on it, especially when your client's friends were legitimate business owners, who were themselves in danger of losing their inheritance and freedom into the bargain.

If the cops nailed Joe, they would certainly go after David, and there would be reasonable ground to start building a case based on this trial's success. David wasn't just being protective toward his employee/lover, who had proven their loyalty; he was also securing his own freedom into the bargain.

Terrence knew that if he failed in this case, it would hurt his career, if it were publicly made aware that his clients didn't get their money's worth. The newspapers and media were eagerly waiting outside for the result.

You see, there is only one rule, if you accept the case: you accept full responsibility, so it is nice to have powerful and important influential friends.

Finally, Terrence opened his eyes and reached to turn off the tap.

Replacing his glasses, he straightened his tie and returned to the courtroom, sitting back down in his chair next to Joe, who was looking a little concerned. David was looking at them both from his seat, with the other spectators.

All rose as the judge re-entered from his chambers, calling the court back to order, and for Terrence to continue.

Terrence gave himself a moment before he was finally ready to step out and give his closing statement; to lead the court, judge and jury his little dance. Hoping that they, and everyone else in court, could keep up with the steps.

To pull off a miracle, it has to be not only spontaneous, but a little theatrical in the process. Perhaps a bold beginning – a sudden dramatic surprise; raising your head and voice, tipping the scales of justice ever so slightly, but enough to capture the plausible of human imagination. Something is going on, but you don't really understand how you're being fooled.

In the end, reasonable doubt will always prevail.

A handshake on the courthouse steps later, and a brief statement to the local press on how justice has been done, and an innocent man was let walk free.

Terrence was straight to his car, enjoying a pleasant drive back to Ravenfall.


The sound of piano music was dramatic, but somewhat calming, as it played out of the small stereo system, filling what appeared to be an empty, plush office.

Very few people recognize the benefit of having a cold shower in their workplace. The icy spray on the body awakens the senses whilst refreshing the pores. The flesh then becomes stiff and goose-pimply, whilst inside the whole body comes alive.

Dressing quickly in his very fine, expensive suit, he took a bottle of pills from the cabinet. Tipping three capsules into his hand, he knocked them back in one go and swallowed dry, before taking a shot of mouthwash.

Returning to his desk, he logged into his laptop and began to look over the many files and upcoming cases. Business was never better, and when it came to criminal law, there was no shortage of clients.

Logging into his online bank account, he found just what he expected: the numbers added up to the full total he had billed for his services.

*Rule one: A man has to get paid, because he doesn't work for free!*

Sitting back in his chair, his eyes shifted from the screen and his mind began to wander.

There are two things in life that you can never forget: who you are and where you come from. These are the seeds from which you dig yourself, through the earth to reach the sun.

Both his parents had been as ambitious as him, but never made it as far. Meeting in the same law class, they had shared lunchtimes and dated in the evenings, finding a genuine connection of love and affection. Things had started out great, as soon as they both left college and found work together, in a Big City Tax Attorney's office. Soon after, his mother had become pregnant with him, so the sole financial burden had been placed on his father, and soon they found themselves in a difficult way. Moving from their fine apartment uptown to a common little flat in the narrows, his father had started to stay out more and mix with the wrong people.

When it comes to matters of law, there are some doors in this world which should not be opened lightly, without knowing what's on the other side. Making certain acquaintances brought risky opportunities for services required, by what was starting to become known as an organized crime syndicate. They were always on the lookout for bright young talent.

Stepping over certain lines, however, you soon found it dragging on your heels. Soon, another foot stamps down hard, stopping you in your tracks.

An investigation and the threat of charges had been placed before the law firm, including accusations of conspiring to defraud the government in certain tax returns.

Breaking the law cost his father his career, driving them to slave hard now, to provide their son with a decent education.

Terrence had learnt from his father's mistake, choosing to start out small to begin. And, though the offers had come, he'd been wise to pass them over, until a sure thing had come his way.

When it came to the law, every man was equal, and privy to the same rights. Repeat customers, however, are always where you find the real money.

The buzzer to his intercom sounded, and the voice of his secretary came through in a somewhat urgent fashion: "Mr. Terrence, you have…"

His office door immediately began to open, and the introduction followed as his visitors stepped through, closing it behind them.

Mr. X was now dressed sharply in a new suit, while my sister Bethany had donned a pair of clean jeans and a shirt, along with her usual jacket, which was now a little cleaner.

"Sorry we didn't have time to make an appointment," she said, stepping across the room to stand in front of his desk.

"I'd rather you had. My day is a little full," Terrence said, reaching to close one of the files on his laptop.

"We could tell, stumbling over all the other appointments cluttering your empty reception," Mr. X charmed, removing a fresh grape from a bowl on the table, and slipping it into his mouth.

"We are interested in Harry's trust fund: the one he set up for his grandchildren," my sister said, getting straight to the point.

Terrence was not appreciative of such direct questions. "Such matters are privileged, between me and my client," he responded. "A lawyer's ethics bind him to protect his client's position."

My sister smiled and moved over to the window, to look down on the expensive car she had passed on the way in. "You're a clever man, Mr. Terrence; we managed to catch your performance earlier." She glanced at the laptop screen. "Dirty deeds at an exorbitant price. How people like you sleep at night I don't know."

Terrence was offended greatly by the remark. "That's a little bit hypocritical, considering your chosen line of work!" he replied. "Even you must appreciate that everyone deserves to have their rights protected. It's why people like me exist: to make sure those rights are preserved."

Mr. X was now looking along the walls to the many law certificates framed there. "I suppose the toughest part for you is making yourself believe that you're working for an innocent person – while the hardest part of being the client is not knowing whether guys like you have their best interests at heart."

Terrence did not respond to this statement. He just closed the lid on his laptop as my sister passed him, and made her way back to the front of the desk.

"Tell the truth: were you actually considering making a deal, before your client's friend – the man who bankrolled your services with his father's money – had his little chat with you?"

Terrence looked charismatic, and hid behind a somewhat fearless demeanour. But, when you looked into his eyes, he didn't really look so tough – particularly to one who made pain and suffering a career. Mr. X was sophisticated as well as dangerous, and capable of sizing up another man just by spending the shortest time in his presence.

"Sometimes, the best deal is the only deal, unless you've already shaken hands with the Devil. In those circumstances, a man's conscience has to be clear," Terrence finally replied, coolly.

My sister nodded and went straight for the empty chair in front of the desk, not waiting to be asked. "There's an old military saying: *'Fifteen years is better than fifteen bullets'*."

Terrence leant forward, resting his arms on the desk and interlocking his fingers. "I take it Harry knows you're making these enquiries? I don't blame him for taking steps in this particular situation," he said, looking from my sister to Mr. X. "I can't honestly say I would be doing the same if I were in his position."

My sister had a thought suddenly come to the front of her mind. "How are things going with your daughter?" she said, suddenly changing the subject. "Have the police got any closer to finding the persons responsible yet?"

Terrence again said nothing. It was personal family business, and nothing to do with their reason for being there that day.

"I bet you don't often – if ever – find yourself on the other side: *being* the victim instead of representing them, those accused of criminal acts against people like your little girl, Abigail?" my sister continued to taunt, sitting back and crossing her legs, interlocking her own fingers.

Terrence recognized the hostility, but managed to keep his cool. "There may come a time when you find yourself sitting in that chair as a client, yourself," he retorted, somewhat smugly.

"I guess we'll have to wait and see," my sister said, unfazed by his statement.

Working in the law is like a chess game: you can't afford to make the wrong move. Since my family worked for Harry, Terrence knew it was in his best interests not to antagonize the people who made his little problems disappear permanently.

"How is it that you believe Harry's trust has anything to do with this matter?" Terrence asked, now impatiently looking at his watch – perhaps thinking of going for an early lunch.

"The person we're looking for doesn't just make simple homemade devices; he is a true expert, and these sort of people cost a lot of money," my sister said, matter of fact.

Terrence nodded in agreement; "Indeed. A man with these sorts of skills has to be on file, or has caught someone's attention. I myself have made some enquiries in the city, but to no avail."

The fact that Harry's business was coming under attack

suggested revenge, but since somebody was going to great lengths to conceal their identity, it also suggested another motive, which raised the question: who had anything to gain financially from Harry's death? He had no other surviving relatives than the baby twins now, and he himself had no real money worth killing over, since most of the lottery money he'd received had gone into constructing the mall.

"There is still the trust," Mr. X suddenly broke in. "When Harry's daughter and son-in-law died, not leaving a will, the assets – which is to say the remaining lottery money – automatically passed to their children."

Terrence's mouth now curled up at the sides. "Surely you don't suspect them?" he asked, but found the joke was lost on his visitors. "You obviously don't know much about trustee law, so allow me to enlighten you, and I'll keep it simple."

My sister detested the sarcasm, but listened nonetheless to what the man had to say.

As the children were both still young, and now in Harry's care, he had applied to set up a trust in both the infants' names, over which he acted as the trustee until they both came of age. "I was instructed by Harry to set up a discretionary trust. It gives him power over the distribution of the money – for the benefit of the children, naturally, such as their education," Terrence explained. "A trustee cannot benefit from the trust, except expenses, though can be named as beneficiaries."

This was where my sister's interest began to peak. "So, if anything happens to the children, the money goes to Harry?"

Terrence didn't like what she was now implying. "It's not quite as simple as that; the law regarding trusts is very complex," Terrence reiterated. "Besides, Harry was the intended target!"

"That's my point: Harry was nearly killed in that explosion. If he, the acting trustee, dies, what happens to the money then?" my sister asked, leaning forward now with impatience.

There seemed to be a short pause, and the room went deathly silent. Even Mr. X was now taking a big interest in where my sister was driving this conversation; he was actually impressed she was able to hold her own against this vile lawyer. The use of a lot of legal terms could make a person very ignorant, but it seemed she may well have discovered a possible motive.

"Every trust requires at least one trustee. Harry, at the moment, is the only appointed person; another person would have to step in and take over upon his death," Terrence now answered. "The successor trustee is usually appointed by the original, but Harry hasn't arranged this, so the courts might appoint one – usually a surviving family member, if there is one."

There is an old saying: *"Every conspiracy theory contains some grain of truth."* And justice, or vengeance, doesn't discriminate between friends, enemies or family.

Terrence considered for a moment, then shrugged. "But there isn't..."

"Well... there is, of course, one other surviving member – somebody we've perhaps overlooked," my sister said, turning to Mr. X: "what about Martin's brother? He's currently incarcerated, but he surely learned of Martin's death, and most likely about the lottery winnings."

The room once again became very quiet; the answer seemed to have dropped out of the sky. Way to go, Bethany!

Terrence decided to make a phone call, whilst my sister and Mr. X got together discreetly, to discuss this sudden revelation.

How they could have missed this possibility ate at my sister. The more they started to put the current pieces of the puzzle together, the more it began to make sense.

True, the man was in prison, but that didn't mean he was incapable of arranging things on the outside; contacting the right people, with the right skills. The man was in the perfect place to learn of such people – on the grapevine, so to speak.

Finally, Terrence had finished his call, and now had a rather unsettled expression on his face. "It seems that Martin's brother is a possible suspect." He returned once again to his seat. "He is, in fact, being granted conditional parole, in a couple of days' time."

A look from Mr. X was enough for the pair to excuse themselves from Terrence's office.

They made their way back home to the butchers' shop, to share their findings. Sitting in my father's office, I sat and listened to everything, and even I thought it was probably a certainty that we had found our bomber's client. If it was Martin's brother, he had a very good reason. A hundred-million good reasons.

Who would suspect a jailbird – a man locked away from the world?

But still, the brother was only a possible suspect at the moment; it was unprofessional to jump to any rash conclusions. Going after the wrong person without any proof wasn't going to resolve anything. It was going to be necessary for my father to go away and check out this theory, while my sister and Mr. X kept going after the bomber.

This usually meant I would be left behind in the shop, with my mother, missing out on the action and any further training.

However, I couldn't have been more wrong!

What was soon to follow would decide my future as a professional contract killer! Not to mention the fate of Uncle Harry...

# CHAPTER 21

### Tuesday 12:25 p.m.
### The town of Wallonfield.

Some people are only comfortable with the notion that each person chooses and creates their own destiny, but a lot can change in the time between childhood and adulthood.

As we grow and evolve, our outlook on life motivates and influences our decisions, though we can't always expect to get it right. We then end up saying: *"This isn't how I expected it!"*

But that is not necessarily a bad thing all the time; some surprises can be quite pleasant, as to live an unpredictable life is like travelling a path, from which you never know where you're going to end up, or whom you are going to meet.

It was still early when my father and I arrived in the town of Wallonfield. It hadn't taken us long, since we'd planned the journey in advance, and were lucky not to have run into a lot of traffic.

The morning sky was beautiful and uplifting, much to the

benefit of my mood.

It was here that we were going to spend the next two days, as a training ground for various simulations of my future career.

Checking into a motel, my father put us both down as aliases, as we only use our real names when conducting the other side of our family business. We had gone through our cover story whilst driving up from Ravenfall; this was only a brief stop on our way up to a cattle show – suitable for a butcher and his daughter.

Once we had got into our room, my father started to quiz me about everything we had just gone through since getting out of our vehicle and heading into the reception office, asking me specific questions:

(i)  Did I notice how many keys were hanging on the pegs?

(ii)  Was the register at the front counter or kept in the back?

(iii)  Was the back-office door open or closed?

To be honest, I hadn't taken any of these things into account. I had just kept smiling at the helpful lady, who seemed very professional in her role.

"Which can be a problem for us; she's the kind of

person who pays a lot of attention to details, making it difficult for us to go about our work unnoticed," my father said. He went on to explain that, at times, it was necessary to know everything about where you stay, and how many were in close proximity to you.

There were two keys missing from the hooks, and two other vehicles in the parking area, meaning there were two other parties staying at the motel. I could immediately recognize that he was building up to the topic of potential witnesses.

So long as we kept to ourselves, and did nothing to draw too much attention, we'd be fine.

We then took a brief stroll around the building, taking in the environment, making notes on quick exit routes and any potential hazards. You had to be able to think quickly at the last minute, when having to get out of difficult situations.

But I questioned this: we weren't in any danger; there was no contract on us.

"It is only professional to take everything into account," my father reiterated. "Remember what I told you about taking everything in?"

I nodded, remembering that every day from now on was a learning experience, and unless I paid attention, my training wasn't going to go be very productive.

Once the lessons were over, I did sort of need a break from everything, so I took a walk into town; even a young person needs their own space from time to time.

It is not always wise to venture out into strange surroundings by yourself. But, as humans, we all are filled with curiosity in regard to places and people. The only true way to live a full life is to never be afraid of it. Caution and fear are two different things, after all.

My father gave me a very important lesson before I left: *"Everything comes down to details."* Even the smallest and apparently most insignificant things brought everything into focus.

Training the mind is a matter of continuously keeping full awareness of your surroundings. When it comes to location, knowing everything – even down to the smallest detail – makes all the difference to one's own survival and professionalism. The eyes and the ears are the brain's greatest tools; you should always be able to see and hear it coming before it reaches you.

There are, of course, many other things to take into account: distances to and from a location; the number of vehicles parked in significant areas; the number of streetlamps... Darkness and blind spots provide good cover, but never doubt what is possible.

As I walked through the streets, taking in the whole

town, I noted the narrow alleyways, the buildings tightly close together, and windows which gave a good view. Perfect scenario for ambushes and sniper fire, of course; the only time you would ever hear a shot is when you yourself are not the intended target.

The town itself seemed not so welcoming to visitors; very few wished to make eye contact. Walking down the street alone, the locals passed by me like ghosts.

It is often the shadows at the corners of the human eye where nobody ever seems to notice a living presence.

Except the one who had been with me for the last five minutes.

Turning the corner, I ducked into an alley quickly, allowing the figure who was following me to pass by, so I could get a better look.

It was a young guy, very tall and fit, and strong enough to lift any girl off her feet.

Approaching him now from behind, I kept my distance.

He stopped suddenly.

"The hunted has become the hunter," he stated, turning with a slight grin on his face. He was very handsome, but something in the eyes suggested he was mischievous.

"Nobody likes to be stalked as prey; it never works out well for the animal," I countered, crossing my arms defensively.

Looking him over more closely, he seemed respectable, given his attire, but I wasn't sure how to play this at first. He wasn't exactly a threat; more than likely a curious local, with very little to do with his time. So, I figured that he just wanted some company.

"I should apologize for my behaviour; I'm not very good at approaching strangers who visit our quaint little town," he said, slowly coming up to me a little closer, minding the distance I was constantly safeguarding with my eyes.

A girl could never be too careful.

"My name's Gavin. It's a pleasure to make your acquaintance." He extended his hand, waiting patiently. "I didn't catch your name."

"That's because I didn't give it!" The statement landed harder than I had meant it to.

I wasn't really in town to make new acquaintances, but then I couldn't just shun this guy and tell him to mind his own business. That would be drawing more attention to myself, and lead to the question of what I had to hide.

As a young girl of seventeen, it was only right to be cautious, even in casual meetings such as this, but it was a norm in society to be approached by others. If I didn't want to stand out, I had to behave according.

"Well, since you seem like a gentleman, I should be no less the lady. My name's Izzy." I now offered my hand,

and found his touch to be gentle.

He smiled now, and it appeared to be a trusting gesture. "I'd be happy to offer my services: to show you all the best this town has to offer."

I looked at my watch. I should really have been making my way back to the motel.

My parents had taught me to be cautious; one never knew what might result from talking to a stranger on the street. But he had offered politely.

Anonymity was the most important craft to be mastered when having to be social, and this would actually make good practice, as I didn't get to meet many people outside of Ravenfall. The visitors, and those merely passing through, were but mere glances, normally. I wasn't usually into temptation, but my female intuition usually paid off.

"Just what exactly did you have in mind?" I asked, with a hint of teasing skepticism. A man was only as good as his word.

As it turned out, the current exhibition at the local gallery was very interesting to the eye, even to a girl from a small country village. I never thought I'd be spending that afternoon at an art gallery; it wasn't usually my thing.

But, in some strange, warped way, I could not draw my attention away from the artwork. All of it had been created by an artist who claimed to be clairvoyant, whose work depicted strong visions he'd foreseen regarding people close to him. One in particular was of a girl – his sister – lying in the street, badly disfigured, due to being crushed by a truck as she'd been crossing the street. It gave me the shivers to think something like that had actually been predicted on canvas – to then, only a few months later, actually become true. The ability to predict the future was both interesting and frightening at the same time.

Looking at the other paintings, a dark part of myself was curious whether the real reason such misfortunes had occurred was because they had been arranged, rather than predicted – a horrible thought, I know, but not unheard of, either. The artist was making good off of this work, only because of the circumstances occurring after their creation. If the predictions hadn't come true, no one would have taken any interest. You would have to admit, it was a sure way to get his name and work quickly noticed in such a short time – not to mention a comfortable inheritance. After all, another misfortune had befallen an aunt, who had left him a nice, sizeable sum, so that he could continue in his chosen lifestyle. It seemed that good could come out of tragedy.

I kept these thoughts to myself, of course, not wishing to give my new acquaintance the wrong impression. In return, he hung back and allowed me to keep my own space.

This also gave his eyes the opportunity to explore more than just the canvases.

I caught him sneaking a peek now and then – not that I was offended, necessarily, just curious whether he liked the complete package or not. It didn't really do any harm – and I did feel a slight attraction myself. That was why I agreed to his suggestion that we partake of tea in the local café nearby.

Taking a seat in the front corner booth, we ordered and he took me through his family's story. His father ran the local bank and his mother worked at the town hall, leaving him plenty of free time to pursue his many interests – such as entertaining attractive young ladies!

When it comes to the art of seduction, there are not too many guys who are able to carry it through, assuming a confident enough attitude to make a girl return the same gesture.

He actually had such an inquisitive mind, it challenged my own capability to maintain a believable cover story to the full, not allowing the slightest slip to indicate any dishonesty on my part. Still, as time went on, I started to enjoy our conversation. He was very easy to talk to, unlike most boys, who struggle to build up a rapport with the opposite sex. Most guys just like to drool over women, never taking the time to sit down and have a proper conversation; so far this week, this was the second time a guy had made the effort.

Of course, that didn't mean that I was going to excuse myself and pay a trip to the ladies. The chase was still entertaining, nonetheless, though I did find his piercing stare to be somewhat intrusive, making me ever so slightly shy. I recognized the desire in his eyes; he obviously liked to play the dominant male, but left just enough freedom for a woman not to feel totally trapped.

Which was just as well, as time was getting on... and my mobile was sounding in my pocket.

My father's voice sounded slightly concerned.

"I'm fine. I'm just taking in the local culture." I gave Gavin a mischievous smile. "I'll make my way back now and fill you in."

Hanging up, I reached for my coat, catching him once again look me over approvingly, as my body curved a certain way. Being desired makes one feel appreciated, and there was no crime in that; it's better than never being appreciated.

And, at times, being the envy of others... Two of whom appeared to be local girls, who had been staring our way since we'd arrived. They weren't that much older than me, but clearly not his taste, as he had not returned their smiles when he walked by their table.

A lot of guys look past girls if they feel they don't visually exhibit certain appealing traits. I won't go into great depth on this; I'm sure you have a pretty good idea already.

"So, have you got any plans while you're in town?" he asked quickly, as I got up from the table to excuse myself. It was obvious he wasn't about to just let me go. We had shared so much in such a short time, and built quite a connection.

But then, I didn't want to seem too eager, either. "I don't have as much free time as you, unfortunately," I said, making for the door.

He suddenly called out to invite me to a party, taking place tomorrow night at the beach. I considered it for a moment; there was still time before we moved on. But I was there to train, not socialize. Before I could say anything, he had come over and pressed a card into my hand with his number on it, saying nothing further.

I gave him my best smile and left quickly, to return to the motel.

Looking down at the card he had given me, I was conflicted over whether or not to throw it away. He had been very friendly, but whether I wanted to take it further I wasn't entirely sure.

You can always find new friends, but real love leaves

you wanting. Many girls are always on the lookout for a potential suitor; then there are those who wait for the right signs to appear before their very eyes. It all really just comes down to sheer instinct, to tell you love is at hand. Then again, hormones can play tricks on you.

Even sitting there as we had been, talking, I kept thinking back to my time with Laurence on the train. Apart from that brief moment in the hospital, we hadn't spoken since.

In reality, love just doesn't come down to a friendly face or a great fuck. It was undeniable that our brief, lustful encounter had been great, but the way things were, it wasn't as if I was expecting him to turn up, flowers in hand at my door. It's not exactly easy finding the right sort of guy outside this profession, who could handle having a killer as a spouse; might go down badly at cocktail parties! When I asked my mother why she had decided to stay with my father, knowing what he was and what he did, she had simply answered:

*"If everyone were to look upon you the same, it would be a lie, because you only show your true self to that special somebody who you see in the same way. That is true love, and life can be awfully difficult unless you have love. One should not deny themselves love, as you deny yourself a full life."*

To love and grow old with somebody is a great comfort, even if you don't have the most extravagant life or much money to your name.

I started to think about Uncle Harry and the two twins. They were real lucky ones: coming of age they'd be millionaires, set for life, with very few worries in this world. It was just a shame they had to lose both their parents as the price. Uncle Harry was at least doing right by his grandchildren, and they were perhaps giving him something in return.

It is important, when your time comes, that you leave something behind. Otherwise, what meaning is there really in a life, if there is nothing to carry on as a legacy?


Back in the motel, standing on one side of the room, I practiced my drawing technique with my father's gun, already feeling my posture improving with each effort.

You have to be confident, when carrying a firearm, that you are capable of using it when the time comes. If you're not, then you shouldn't be carrying it.

I had to get it locked mentally in my head: the possibility that I would have to kill. But the question of whether or not I could take a life was something I hadn't truthfully made up my mind on. Surely even my father and sister must have struggled with these issues. Doing so proves that there is nothing unusual or mentally irregular in our family's character.

Inside my mind, I tried to picture a target before me, wishing it were the bomber, who had now been identified, thanks to some associates of Mr. X.

My father had received the information on his app, just as I had got back. Looking through the person's history, it didn't surprise or shock me in the least.

In this world, there is a disease which is spreading its way through our society, infecting one person to the next, causing a sickness of desperation and madness. I was contemplating life as an assassin, a tool, to rid the world of bad people such as this. Not everyone of their nature has goodness in their heart.

Continuing with my exercises, I began to think about the bomber, the lives he had taken, and for what reason. Was it just the money, or did the guy get off on it? Like mine, his life must have started out pretty normal, but then unexpected things had happened and a monster had emerged. You clearly don't always pick your own destiny; it sometimes picks you.

Aiming the gun at my reflection in the mirror now, I coolly pulled back the hammer and took a deep breath, exhaling as I squeezed the trigger.

*Click!*

It was that sound that had made the spiralling of uncertainty come to a complete stop.

This guy – the bomber – was mad at the world, because his life was pulled out from under his feet; now there was just a big, empty spot in his heart. He had no love, the world had treated him so badly, and the struggle had only led to one conclusion in the end, when each of us chooses to face what destiny has placed before us.

When we all face the true evils of this world, which either corrupt us or force us to fight back. Which side of the line you choose to stand on defines you, and justifies your actions.

Looking deep into my soul, I wanted to help humanity by ridding it of evil, and though to some it might appear wrong, it takes a certain cool, a steady hand, to pull the trigger.

And, once you cross that line, you have to accept the consequences.

You don't always get to pick what you're good at, and you can't always choose who to love. But it is up to you whether or not you accept your destiny.

# CHAPTER 22

### Tuesday 6:46 p.m.
### Ravenfall – the emergency ward.

The hospital security guard was doing his rounds down in the arrivals bay when he noticed a vehicle – a dark, medium-sized truck – parked just outside, with the engine still running. The figure of the driver was hidden under the raised bonnet, his head tucked inside – tinkering with the engine, it appeared.

Approaching from the side, he looked to the man in blue overalls, who looked around and smiled pleasantly. "I'll get this fixed and be out of here in just a minute. Damn thing's always giving me trouble! I should really have traded it in months ago."

The security guard minded him carefully. He did not recognize the man as hospital staff, yet the vehicle had a medical parking permit, and the man had a special I.D. card around his neck.

"I think that should do it," the man said cheerfully, and looked to the guard again. "Would you mind giving the ignition a try for me?"

The guard just nodded and peeked inside the cabin. Glancing in the back, he saw something he recognized: a boot, with the owner's foot still in it – the rest of him covered by a sheet.

The single shot to the back of his head had been muzzled by the silencer attached to the pistol. The guard's body collapsed against the truck door.

Slipping the weapon inside his overalls, Andrea the bomber looked cautiously around, ensuring they were once again alone, before closing the bonnet and moving to the back.


My sister Bethany and Mr. X had taken up position in the reception area, while Harry's men covered his private room.

Mr. X was going over the dossier his contacts had put together on their suspected bomber, and his history wasn't pleasant – but then, they never were.

"We're not expecting a crazy person with a bomb strapped to his chest," he said to Bethany: "the man wants to spend his money, and Harry is not a target worth risking his own life for."

My sister nodded, though she disagreed with this current plan of action: acting the part of the hunter who didn't stalk his prey, but waited in the brush to spring his trap.

"The only good hunter is a smart hunter, with patience and the right sort of bait," Mr. X quoted, smiling to one nurse who walked by them. "Sometimes it's just a matter of staking out a goat and waiting for the wolf who comes sniffing."

Bethany was familiar with these tactics, but the particular goat in question was their client, and making a sacrifice play was out of the question.

Their attention was suddenly drawn to the receptionist, who was talking to one of the male orderlies, asking if he had seen the security guard, who was not answering his radio. On impulse, before Mr. X had time to say anything, my sister decided to patrol the outer perimeter of the building.

She soon found the black truck with the corpse inside, and the guard on the ground beside it. Taking out her mobile, she spoke quickly to Mr. X, telling him to put Harry's men on high alert.

It was a complicated decision whether or not to make an anonymous call to the cops, to have the building evacuated. There was no real certain proof that there was a bomb there. If there was, flashing lights and sudden evacuation might cause the bomber, were he close by, to set it off. No, for now they had to remain covert. Public safety is a factor we always take into account, and the last thing needed at that moment was a panic; for now, they had to keep their suspicions to themselves. Stopping by Harry's room briefly, they checked in with Victor and Hector, before quietly going about the search – luckily, nobody was really paying them any mind.

The timeframe to carry out such a covert investigation couldn't have been better; most of the staff members were on a break.

You could very easily walk into a place such as this with a bomb, and plant it anywhere; a hospital was a perfect target of opportunity. And this guy liked to make statements. It was also now a certainty that the man was armed, and willing to kill innocent people who got caught in the crossfire.

Mr. X, being wise beyond his years, was compelled to take a look in the maintenance area, one floor beneath Harry's – exactly under his room, to be precise.

Stepping through the door, he glanced at the shelves and boxes, and various work tools and equipment; everything there appeared to be what you would normally find in such a place.

But then, the hairs on the back of his neck began to stand on end: a defensive mechanism which had saved his life on more than one occasion!

He dropped to one knee, just as the sound of a shot echoed in the room, and a bullet struck the shelving just above his head.

He returning fire as a shadowy figure came into focus: a man dressed in blue overalls, crouched behind some boxes near the back.

Hearing the shots fired, my sister entered behind Mr. X, returning fire so that he could find better cover for himself.

Then, everything went silent for a moment.

Was he gone?

Suddenly hearing a noise that sounded like a door opening and an alarm, it was a fair guess that the man had not liked the odds and made for one of the emergency exits.

The bomber's presence and sudden departure left no doubt that a device had been planted, so they began to search the area.

Mr. X ended up over by the gas cylinders, finding one which did not sit right amongst the rest; there appeared to be a metal plate screwed over one of the largest air tanks? Could it be that our bomber had a strange sense of humour, putting a killing device in a lifesaving one?

My sister came over, and she too thought it to be a little large for holding oxygen. She took out her knife and scraped at the surface, finding it a different colour underneath.

Removing a multi-tool from his pocket, Mr. X slowly started to unscrew the housing plate. Carefully checking around the rim, he finally removed the cover, revealing their worst fear.

"Can you defuse it?" she asked, looking at the explosive device inside.

"Didn't I tell you? It's one of my many talents," he charmed, taking three deep breaths.

A job like this required a man with steady hands.

But, for the first time, he found the tips of his fingers itching and twitching. The device could be booby-trapped in various ways. He couldn't get a hold of himself for some reason – and it was actually the most obvious: twice now he'd nearly been killed on this job; he didn't want to try for a third. Luck was going to run out sooner or later; it was probably best not to tempt fate.

Straightening, he turned to my sister: "I need you to slap me, hard, across the face!"

She looked at him for only a second, before obeying his request. She found some satisfaction as the palm made impact with his cheek. The man had needed something to steady his nerves, and how could she refuse? If it was that easy to defuse a bomb, everybody would be doing it!

Returning to the bomb, Mr. X found my sister talking quietly into his ear: could they not just load it onto a vehicle and drive it out of there; dump it where it would do no harm? He ignored her.

Mr. X found what appeared to be the detonator, in a simple brass tube; there were two wires coming out of the top: one red and the other blue. One would fire the detonator, causing a very big bang; as for the other, it could be a dummy or a booby trap.

It seemed so simple – and that was what made Mr. X anxious.

The bomber would not leave two wires to chance, even if it were a fifty-fifty call. He decided to carefully take a look under the metal tubing of the detonator, which was loose, finding what he was half expecting to see: a classic trembler switch in the shape of a cross.

There was no chance of moving the bomb out of there.

Replacing the tubing, he pulled carefully away and took a couple of deep breaths again, finding his head was starting to sweat.

There was still time to run. The fire alarm could be activated and maybe some would be saved. This job wasn't paying enough to risk his life; taking lives paid so much better. Trying to be a hero and do the right thing only led to an honourable funeral before your time. He'd never been in this situation before, with the lives of so many people in his hands – and this time he didn't have to do a damn thing to cause their deaths.

He looked to my sister, who reached for the cutters. "Give it to me; I'll take it from here," she said, tentatively.

He held on tight, not letting them slip from his fingers. "I don't remember asking for a break. Just a little breathing space."

She let go and moved back toward the wall, admiring his bravery.

Disarming this bomb would save many lives, but not necessarily give him a first-class ticket to Heaven. It was society and governments that made people like him and the bomber, though so far even Mr. X hadn't crossed too far over certain lines. He was a professional with blood on his hands, sure, but that blood was not innocent; it still reeked, no matter how much he sanitized, from day to day.

My sister knew precisely how he was feeling.

It could be that they were both living on borrowed time, so what more was there to fear?

Two wires: one tripped the detonator; the other a booby trap. But, which was which: red or blue? One snip and they would have the answer, either way.

Shifting over the cylinder, his body now shielded the opening – not that it would protect my sister from what might come next.

Ten seconds passed and she heard a snip, followed by complete silence.

She stood for a moment, still waiting and waiting, realizing that nothing was going to happen. But still Mr. X had not turned to face her. Leaning forward, she moved up once again behind him and peered over his right shoulder, finding that the blue wire was still intact.

*Red! It was the bloody red wire!* Well, it usually is, isn't it? At least, that's how it is in the movies.

Such a climactic moment – even though you were probably expecting them to succeed.

What my sister hadn't expected was for Mr. X to suddenly spin around and plant his lips over hers, or that she would drop her own gun to pull him very close, in a tight embrace. Their bodies close together, they kissed warmly in the dark.

Where they went from there, I'll choose not to say in any detail.

If you had been in a close death situation and survived, what would you do? Bearing in mind that they were both alone, with a disarmed bomb, and not likely to be disturbed for some time, I think the imagination should provide sufficient enough an answer!

# CHAPTER 23

**Wednesday 9:14 a.m.**

**Baymorre County – the local penitentiary.**

Though it was actually man who invented the concept of time, so few of us use it wisely.  And those who do not appreciate its freedom so often have it taken away.

It can be a strange thing, looking through a file, at the life of another person.  The history and snapshots in a dossier contain everything you ever need to know.

Sitting shotgun in the truck, I looked through everything over and over, and found our potential target, Martin's brother Henry, to be a man of very little character, even for one who had served his country.

My father sat quietly, staring out toward the prison gates, whilst I continued to read through the paperwork which had been put together by Harry's main source – namely Mr. Terrence, whose contacts had been very helpful.

Some people think criminal behaviour runs in the family genes.  Well, maybe that's true; maybe it is an inherited trait.  No matter how good you start out, or how normal you seem in the beginning, your family history always catches up with you, sooner or later.

Martin's brother Henry had left home at an early age to join the armed forces, in order to get away from his abusive father, who had been a police sergeant in Ravenfall at the time. He had left his mother and brother Martin to fend for themselves, regretting it terribly on his return, finding his mother a miserable coward and his brother badly scarred.

Having it out with his father, both men had got into a bad fight and Henry had ended up killing his father with a knife, right in front of Martin's eyes.

The criminal court had sentenced him to ten years, which had set off a chain reaction in Martin's life: a life of bad luck and crime, which led to his own untimely end.

Fate is just cruel, and consequences for one person always have an impact on others.

My father was skimming the pages of a local newspaper, when he came across an article of a young woman found yesterday morning, raped and murdered, not far from Wallonfield. No matter where you went, murder and cruelty always showed its ugly face.

We had left Wallonfield early that morning, so we could drive to Baymorre County Jail and wait for Henry to be released, then from there follow him around for the next few days. If Henry was behind this plot against Uncle

Harry, we were hopeful we would soon find out.

The sound of a buzzer rang out over the large car park, and the large, steel doors slowly opened on both sides, revealing a thin figure of a man, lazily dressed.

Since nobody was there to welcome him back into the free world, Henry wasted no time in kneeling and kissing the ground beneath his feet, before making his way down the road on foot. As they followed at a safe distance, he finally reached a bus stop, lighting up a cigarette and waiting patiently, while others walked past, glancing in a distasteful manner.

I looked at the picture in the file, then once more to the man whose time in prison had cost more than years of his life. His skin was pale and his eyes slightly sensitive to the sunlight, whilst his posture was that of a frail old man, who had difficulty keeping his head up straight when he walked. He spat the taste of the stale tobacco from his mouth and threw the unfinished cigarette into the street, as the bus now approached.

My father started up the engine again and waited for the bus to get underway, before we started to tail it from a safe distance.

There's not much a person wants when recently released from jail. Getting off of the bus, Henry had made straight for the nearest off licence, then booked himself in at a local hotel, putting a *"Do not disturb"* sign on the door. He would probably not stay in for too long; a man recently released from lockup would be looking to go out and enjoy his freedom.

Registering ourselves and getting a room on the same floor, we waited patiently until he left. My father then followed, while I stayed behind to set up a few surveillance devices in his room.

During the past few days at the previous motel, my father had taken me through a course on lock picking, using our own motel door and the usual pick tools. In truth, it is not the easiest skill to adopt, and it had taken me eight minutes just to get Henry's door open, pausing and moving off now and then, so that nobody saw me going in.

Once I had gained entry, I planted a small camera and put a tiny audio bug under his bed – this way, we could keep better track on a day-to-day basis.

I returned to our room and checked the image on our compact monitoring system, finding everything I had set up was working efficiently and would be ready for his return.

Surveillance has to be the most important part of the work – but it's also the most boring, following or waiting around for people. It's uncomfortable in a vehicle, and not particularly different either in a room, where it's so easy to get cabin fever. After about an hour, I decided I wanted to rejoin my father, wherever Henry's travels had taken them both.

The guy would no doubt be looking for liquor and a date, though it wasn't easy for a guy to hook up with some babe on the same day of his release from jail.

Calling my father on his phone, I found he had tailed the brother to an exotic dance bar, just on the outskirts of town. That would be no problem for me…

Using my fake I.D. at the door, I walked straight in and took in the entire venue.

The clientele was mostly men, and in places like this it wasn't bad manners to stare.

It was typically the sort of place where you were happy to part with your hard-earned cash. Such beauty and entertainment always came with a price; the more greenery, the better the scenery! Some of the girls were attracting a lot of attention, and getting well paid for their time.

I noticed one woman moving through the crowd, giving a smile and a wink toward me – and not just in a friendly, welcoming manner.

I actually found the beat of the music to my liking, though some of the looks I didn't care for much!

Particularly from certain tables occupied by gents the age of my own grandfather!

Finally, I found my father sitting in a booth in the far corner, giving me a questioning look as I slipped in beside him. I saw Henry seated at the main stage. None of the other patrons paid us any mind.

I couldn't imagine something like this in our local. Strip clubs, illegal gambling, prostitution – we'd worked hard to keep it all out of Ravenfall. It was things like this which ruined a town; once one starts up, others are bound to follow.

Not that I hold anything against these girls; they're just trying to make a living, and they do pretty well financially, whilst providing a service to the community. Like any eco system, not everyone has to like it, but if you close it down a lot of people are out of money. One way or another, they're all in it together. Sometimes it is best not to disturb the balance of the universe!

My father had everything covered, so I decided to check out the rest of the place, finding more smiles from the clientele now being directed toward myself. Surely they could tell I wasn't staff? I was fully clothed – and not even of legal age! Men could easily get bad ideas about women in establishments such as this; they come to live a fantasy – and their tastes are obviously not too particular.

On the bar counter there were the usual bowls of tempting pretzels and nuts. My mother, however, always taught me to be careful of buffets and complimentary snacks: people touching and breathing all over them. *If it's not wrapped up, it isn't safe to eat!* Thankfully, I was only thirsty, and the barman was too busy to even question my age.

I ended up talking to the woman I'd first seen coming in, now standing at the bar – a regular performer with long, red hair and very lengthy legs; she must have been one of the best-looking women in the whole place. But they weren't paid to stand around and socialize for free; tactfully slipping a note from my wallet, I placed it down on the bar.

"Nobody gives so generously without wanting something back," she queried.

I hated to disappoint her, but what I had in mind would require her clothes to remain on her body. "I just want a little information – not too much to ask." I gave my best smile.

Picking the money up and looking thoughtfully at me, she smiled seductively. "You'd be surprised the things people ask for, sweetie." She took me by the hand and escorted me to the private backrooms. Closing the door shut behind us, she sat me down in the chair and took my drink from my hand, preparing to perform one of her special routines for me.

"You want something to help you relax?" She took a small baggy from the left cup of her bra and dipped her finger in the white powder.

"They let you do that stuff?" I asked, expressing no interest in partaking.

"Not exactly; not really compatible with the liability insurance." She tasted it with the tip of her tongue. "But, what they don't know doesn't hurt them... or me." They obviously didn't waste time replacing girls who were bad for business.

"What made you want to get into the business?" I started to talk casually as she danced, but kept herself respectful.

She was slightly amused, as though I was enquiring for a school project. "Well, it beats working the streets, money is good and I don't have to take my work home with me!"

I guess being a stripper doesn't make a girl a whore, even if she does flaunt herself for pay. And, she was very skilful in the way she used her body – practically the best in the house.

A lot of girls who were new to this line moved like zombies, and were too modest when it came to freely revealing their assets. But sometimes just having the right vibe was enough, even if you didn't have all the moves.

This woman, however, had her technique completely down!

Though this was all new, I wasn't at all bothered at having her now slip her clothes off in a sexy way; it was curious – perhaps even exciting. And certainly a surprise, even to me!

She started to place her hands over me. For a moment, I began to think about my father out front, watching our target. I should have been getting back, but I was finding it educational, as I questioned her further about the sort of things her clientele asks of her each night.

It's a funny thing, but guys always seemed to want to know the girls' real names. Personally, I would have thought that would spoil the fantasy.

And, that's all this was, at the end of the day, no different than theatre or television: every woman in the place was playing a part, and some were very talented.

The really naughty patrons paid for two at a time, and they always wanted to see the pair make out with each other. I once knew a boy at school who said that girls who kiss girls aren't gay, just providing entertainment – which kind of spoilt the mood, considering we were on a double date. Not exactly the most romantic, but at least my friend Jess won her bet of which of us was going to lose our virginity first.

"How does a woman of your sexuality do what you do?" I pressed, as delicately as I could.

She wasn't offended by the question; it must have been common knowledge among all the other girls.

"That's easy, honey: I just pretend they're all chicks." She sat down on my thighs and wrapped her arms around my neck. "It's all a state of mind."

Placing her lips over mine, I admit I did find myself becoming sexually aroused. But I pulled back; it wasn't the place or the time for these sorts of discoveries.

Thanking her for her time, I made my way back to the stage area, still with a lot of thoughts running through my head.

There's nothing wrong with a man *or* a woman appreciating a woman for how God made her, or how he shaped her form: voluptuously, to boil a man's blood. Attraction is a natural human emotion, and so is lust. Though the latter is said to be a deadly sin, it is probably the most common to be found in any teenager's thoughts. And I don't ask God's forgiveness just for being human!

I began to think of this as an in-depth study into the male psyche. Just how vulnerable they could be at moments like this! It was perhaps an opportune moment to strike undetected.

As I returned to my father's side, he remained still,

saying nothing, as he watched Martin's brother drinking and enjoying himself with one dancer; the guy had been away a long time!

Whereas I guessed the guys with rings on their fingers were just happy to see another pair of tits.

A man in a dark leather jacket approached the brother and whispered something in his ear, which made him draw his attention away from the stage now. He soon followed the guy out back to the gents, and remained there for a few moments. No guesses what kind of transaction was currently being undertaken. The guy was either a pimp or a dealer, and whatever the guy was selling, he already had a new, eager customer.

There was nothing in the file which mentioned anything about him having any addictions, but that could have started on the inside. Even if you weren't a junkie before you went in, chances are you were upon your release; he might have developed a need whilst serving his sentence. It wasn't difficult to get drugs in prison, and they were in great demand; the obvious reason why prisoners were so desperate to do drugs was that it helped burn the time. Then, before you knew it, you were getting out, just as you were coming down off the high. The moment you passed through the large gates, stepping out once more into the real world, you went straight to the best source to get more.

This could be to our advantage when – or if – we had to complete the contract. You see, dead bodies found under suspicious circumstances make a lot of noise, but people die from overdoses every day, and not much work is done or many questions asked by the law, especially if a recently released offender.

This sounds very cold, I know, but it's the way it has to be, and it happens more often than you could ever imagine.

The man had a dark past, and it wasn't getting any brighter.

At the end of the night, Henry crawled back into his hole and started fixing himself up with a spoon and lighter, cooking up the day's special and depositing it into his arm with a syringe.

The guy was clearly not looking to improve his situation on the first day of his release. It seemed that he was just riding it all out.

But, waiting for what? His own newspaper article in the obituaries?

These thoughts bothered me, and they should have done, according to my father.

We heard back from Bethany about the bomber's second attempt, which had been thwarted at the hospital.

It made me mad: two other innocent lives had been taken by this man, just to achieve his objective. Speaking as a professional, that was only ever a last resort, when needed.

Uncle Harry did not want to risk any more lives, and was immediately discharging himself from the hospital, to return to his home. I wasn't sure if that was wise, but my father assured me that Uncle Harry knew what he was doing. Besides, he had Victor and Hector – the two best men – on the job, and he trusted them with his life.

Suddenly, a noise drew our attention to the monitor: Henry's phone was ringing.

A conversation was now in play, though we were only able to make out what the brother was saying to the party on the other end. A time and location were given for tomorrow – perhaps a meeting with our mystery bomber?

If so, the fuse was about to be disconnected from the shoulders up – permanently.

# CHAPTER 24

**Wednesday 7:00 p.m.**
**Wallonfield Beach.**

In life, there is that which we expect and there is the unexpected. There are no real promises given either way, at the beginning. And why would we want to live life that way? Each day, every week, from one year to the next, you'll always find something new. But, do we all appreciate this?

Life-changing events can either be exciting or dangerous, for better or for worse. Most people actually choose never to get near to going beyond their usual humdrum existence. But, when the opportunity does arise, some are only too happy to deviate and embrace the different, which can define and lead us to our fates.

I'd been on other dates before this — only three times, actually — so I wasn't that nervous. What mostly concerned me tonight was missing anything to do with the job while I was away. My father, however, was actually glad I was going out and doing what girls my age do. And, since nothing was going to happen until tomorrow, I wouldn't be missing much. Henry would no doubt only be going back to the strip club, or the local bars.

I hadn't packed anything fancy, since social engagements had been the farthest thing from my mind at the time. I opted for a pair of black denims and a red shirt, along with my jacket. Looking in the mirror, I decided the look was casual, but acceptable enough an effort.

Some people are so self-conscious of how they are perceived by others; we are often influenced in how to dress and behave – all motivations driven solely to please or fit in with our peers.

Punctuality is always the best way to make a good impression on other people's parents – especially when it comes to their spoilt, over-privileged offspring making friends with the underclasses.

I hadn't long stepped through the front door before Gavin's father – an elderly man dressed in a white suit – began asking me about my family's business.

"We own a butchers' shop in our village," I said flatly. He seemed a little disappointed that we didn't own a franchise, as maybe his son had led him to believe.

Introductions to the mother had been very brief, as she was heading out of the door in a stunning dress; they were off to some special local dinner. She reminded him to lock up after them before going out.

Gavin's beach-house home was plush, and all the furniture and ornaments looked very expensive – the world of banking and finance certainly paid well. It seemed to be a home of perfection; the only thing which seemed a little out of place was a tennis racquet, lying on the coffee table.

"Do you play?" he asked, picking it up and holding it like a professional. "There's a great court at the local club. Maybe we could have a match sometime." He started to swish the racquet in the air, in an attempt to show off his power.

"Not really my sport of choice; I'm more into impact sports," I said, with a slightly macho tone.

He continued to shadow-play, darting now from side to side like a lunatic. "You should really see my backhand," he said, drawing it back and swinging around recklessly, knocking a tall vase off its resting place. The clumsy act caused it to fall to the floor and shatter into pieces.

He chuckled and covered his mouth coyly, as though he were a little boy. "Like I said, it's a killer," he chuckled, hugging the racquet to his chest. It seemed the only thing not damaged was his pride – and his unique sense of humour.

Excusing himself, he went to get a dustpan and brush from the kitchen.

These people were the classic representation of clean

living, and the ever-growing buzz of ambition, all bought at the expense of a job which called for a crisp, pressed suit and the use of fancy words and figures, which rolled so easily off the tongue, like a snake seducing its prey in a trance.

I did not, however, sense any snobbishness from Gavin, which was refreshing, considering he came from a wealthy family. The parents seemed to indulge his needs, but he didn't at all seem content in these surroundings, or with what they possessed.

Having been raised in modest accommodation, everything in that room should surely have great financial value, yet he paid the vase no mind.

I wasn't sure whether his parents would have acted the same way, sweeping up the pieces as though they were mere biscuit crumbs.

"Was it expensive?" I asked, casually.

He shrugged it off, collecting up the pieces. "Nothing that my father can't afford to replace – like a lot of things in his life and business." There was a slight anger attached to his last statement.

I found myself becoming more inquisitive, wanting to get inside his head. Everything he had was more than I had, yet there was clear resentment in his manner. "Did you go to school around here?"

"No, he sent me off to a boarding school, and soon it's off to university." He climbed back up to his feet. "My father wants me to go into business and commercial banking, so I can be like him."

The resentful statement had not been a surprise, and I found myself wanting to press a little harder. "Isn't that what every parent wants?" I said, with a touch of humour. "Their children following in hereditary principle?"

Emptying the broken crockery into the waste bin, Gavin looked scornful. "My father says he believes in me, but I find myself doubting I'll ever live up to his expectations," he said, looking to the family portrait over the fireplace. "Not that I'll hold that against him. It's just that we're not all born with the same genes – and that's not always a bad thing, when it comes to this family's heredity." When he spoke like this, there was a little apathy to be found in his tone.

There comes a point in everyone's life when they want their existence to mean something, and wish to do their family name proud. Most children look up to their parents, fearful of letting them down. Then there are some teenagers in situations where they feel emotionally neglected, treated as though they are a human bearer bond, rather than a member of the family. Maybe this was a man who was looking to live his own life, and chose not to continue their legacy.

"So, what would you prefer? To leave the family nest?" I enquired, tentatively. "Go off and explore the world; experience new sensations; broaden your horizons?"

He suddenly broke into a wide grin. "I think you and I have a special connection! I felt it when we talked last."

I wasn't really sure to what he was referring. So far we had just been talking casually; I hadn't thought anything too deep had emerged between the two of us. My observation may have been accurate, but the way he was now approaching and invading my personal space, it was as though he thought the appropriate sparks were flying over our heads.

Placing his hands on my shoulders, he lowered his head to whisper: "New sensations and experiences make us grow and mature, but we still remain primitive sexual beings." He lowered his head, to bring his face close to mine.

I can't say I wasn't flattered, and a little drawn to his attempt to progress this mating ritual, but I wasn't quite ready to get this intimate, so I weaved quickly away, moving across the living room. I picked up the racquet.

"You may have a killer swing, but my left hook is truly to die for." I swung the racquet round with slight grace. "So, just remember those manners."

The warning had been light, but he got the message

quickly, raising both hands defensively. "My mistake. I'm willing to be patient; take things slow."

He was very sure of himself, but I wasn't totally convinced. I decided some things were better left unsaid for now.

We humans are so complex; even breaking down the D.N.A. code, you can never fully understand how we are each put together. Though, the way his eyes were wandering over me, it wasn't hard to believe that he was trying to undress me with his imagination. I just hoped he was self-controlled – otherwise this could be a very disappointing evening.

We came out onto the terrace and found a row of lanterns, leading down some wooden steps toward the beach. A slightly dim strobe light and retro music lifted me into the party mood.

Everyone was staggering in the sand, or being held up around the shoulders. Clearly, this party had been going for quite some time before I had arrived.

The rising blood alcohol level would soon have them all seeing pink elephants!

A bottle was immediately placed in my hand and we moved through the dance area.

*Nobody goes to a party and just listens to the music!* Those who were still capable danced and twisted their bodies to the beat.

It was very different to the nightclub scene, given the breeze on my face and the slight smell of salt in the air; it gave us a unique form of freedom.

Being young, you think the only way to be human is to be rebellious. To be your own free spirit is to embrace life. Freedom is always better than slavery.

Gavin led the way, taking my hand as we began to bump, shoulder to shoulder. Typically, a lot of the guys were looking for a little female attention, but from the way in which he was holding me close, it was clear that I was already spoken for that evening.

As host of the party, social gatherings like this usually brought conversations and introductions. But we mainly just kept to ourselves, as we walked through the crowd. In turn, nobody was paying him any mind – rather bad manners, considering they were all his guests. My first impression of him as a people person was starting to dissolve before my eyes; it became clear that he didn't really know any of these people, most likely just casual acquaintances.

As before, in the café, a girl not much older than me had tried to get his attention, but scolded him and flipped him off when he paid her no interest. My intuition told me that she was no stranger, and I started to wonder if this guy liked to hook up with random girls a lot, have a laugh and a good time, but never really looking for a real relationship. I began to suspect that this guy was the sort who constantly required some mindless stimulation, whether it was art, girls, booze or, of course, drugs.

Well, the last were bound to pop up, with at least one person handing them out like appetizers. One pill was even placed in my hand. I merely pocketed it, as though to save it for later. Gavin didn't hesitate knocking one back, but that didn't bother me; each person's life was their own and you had to respect that, even if you didn't agree with their choice of lifestyle.

Moving out of the crowd, we sat now by one of the small dunes close to the water. He seemed happy, and curious of whether I was having a good time.

"You want to try something else?" he asked, pulling a cellophane bag from his pocket, containing a small amount of cocaine.

Our relationship took an immediate nosedive into solid concrete.

I thought back to the scumbag we had interrogated trying to locate the bomber, and the stuff I had emptied over his head.

The dark flame which lit up in his eyes as he opened the bag, and poured some onto the back of his hand, was a reveal to a slightly dark side of his personality. Taking a long snort, he threw his head back with a satisfied grin, his eyes closed to savour the full sensation, before pouring a second helping for me.

"I think we should be getting back to the party," I said, refusing the offer as politely as I could.

The expression on his face displayed disappointment, as though I were putting a dampener on his evening. "Not your thing? I'm surprised."

He took another hit through the other nostril. "It's not as bad as you think."

For reasons I have already explained previously, he was completely wrong on that count. Then again, I was still his guest, so I refrained from going into those details.

It really shouldn't have shocked me – after all, I had only known him a short while – but the way he was sliding across to me, and his hand reaching up to comb back the hair from my face, his intimacy was crossing a boundary.

Could it be that the guy had just got out of a relationship, perhaps with that girl? If so, I wasn't about to console him with my body, particularly as his eyes now looked upon me with only a lustful desire, rather than affection.

They were different from Laurence's: seductive with a hint of danger; I'd be lying if I said I hadn't considered the possibility of sex. But everything now felt a little off, feeling the energy coming out of him.

"I know you want this, and you're strong enough to handle it." He moved in closer, so we were eye to eye. "I can be very gentle, so you don't have to worry."

I laughed as a reflex; the guy actually took me for a virgin. I was neither stupid nor adolescent.

I liked him – I really did – but right then I couldn't find myself wanting to take this any further. Being there at that moment, it just didn't feel right. Unlike him, my head was still straight; I knew what I wanted and didn't want – my choice, my body and my decision.

Before I could move away, however, he took me in his arms and crushed his lips heavily against mine. It felt rough, with no real passion, his hands pulling me in and wandering.

A kiss shouldn't feel inappropriately awkward!

When luck comes your way you have to grab it, and guys aren't always prepared to wait for the honeymoon. But it wasn't really a turn on; the touch wasn't gentle on my breast. Some people say that you can't fully appreciate pleasure without enduring a tiny bit of pain – it's the most suitable balance of natural ecstasy. But, to me it was uncomfortable, and made me pull away quickly, finding immediate relief in being free of his grip, and a new sensation starting to creep up my spine.

The guy was sending me bad vibes; his eyes now seemed cold and dark. The way he moved his hand around my waist sent a shiver through my body, and the reaction seemed to pleasure him, surprisingly. The guy was getting a little over-confident and frisky for my liking. I broke away to move back toward the group and music, starting to dance in the crowd.

I could see slight disappointment on his face, not being able to keep me all to himself. I was starting to believe that it was often like that with this guy.

People who are incapable of hanging onto things for very long don't really understand the concept of value, whether it is an object or a person.

I wasn't sure what was going to happen next – maybe he would cool down and we could take it back down to a more comfortable level. But I could see once again impatience emerging through his eyes as he approached, bumping shoulder to shoulder, to make his way over to me.

He had the wrong idea about tonight – and about me, for that matter. I was starting to get a very bad feeling about what this guy was into; the kind who denied himself nothing, taking what he liked when he wanted. It was clear now that chasing a fuck was half the fun. Only I wasn't in the playing mood.

He was right about one thing: I was strong. And this had gone as far as I was prepared to let it go.

There are certain religions that believe a woman's body is a sacred altar, and mutual pleasure was a pathway to Heaven. But the only connection I was willing to make was of another kind.

The only thing I was going to give up that evening was a well-placed knee…

…harshly up into the groin!

He immediately crumpled, and I grabbed his shoulders and spun him down to the floor, while the music and crowd continued, without even noticing. I had quite literally killed his hard-on!

You can't really blame me, can you?

Retrieving my jacket, I decided to leave the party, moving on down the beach, hearing the music fade away.

The evening had turned into a disappointment. It was clear then that some people aren't meant for each other, even if they like similar things.

I was, however, mistaken to think that it would be over that quickly…!

Before I knew it, arms had bound my own from behind, and drew me back and down, sideways to the ground. The hot breath and the feel of his coarse lips were now at my neck.

They were retracted following my reverse elbow strike to his gut.  Rolling, I delivered an edge-hand strike to the side of his neck.  He withdrew in pain, only to receive a palm strike to the nose and the heel of my foot to his chest, sending him back into the sand.

Jumping angrily to my feet, I came forward, leading with a double flying kick.  It caught him in the shoulder as he began to rise, knocking him down once again, stunning him good and proper.  As he was on the ground, I executed further kicks to his body, until I could see that he was well disorientated and no longer a threat.

Rising over him, I looked down on this guy with disgust, and finally saw the image of a true predator, who had made the mistake of fucking with the wrong girl!  I lifted my heel and placed it over his throat.

But then I thought better of it, hearing the music again in the distance: I couldn't have him turning up dead, not after being seen with me at the party.  It was best that I just leave him there and make my way back to the motel.

So, without looking back, I headed off of the beach and back down the road.  I had quite a walk ahead of me, and quite some time to think.

# CHAPTER 25

**Wednesday 8:16 p.m.**
**Wallonfield Highway coast.**

There are days when you feel you are living a charmed life, and others which are given on borrowed time.  But, sooner or later, luck runs out and all favours are called in.

The things you think you know, and the things you come to learn, are all a part of the process of life.  Observing life without living – which is to say, experiencing the good and bad – is a lesson not worth following, if you're not willing to evaluate fully the choices which lead to each individual consequence.

Everything had been fine, and then Gavin had to go and mess it up with that junked-up, dominant male bullshit!  I honestly thought I knew better than to have allowed myself to get pulled in like that, with that sort of man.  How could I have been so naïve?

At this time, I was ready to call it an evening and catch my bus back to the motel.  Whether I was going to bring this up with my father, I hadn't decided.

Then, it suddenly occurred to me how close again I had

come to taking another human life, out of anger, just as with Abigail in the nightclub. I had nearly found the answer, but chose not to follow through, and rightly so: a contract was one thing, cold-blooded murder quite another. He may have been a complete creep, but that didn't give me the right to spill his blood in the sand. Again, I had found my control.

Putting my hands in my pockets, I felt the pill that had been given to me, removing it and looking thoughtfully at the object with some ambivalence.

Was Gavin's nature any worse than those people taking things like this? He used and maybe even abused women for pleasure, and they used drugs to achieve a heightened state of pleasure.

My mind started to think about the bomber. How much pleasure did he get when setting off his devices? I knew I wouldn't have achieved any pleasure taking Gavin's life, and that brought me some relief and comfort.

Officially, we don't think of killing as a drug, or an addiction, but it is dangerous to get high on the feeling of killing and death. That's why it is so important to have other vices, to maintain a psychological balance. It is often the reason why some in our profession turn to drugs. Sometimes, it's hard to find the time to be at peace with your own mind.

I'd had the man's life in my hands (or under my boot), and for a split second almost crushed it right out of him, with little more effort than killing an ant.

I needed my mind clear of these thoughts, so I considered the pill. Since I was in a bad mood, I felt I needed something to perk me up; maybe what I was holding could offer some insight, as well?

*What the hell! You only live once!*

I had heard that the first time you take drugs is the closest chemically you can get to God, without passing through the golden gates of Heaven. Taking ecstasy was supposed to make you feel good, but it had the opposite effect in my case. My head started swimming and my eyesight became blurred.

Before long, all I could see was the shadowy outline of trees; the branches had become dark and empty. My mind faded, as if everything around me was becoming an illusion.

I can't say that I wasn't scared; all senses and emotions had left me. My heart had started to beat slower in my chest, and all the feeling just seemed to run out of my arms like sand, until I was numb.

It finally hit me that the pills being passed around were not E.

Before I knew it, my imagination brought terrible visions

of bodies lying naked in the sand. What they thought was going to be a night of love was turning into a mass flurry of violations, their screams smothered by hands.

Then, a familiar face came back into view…

Shaking it clear from my head, I started to breathe more deeply, hoping that this experience wasn't going to last too long.

Finally reaching the bus stop, I sat down and allowed the drug to run its course.

My pulse was slow and my body wanted to fall asleep, but my will was strong, focusing on whatever I could to prevent the darkness from taking me.

Lying face up on the ground, next to my right leg, was a copy of the local paper, slightly dirty, but the front page was still decipherable. The lead article was on the girl who had been found raped and murdered. They had placed a photo now with this article, depicting the victim – a brunette aged around nineteen – with what appeared to be some local group or organization.

But there was one face which drew particular attention: a man standing just off to her right side, holding one end of a banner which read: *"Wallonfield Arts Society."* The face was unmistakably that of Gavin, dressed very smartly with a familiar grin on his smug face. Picking it up, I read quickly through the summary.

The girl, whose name was Janine, had been found partially naked, with ligature marks around the neck, indicating that she had been strangled. The police toxicology reported that she'd had drugs in her system: a mixture of cocaine and another drug, which produced symptoms similar to those I had just experienced.

By now, my imagination was starting to run away with me. Could it possibly be that Gavin was the man responsible for this killing?

Considering what had almost occurred with me, I started to piece the facts together.

He had a unique sexual charm, which most girls would have found very appealing, though it was also clear that the guy liked to take advantage of girls. Maybe, when they refused him, he chose to get violently physical. I again recalled that sudden change in his expression; the dark lines of cruelty; the strange sense of fear suddenly overcoming me... warning me.

My senses had saved my life, along with my fighting skills – unlike this girl, who had not been so fortunate, or had not possessed the same will to survive.

I truly believed now that he had committed this crime, with calculated viciousness.

Why was God granting him the mercy he had never shown his victims?

No, no! *I* had been the one who granted him mercy and tolerance, despite his attempt to rape and most likely murder me.

I was now regretting leaving him in the sand, left alive to prey on other victims.

Jumping to my feet, I reached down and picked up a wooden plank from the ground, hammering away at a nearby signpost in anger. Then, I started to turn the anger against myself, for being so foolish to have put myself in this situation – no better than those people back at the beach.

I screamed and dropped it at my feet, clawing at my face. I collapsed onto my ass again, unable to get rid of the dark thoughts forming in my mind.

There would be no justice tonight, and very little come morning, for those who remembered – and, if so, would even be brave enough to report it to the law.

Sitting there in the dirt, I looked up to the sky and the stars shining down on me. My head was now a little clearer, along with my mindsight. Despite my little drug-fuelled rage, I was starting to have a moment of clarity.

Some pills were painful to swallow, but at the same time this one had tested my own strength; right then, I wasn't about to just walk away.

What was I supposed to do? Let this crime go

unpunished?

Before that night was over, my hands were finally going to be stained with blood – I vowed that, right then and there. And, this time it was going to be a human animal, a monster whose blood was going to run red – if that even was the colour to be found in his veins.

Returning to the motel, I found that my father was out tailing Henry, who was probably up to his usual tricks.

Looking in the case under the bed, I found my father's gun was still in its holster. Tucking it into my waistline, I called myself a cab before leaving the room again.

Following your instincts usually leads you to the right place, and helps you to do the right thing.

I still remembered where the house was on the street, and immediately made my way stealthily round back, to gain entrance through one of the patio doors. My lock-picking skills had improved in such a short time, and I already knew that they had not installed any security features on the doors or windows.

Making your way through a dark house is risky, since whoever lives there obviously knows it better than you! The first thing to remember – and I see it all the time in those bad movies – is to never enter a room with your gun held out, in an extended arm; it's best to keep it drawn back, close to the body, always looking down the barrel to clear the corners, with little chance of being caught off guard.

The parents were in their bedroom, sound asleep now.

Usually, it's best *never* to do a contract whilst under the influence – although there are some who think it's good to get a little pumped up, as it helps them work better. But, not having all your faculties about you leaves you sloppy and open to mistakes.

This was technically going to be my first job, so already I could feel my heart pounding in my chest; I could feel the adrenalin already counteracting my nerves.

My hands were shaking as I entered through the slightly open door, and I immediately saw my target passed out on the bed. Thankfully, he was alone, a bottle by one side and the T.V. remote on the other. The station played nothing now, the T.V. just giving enough light to the dark room, which was deathly quiet.

I remembered my mother telling me that the first time was the hardest, and being there now, doing this on my own, brought new conflict to my mind with each approaching step.

You don't ever kill anyone in this business without a contract, or a good reason. Well, no woman in this town –

or any other – would be safe as long as this monster roamed free.

But then it hit me: I had no proof that this man was the killer!

I was there on a personal vendetta.

My own unpleasant experience with a sick rapist had cost me my judgement. Now my head was starting to clear, I rationalized that maybe I had found the right man, but it was my responsibility to expose him.

But how? With no real witness and detailed accounts, such knowledge was worthless.

Quietly, I started searching the room.

I finally found a book, hidden behind some folded bedsheets in the closet.

How little we know what goes on inside the head of a person, until they write it down on paper, in a detailed account!

Looking through his diary, from one page to the next, was like reading the most terrible confession ever written – as though the author was incapable of anything other than committing atrocities.

He had killed half a dozen other girls!

Not all locally; some in other towns and one in another country.

I could make no sense of this man's perverse desires

and reminiscences. It is said that only God is capable of looking into a man's soul. And, in this case, such a dark, indescribably foul thing it must have been.

An uncontrollable hatred came over me, from the terrible knowledge I had just gained. My hands sweated, and itched terribly to pull the gun once more from its holster.

I took the gun in my hand – before I realized that there was no silencer attached.

It was going to make an almighty noise when I pulled the trigger!

First mistake: I'd failed to check my weapon before going out on an assignment.

The gunshot would awaken the whole street, and it would be spotted easily in the dark; the muzzle flash would be seen from outside through the window, even with the curtains drawn.

My lapse in concentration due to the narcotic I'd taken earlier was now bringing my father's voice forward from the back of my mind, everything he had taught me repeating over and over.

If I'd thought this through more carefully, with a clear head, I wouldn't have been standing there right then.

There were so many factors going against a successful kill. Yet, despite all these problems, I had to get over it and complete the job I came here to do!

Reaching down, I took one of the pillows and tightly folded it over the end of the barrel.

I don't know why, but I could suddenly smell a dozen different fragrances all over him, as though he had bathed in many bodies that very night. Whether or not he had killed anyone, I couldn't concern myself with at that time. I could see, even just watching him sleep, that he had gone into some scary place, reliving all the bad things he had done, and the faces of those he had hurt.

I had to do this fast, and get out again just as quick.

Squeezing a little pressure on the trigger, I could see the hammer drawing back.

But it would go no farther. My finger had stopped in mid-motion.

What I was about to do could never be undone, and would not necessarily be justified, even in God's eyes. It was not for me to judge and carry out punishment this way. It was my own emotions forcing my hand, not the act of a neutral executioner. I would not just be striking a mortal blow to him, but myself also, into the bargain. Though the killing seemed just, it was going against everything my father had taught me. It was not our job to fix everything in the world; at times it was necessary to look the other way.

You understand; there must have been a time even you

have chosen to look away yourself?

Was it really too late to back out? To go out the way I came in, leaving no trace.

Looking down, I kept imagining him suddenly waking up and making the decision for me, but he was too out of it.

No, I couldn't bring myself to do it, even if he deserved a bullet.

Withdrawing, I reholstered my gun and stepped back, wondering what I should do now. I could still get the authorities involved. But the only evidence I had was written on pages which could arguably be the ravings of a sick mind, which only fantasized, without having actually carried out such acts. There were no names or real descriptions revealed of any of the supposed victims. It was clear to me now that there was no way to prove these horrible secrets were anything more than a man's darkest desires, penned like some gothic novel.

Besides, although he had tried to act out the same with me that very night, there was no way I could go to the law, considering my father and I were here on our own business!

It sickened me to have to spare this man's life a second time, but I would not kill out of an emotional response; it was not what my father had taught me.

So, finally, I replaced the book where I had found it and

left the monster sleeping soundlessly, taking my leave the way I had come, leaving not a trace of my presence behind.

If justice were to be served, it would come another time.

# CHAPTER 26

### Thursday 7:45 a.m.
### The Big City – Mr. X's apartment.

Death comes to us all, but sometimes too soon.

When murder is a mere exchange of life for money, its value is depleted. No matter how much you make, you find yourself questioning the true price... of both the life you take and the soul you destroy inside yourself.

A life is what you make of it, and sometimes it's too late to turn back the clock. The possibility of a different future is a hard thing to see on the horizon.

Picking up her watch from the bedside table, Bethany slipped from the bed, gathering her clothes from the floor, keeping her movements quiet, so as not to disturb her part-time lover. They say that dreams are a luxury the guilty cannot afford, but from the way he slept, his mind seemed at peace with itself.

Moving quickly into the bathroom, she started the shower and stepped inside, letting the warm spray tingle her body.

You're not really alive if you've never cared about

anyone but yourself. It's difficult for some people to allow such feelings to affect their decisions. It is even extremely rare to find another you can relate to and trust.

Having somebody pressed up against you, even for a short while, is an experience like no other, connecting perhaps one tortured soul to another.

People often dream about meeting someone they can spend the rest of their life with, but in a dream the fantasy always masks the reality. There are few people who can say that they love somebody for being who they are and what they do – especially when it involves killing people for money!

The most difficult situation in a relationship is discovering that the person you have been holding out on have themselves been holding out on you, for the same reason.

Should we be happy in these circumstances? Should we be grateful?

Coming back out of the bathroom, she dropped the towel from around herself and started to dress in front of the mirror, looking at the few scars on her body.

They were not as bad as those decorating the body now lying in the fine bed linen, face down. Some people just like to throw themselves in danger's way, I guess. But even hard men have soft spots, if you press in the right places.

She once asked our mother how it felt to really love, and the answer she got back was simple: *"It's the reason for living!"*

Sitting down on the edge of her bed, Bethany felt she knew him perfectly, which was the greatest tragedy, as he would never truly belong to her, as long as they remained in this occupation. But she would never ask him to stop, and he would never commit to settling down; too many demons remained beneath the skin. But they did not scare her in the slightest.

That was true love: knowing the worst thing about those you care for and accepting their nature, just as you accept your own.

Moving around the apartment, her curiosity got the better of her. Rifling through drawers, she found a family photograph in the desk. It appeared to be of him at around the age of ten, with his sister and parents. The father looked to have a strong and somewhat cold demeanour about the eyes – she imagined that, for some reason, he had become withdrawn, as he was standing slightly off and away from his family.

Some people can come to love killing so much, it can become an addiction, like anything else. Everything else in their life becomes weak and meaningless by comparison.

"What are you doing?" Mr. X's voice startled her a little. He was out of bed now and standing in his boxers, looking disapprovingly her way.

"I never took you for a sentimentalist," she said, indicating to the picture. "You look a lot like your father, though he wasn't as good a dresser."

Mr. X came over and took the photo, looking at it carefully, as though he hadn't seen it in a long time.

The sins of evil weigh heavily at times, and make us appear older than our years, driving the lifeforce from our body.

"He never cared much for the material things in life. All he could ever afford was the rent on our shitty apartment and the food to put in our bellies," he said, replacing it in the drawer. "So, I had to work my way up from the gutter, to take the jobs nobody else wanted, so I don't have to live like that anymore." His voice seemed cold and distant now. It seemed his protective barrier was back up.

It was difficult at times to mix business with pleasure, but my sister wasn't about to just let it rest.

"All the suits, the gold jewellery, make up for a whole childhood of depravity?" she asked.

Our family has always appreciated the simple pleasures in life – this was where the two of them differed again. He needed this place and his possessions as a comfort blanket; the image of a man who was not the shadow of his father.

"Don't try and psychoanalyze me!" he snapped harshly, moving over to the kitchen.

She laughed against the cold brush off. So typical: the man had a serious complex to always be in control. But, of course, my sister would never dare try and psychoanalyze him.

"I don't think you're worth the effort; you won't let anyone get behind that thick, iron wall you've built up around yourself," she said, following after him slowly.

He set to making himself a fresh pot of coffee. "It's not like we have some pre-nuptial agreement," he countered, removing the soya milk from the fridge. "I don't like to get sucked into these conversations."

My sister sat across from him, taking her own cup and leaving it black. "Just what are you afraid of?" she asked. "Getting too close?"

"I'm not afraid of anything, except allowing myself to break a code I've lived by my whole life." He took two slices of bread and slipped them into the toaster. "Every man has his reason for doing what they do, living the way they do, and it's his own business."

It was clear that he wasn't going to let her in, so she let it drop for now, and allowed him to make some phone calls.

There are some enemies you cannot fight without a specific kind of weapon, but so far his network of informants wasn't doing him much good. He was still having trouble tracking this bomber down; knowing who he was didn't necessarily lead to where he was, and nothing useful was coming back from his network. She could tell it was beginning to trouble him. He knew that they were now potential targets, too, which is why he had taken to locking his car up in the garage.

Hanging up the phone, he began to rub his eyes. It was the first sign of mental fatigue she had ever seen on him – at least, out of bed. He hated to admit it, but he was at a loss.

My sister said nothing; she just poured another fresh cup of coffee.

There is a certain appeal to committing yourself fully to being a loner, but then there are times outside the act, when you genuinely crave companionship. This current show of pride and individualism was half the evil preventing him from expressing himself truthfully. The signs of insecurity were preying on him, and he didn't like the feel of it.

When the risks are too high, the only course of action is retreat; if you think you can't win, you have to walk away.

The alternative is to leave your fate to chance, which is risky – especially when the odds are greatly stacked against you.

"I think we should part ways now," Bethany said, getting up from the couch, moving to get her jacket. "I'll see to it your bill is paid."

Mr. X was shocked by this statement. "Are you losing confidence in me?" he queried, in a somewhat uncharacteristic fashion.

She recognized the tone to be arrogant and hard-headed. "I just think we are going about this all wrong. I know it's the age of technology and networking, but clearly this guy is too good," she said, catching his scowl.

Mr. X clearly took offence to the suggestion he had finally been outsmarted, for the first time in his career. "I've never failed a contract and I'm not about to start now!" His professional pride was still in the game, and he wasn't ready to show his hand, or just fold on a simple whim; it wasn't really his style to walk away. They both shared this persistence – and a tough, stubborn streak.

"Okay, so why don't we try going back to basics? Let me take point for a moment," she offered, in a non-challenging way.

So far, he'd come up with no key information which could lead to the bomber's whereabouts. Usually it wasn't this difficult; there was always someone, somewhere, who knew something, and he'd put a lot of effort into forming this open network. There was no intelligence, because the bomber had covered his tracks well.

With some contracts, however, you couldn't make up your own rules. He decided to concede, just out of curiosity about what she might come up with that he hadn't thought of. It would have been difficult, considering that he was the best.

Bethany, however, had decided to try an old-school approach, going through everything from the beginning; it didn't hurt at this point to double-check the smallest details. Supposition and bad guesses weren't going to get them anywhere, and a theory stinks without evidence; they needed a solid lead. The bomb from the hospital was a good starting point.

Going down into the garage, they looked over the device, which was now in Mr. X's car; it was harmless now that it had been deactivated. Maybe there was something they could learn from the bomber's work. It was a slim hope to maybe find something: a slip-up, perhaps.

"Guys like this don't make mistakes," Mr. X said in an almost submissive tone, lighting up a cigarette. "It's why he's so good at being a ghost."

Bethany didn't like losing her train of thought, so there

came no reply as she looked over the device carefully. It wasn't that she was treating the bomber like an amateur; rather more looking for the human side.

"He's flesh and blood, not some apparition," she said, finally. "Everyone makes mistakes. He underestimated us at the hospital, didn't he?"

Mr. X took the point: the guy was perhaps a little too sure of himself, and maybe that was the key to finding him. But the old-school way didn't seem to be paying off, either.

Suddenly, my sister called to him, indicating something on the gas tank housing. It suddenly came to Mr. X that these canisters usually had serial numbers which could be traced; they weren't something you could just pick up anywhere.

"I've found something very interesting," she beamed, at a unique mark of yellow paint.

Had the man had an uncontrollable, narcissistic urge to mark his work?

"You can ride shotgun," she said, going around and getting into the driver's seat.

They say that one way to spoil a great romance is to try and make it last forever. And the one charm of marriage is just doing what the woman tells you, without question.

*Fuck it!* Slipping inside, he handed her the keys and just sat back, while she sped out of the garage and headed straight out of The Big City, back toward Ravenfall.

If they acted quickly, they might be able to catch the guy off guard.

Timing was everything, and it was now a race against the clock to end this madness.

# CHAPTER 27

**8:32 a.m.**

**The motel – Henry's room.**

The only truly effective punishment for criminals is keeping them locked up, away from the public.

Therapy sessions and trade skill classes are on offer inside, but few take to them seriously, as they are mostly window dressing; still, they are better than chain gangs, and going to work on the public highways.

There are some things in this world that you can never get over – and you can't move forward in life if you feel like you're always stuck in the past. No matter how hard you try and run, it always catches up with you; people so easily become trapped in a vicious circle.

So often you hear: *"It's okay to be angry with yourself, but don't give up."*

Most people argue that we don't see nearly enough support when it comes to rehabilitation, as not everyone is capable of straightening up their act by themselves. But then, there are some things in life you have to figure out for yourself. It's easy to blame other people, or society generally, for the choices we make, but we are all responsible for our actions. And, until certain matters are resolved, a person is incapable of really healing their soul.

A man also can't sleep the whole day away. So, peeling himself from the sheets, Henry staggered to the bathroom to relieve his full bladder.

Resting his palm on the edge of the sink, he fought back the tornado whirling in his head. It had been years since he'd woken with a hangover this bad.

Tipping some painkillers into his palm, he looked back to his reflection above the sink, swallowing down a glass of water. The haze slowly began to clear.

Prison was supposed to change a man; to make you appreciate what is truly important in life. So many years with no distractions gave you plenty of time to think.

And there is nothing convenient about having to spend so much time in a confined room, with nothing else to do but look deeply into your own soul.

Why do people do bad things to themselves and other people? You might as well ask why we as a species do bad things, on a day-to-day or one-off basis. Even those you might think you know well are capable of surprising.

There is an unrealistic view in our society toward what is known as criminal activity, the atrocities we bring on each other: it is all said to stem from the human gene. Whether it's unexpressed anger toward childhood traumas, or just a dark, lustful desire to cause pain in others, you try to understand it, but instead just allow it to control your life. We are all not above sin; it tickles the soul to a hysterical frenzy, whereby we lose control.

And, prisons are places where you send people you cannot control. Society only feels safe when you put a monster behind bars, and the taxpayer is only too willing to put up room and board.

Inside any government-run institution, it's like living in any other community – only you can't step outside your own front door! If you're lucky, you might get a window not facing a brick wall.

As for Henry's neighbours, the maximum-security wing housed inmates mostly sentenced to the same crime. New arrivals always piqued the interest of certain parties, as entertainment options were meagre. But, as they soon found out, Henry was nobody's punching bag. Those who tried to "befriend" him, for services as a protector, received the same harsh treatment, sending him straight to solitary confinement. It had suited him fine being out of the general population.

Everyone there had their own story, and few ended in the words: *"I'm innocent!"*

Most of Henry's young life had involved some form of

reckless behaviour, bringing about his father's wrath, in the form of a belt or fists. The only reason for his enlisting in the first place had been to get away from his father, but it had done him some good in turn, making a boy into a man.

After he had returned from his four years' service, arriving on the doorstep of home one day, the happy reunion had not been what he had expected. The black eye on his mother's face had sent him into a rage, and he demanded to know what had happened. His mother claimed it to be an accident.

Martin, his younger brother, had once hero-worshipped him, but now resented Henry going off and abandoning him and his mother for all that time. Pressured by Henry, Martin finally came clean, saying that he'd heard his parents arguing, then the sound of something being knocked over. Hearing the front door slam, he'd gone downstairs and found their mother lying on the floor in the living room, clutching her face and crying.

Henry, now being the man he was, decided that when his father came home, he would have it all out with him: this treatment toward them all had to stop! Using his position in the police was no longer going to do him any good; the whole village knew what kind of a man he really was, anyway.

His father had laughed; at least he could keep a job.

And Henry's reasons for getting out were not the actions of a patriot; throwing a career away just proved him to be a coward.

With that, a struggle had erupted, and the two men had grappled in the kitchen. Martin came in and told them both to stop, but Henry had already reached for a blade, as his father turned to look toward Martin.

Henry was unable to remember very much after that. Waking with a bad headache on the bloodstained bathroom floor, he had felt rough hands on his shoulders, flipping him over onto his front, and the lock of cuffs on his wrists. Neighbours must have alerted police to the horrible screams which had come from his mother, when she had awoken to find her husband lying dead, next to her in bed. The chest wound indicated that he had not died immediately, and had somehow dragged himself, or been helped there. Escorted downstairs, he could see his brother Martin and his mother, sitting with one of the female cops, looking on after him, as he was taken out of the house.

He exhibited no remorse during the court trial and, as such, received no leniency in the sentence of ten years – seven of which he had now served.

When asked by the rehabilitation officers why he had not shown any feeling toward taking his father's life, he had retorted, simply that he wasn't sorry, so saying it would have been a lie.

There wasn't much he wanted to talk about after that, so he just kept to himself.

But, being locked up in your own head, as well as behind high walls, was not good psychologically.

Every now and then he could hear the echoes of his mother screaming, and the look of terrible shock on his brother Martin's face. There are some images you just can't get out of your head – not without a little help from certain recreational pharmaceuticals. The feeling of powerlessness makes most feel uncomfortable, but it can also be seductive. Throwing away guilt, seen only to be a destructive emotion, people are free from the restraints of having to worry about forgiveness. With this freedom, uncaged and untamed, we come to want and desire – but there comes a price, which all must pay.

He wasn't sure what he would achieve by allowing his mother or brother to come and visit, so he sent them a letter asking them never to come.

The mail privileges, for those who had somebody on the outside, were like scriptures from Heaven, sent to the bottom of the world. His only contact with the outside world had come in the form of a letter from some legal firm, detailing what had really happened with his brother:

starting with the lottery winnings, then telling of his untimely death.

"Tragedy" didn't seem to be a strong enough word to describe Martin falling down those stairs, or the sudden passing of Martin's wife, giving birth to their children.

And now everything was left to the siblings, under the care of their grandfather?!

Henry knew there was more to the deaths than simple luck and tragedy, mixed into one.  Beyond the walls and guards, the word which came from his hometown had brought forth great anger.  He didn't know what to do.

What could he do, being locked up as he was?

Not long after he had heard there was a strong chance he was up for parole, a certain legal firm connected to his family had been in touch, willing to help him make a fresh start.

Sitting back on his bed, Henry removed the letter of recommendation from its envelope and gazed at the familiar signature.  The words and the long number typed out on the paper now did very little to brighten his mood. Screwing the letter up in his fingers, he let it drop to the floor and laid his head once more on the pillows.

What do you do when you're past all help, and not loved by anyone?  What had he to offer the society which had punished him, for protecting his family?

There was only one reassurance still available to him, and it was always close by. Reaching for the brown paper bag on the side table, he took out the syringe and foil wrap. The prick of the needle in his flesh brought about a calm abyss.

What was the sense in lying to oneself, anyway? All could not be forgiven, and money could not make up for everything he'd lost.

Maybe he was just an evil bastard, like his father. Admitting something like that left no shame stain on the human soul; it was better to embrace the truth and not make life any harder.

You cannot always run away from darkness, so all that is left is turn around and face it. Sometimes it is best to allow it to swallow you whole, leaving not a single trace.

# CHAPTER 28

### 9:00 a.m.

### Ravenfall – the bomber's workshop.

They say that there's always calm before the storm.

Everyone goes about their business, blissfully unaware until it's too late. Even if you did happen to notice, just how far would you get before the shockwave hit you?

It's always the birds who are the first to react, spreading their wings to take flight, whilst the people on the ground spread their arms and feel themselves get lifted into the air. Then, the sound of the flapping wings above suddenly disappears and you go deaf.

As the birds fly away to safety, the bodies drop like stones, some breaking apart as they hit the hard surface.

Everywhere around you, buildings crumble and fall into rubble, and the sight of someone you care so dearly for becomes obliterated before your very eyes.

Awakening in his cot, Andrea the bomber wiped the sweat off of his face and breathed heavily, while the radio at the workbench continued to play.

Rubbing his eyes, he lifted his feet around and onto the

floor, rising to retrieve his pack of cigarettes, and opened a beer bottle, swilling his mouth out.

Andrea had never been a God-fearing man, and never particularly religious when growing up. And, his previous career had shown him things he was unable to erase from his mind; the loss of his love had caused nightmares which were forever burnt into his soul.

Taking his time, inhaling one deep breath after the other, he tried to clear his mind of the images.

Everyone, no matter how sane or insane, experiences moments of doubt, and with no faith to guide you through life, all that is left is sheer willpower and determination.

Looking to the display board, his eyes stared icy daggers at the pictures of Uncle Harry – his one and only prey, who was proving to be more difficult; never before had Andrea missed a target. Twice now he'd been so close to fulfilling his client's ultimate goal of revenge, fuelled by rage. To Andrea, it was all business – but by now his client was no doubt losing faith in his abilities. That hit a raw nerve.

Perhaps it would be more prudent to kill everyone connected. Of course, he'd only charge for the one target. But the effort was going to be considerable; the sort of people he was up against were as relentless as him, and almost worthy of his respect.

It had first made it exciting, going up against professionals, but it had greatly cost him his own self-discipline.

Law enforcement was now also a big factor. He could not enter the village so easily again, as a stranger. He could no longer go about his business without somebody now keeping an eye out.

His window of opportunity was closing, and he didn't like to leave business unfinished.

Now, because of what they had done, he would look to punish the whole village. All he would need to do was drive through the streets in a large vehicle, loaded with his very best mixture, and park it in the most heavily populated area. He could then push the detonator switch from a safe distance, and there would be nothing they could do to stop him. This time he would leave nothing to chance.

He would wait until his target needed to come into the village again, seeing as the worst things in life were only satisfying when they happened to those who deserved it. The rest were just collateral damage.

The red light and buzzer of the indicator on his wall came alive; somebody had activated one of his sensors to the rear of the compound, where nobody had ever come before. Switching on a monitor, he saw a familiar car slowly creeping its way up the gravel.

It seemed that his adversaries had finally zeroed in on him; it wouldn't be long before they were upon him. He had to set to work quickly, fixing them a warm welcome.

Some people take too much for granted, and complacency always trips them up in the end. Anonymity only works if you keep to a good plan and leave nothing to chance. If you obey the rules and keep working to the highest standard, what could go wrong?

But, even the most perfect of designs can be found to have the minutest of flaws. What you miss, and what others discover, can lead right back to your doorstep.

*

Mr. X had to give the gold star to my sister Bethany: finding that mark on the cylinder tank had led them straight to the local scrapyard. She remembered it from before, when we had brought our old oven there.

Climbing out of the car, they approached each container stealthily, guns drawn and ready, each footstep carefully considered – they were dealing with a professional, after all. Although, they doubted he had planted any mines, this being a place open to the public.

Mr. X knelt quietly at the large doors of one container, seeing that it had a brand-new lock, which was easily dealt with by his picking device. Pulling the doors slowly apart an inch, he looked carefully inside. It wasn't that they were expecting to find a welcome mat – more a nasty surprise.

Looking around the edges, he could see no wires.

He was actually disappointed at first. But then he removed something from his jacket, putting the scope up to his eye; he looked down to the container's floor and found that he had very nearly underestimated their quarry: laser tripwire, just inside the doorway.

The only thing an assassin should be cautious of is another killer.

"Clearly we're not on the guest list," Mr. X charmed, opening the doors fully and stepping over the beam carefully, followed by my sister.

The workshop had been deserted, all tools left in their place. But, one thing stood out: the radio on the floor; an unusual place to keep such an item.

The sound of the music was starting to break, and Mr. X had this gut feeling; everything up to this moment had been too easy.

No sooner had he grabbed my sister's arm than a slight beep came from the device, causing a rush of feet as they ran back outside – just before they were both lifted off of their feet into the air, as the whole container became a huge fireball.

Landing heavily, they both coughed. My sister kicked at

the gravel, angrily.

The sound of an engine being started, and the motion of a truck speeding out of the yard, propelled them both onto their feet.

"That's the third time that fuck has nearly blown us up!" spat my sister, running back to the car with Mr. X at her side. "I'm going to end this, and right now!"

Mr. X jumped straight behind the wheel to give chase.

Speeding out of the main gate, the bomber had taken a left, travelling up into the hills. Thank God he hadn't headed toward the village: the magnitude of what was transpiring would have no doubt got the city police unit's attention. So far, nobody knew anything, and if it were possible, they wanted to keep it that way. It was fortunate that they weren't driving through some city or urban environment – that was the worst-case scenario, which they had been hoping to avoid. Trying to take down the bomber in a speed chase was not ideal, as it not only drew attention, but also put possible bystanders at risk.

The trouble with having a nice, fast car is that you are always curious to see what it can do; there was nothing like a pleasant drive in the country, with a black man sitting beside you, firing hot lead into the back of a psychopathic bomber's vehicle!

Proceeding directly behind it on the narrow road, Mr. X

tried to rear-end the back of the truck hard enough to disable the vehicle. But my sister cautioned that such an impact could trigger an explosion, if the truck had been rigged. They had to stop him before he reached a heavily built-up public area, as it was already clear that this man didn't care who he hurt or killed. My sister instead requested that Mr. X try and position their vehicle to the rear side.

"Make sure you aim for the tyres," he advised, trying to control the car at the speed they were accelerating, to keep up.

"I don't know why I didn't think of that," she said, taking aim, but only managing to hit the bodywork.

Mr. X tried to get alongside the truck to give her a better target, but the guy was just too good behind the wheel. The only option was to use brute force, hoping it wouldn't blow up – literally – in their face.

A few heavy shoves were effective, and the bomber's misjudgment caused him to overcorrect, hard, throwing the steering wheel so far that the truck became out of control. There soon followed a distorted feeling inside the cab. The bomber's vehicle had sped beyond his handling and now toppled over a steep embankment, finally coming to rest on its side.

Remaining still in the driver's seat, Andrea could feel a

light breeze on his face, from the windscreen being shattered. Opening his eyes, he looked at his legs, which were trapped underneath the dashboard. A fierce shooting pain cried out from his spine at the slightest movement.

All his life he'd had a taste for danger, and it had become his life's work. Now, everything had come around full circle, to his end. He had failed in his mission, and now there was only one course of action left to take.

The injuries he had sustained were already starting to make him suffer real badly. But it was alright; the pain wouldn't last long: he always carried his own destiny with him. Glancing to his wristwatch, he focused on both the hour and minute hand.

There is supposed to be stillness when a life ends. *If I am to die, then let it be peacefully.* The circumstances in which a person chooses to live often defines how they will leave this world. Dead is dead; the only thing which matters is how they go out.

He felt no fear; he would rather surrender his soul to the next world, than again be locked away in this one. Not rotting slowly away in a cell, and not as the result of a bullet. Death is not a tragedy if it comes full circle, as a symbol of your life's work. In his last moments, all he wanted to do was use his own body and breath to give it one more bright spark.

Taking the crown of the watch in his thumb and index finger, he closed his eyes and once again saw the beautiful face of his fiancée, before he pulled it out, hard.

Approaching carefully to make the passenger side assault, which was the only one available, my sister and Mr. X were suddenly stopped in their tracks, as a huge explosion erupted from inside the vehicle's wreckage.

Initially, for a split second my sister had seen the flash and her heart missed a beat, but she was relieved to find it had only been a small bomb, so no shrapnel or debris came close to them. There had been no screaming prior to it, so the detonation had certainly been caused by the bomber.

They couldn't remain here for long; there was no telling who else might have heard the explosion.

Driving away from the scene, my sister got on the phone to our father, and reported the situation as it stood.

The bomber had been stopped, but they hadn't got the answers they needed regarding the client who hired him. This contract was not yet fully concluded.

# CHAPTER 29

## 9:35a.m.
## Wallonfield train station.

Every decision you make in your life affects somebody, somewhere. The decision to do something – or do nothing – has an impact either way. Every decision leads to some form of outcome, beneficial or not.

When you choose to do nothing, you decide to turn away from responsibility. And, when you choose to do something, you decide to take on a responsibility. Where others are powerless, you may have the strength to see it through. To choose and use a power, for something greater than ourselves, is a responsibility.

But, whether or not you take on such a heavy burden, which is not yours to bear, is where a person truly shows their character.

An assassin who cannot kill is a complete contradiction. This sort of work defines you; it is who you are and what you are.

So, where did that now put me?

Returning to the motel, I handed my father his gun and

told him everything which had transpired the previous evening with Gavin, and what I had learnt and almost done.

"You can never make a kill personal; it makes you no better than those we execute," he said, after I had finished. "This man is guilty, but it is not for us to decide his fate directly; it's emotional and unprofessional."

I could only nod. "I hadn't wanted it to be him; I just wanted to know if it was. Once I had discovered the truth, all laid out in the journal, I thought it would be easy."

My father was clearly worried about me, and how my actions could have jeopardized not only this contract but my own future – my whole life. My inexperience had clearly shown through my actions. Simply putting a gun to someone's head wasn't enough; you had to think through everything, with a detailed plan of action. All I had done was act on impulse – and thankfully had the good sense not to see it through.

My father needed me to go home; he would remain and finish the job by himself, the way it needed to be done.

The worst feeling a person can have is that they have disappointed their own family. It is through the various struggles of life that we discover who we really are. Pain is the one thing a human cannot avoid; it is a valuable life lesson: pushing through the pain and suffering, though challenging, you are able to look deeper inside yourself.

I'd been doing a lot of thinking since I left my father at the motel. Sitting and waiting at the train station, I wondered if there were ever times my father ever thought I would be better doing something else. Perhaps being a teacher, or helping out at the school, just like Mother used to.

By now I had no obsession with death; it wasn't as if I was so morbid as to think about it all the time. The truth was that I was too young to think about it in relation to a career.

Maybe I wasn't cut out for this work; maybe I was just wasting my time. There was still college, and hopefully a career somewhere out there which would suit me.

I didn't want to remain at home now, being around my family, knowing I was not going to continue our legacy.

Maybe what Laurence had said about moving to The Big City was a good idea. It was a tough place, but nothing I couldn't handle; I was strong and capable of looking after myself. Maybe I could get a job in security. Laurence had contacts, they were always looking for females and it was well paid. It suddenly sounded very appealing. But what would my parents think?

The sound of a train arriving across the tracks brought me out of my thoughts.

As I watched the people coming over the walkway, one figure stood out of the crowd: a familiar man with an expensive suit and glasses. Harry's lawyer, Mr. Terrence, was carrying a briefcase and making his way down the stairs and out of one of the exits. What was he doing in this town?

I quickly sprang from my seat and made my way outside, just in time to see him hop into a cab, so I did the same. The driver looked at me strangely when I said the classic line: "Follow that taxi!" Obviously I was too young to be a cop, but he didn't argue – particularly when I promised a generous tip.

We made our way back into town, and the taxi stopped by the same café where I had spent the afternoon of my first day here, with Gavin. Keeping my distance, I took up a surveillance post across the street, and watched as he took a table at the front windows, in clear view. What luck! That made my job easier.

The streets were fairly busy outside; a parade was about to take place soon. That was going to make a difference to the view, but would also provide some extra cover for me, should I need to get any nearer.

There was a man seated on a bench nearby, with a camera around his neck: more than likely a press photographer, waiting for the parade to begin.

I got on my phone to my father, to update him on the situation. He was surprised to hear that I hadn't left, but even more so when I told him about Mr. Terrence. In the background, I could make out the sound of the truck engine; my father was driving, probably tailing Henry.

That's when the thought suddenly hit me... just as it did my father.

We were both proven right, shortly after I had hung up, having been told to stay and keep an eye on Terrence, when Henry turned up in another taxi, my father's truck not far behind it. I wasn't even about to question whether this was just a coincidence.

My father joined me as Martin's brother entered the café.

In the distance, I could hear the sound of drums; the parade was coming.

Through the window, I could see the brother taking a moment, then slowly making his way over to Terrence's table, standing for a moment before being invited to take a seat. They had made contact. We finally had something to go on.

My father got on his phone and got through to Harry straight away, asking if he knew anything about his lawyer being here.

Meanwhile, my attention had been drawn back to the

photographer, who was starting to take pictures – yet the parade hadn't even reached us yet! I looked across the street and realized what he was taking pictures of. I caught my father's attention, and he also found this intriguing.

Uncle Harry knew nothing about Terrence's visit, or any photographer, so we had ourselves a little mystery, which needed to be attended to.

Looking back to the café window, I saw that the brother was rising out of his chair and causing something of a scene, before slipping away from the table and immediately exiting. The look on his face indicated the meeting had not gone well.

Meanwhile, the photographer continued to take pictures of the brother, as he headed down the street. Once Henry was out of view, he started packing up his camera and made his way across the street toward the car park. My father followed at a distance, whilst also careful not to let Terrence see him – but he was too busy talking with one of the waitresses as he ordered from the menu. Clearly, he wasn't going anywhere for a while.

When my father came back, he had the photographer's car registration, but had also read something interesting printed on the side of the van he drove: it belonged to a local pet store.

He would need to catch up with the photographer later, but for now he had to get back to tailing the brother. He charged me with keeping an eye on Terrence, and to follow him when he left the café.

Then, despite the moment's urgency, I leant in and gave my father a hug, truthfully glad that he once again trusted me to help with this job.

I may, in fact, have been the one who cracked the identity of the bomber's client!

When my father left me, he immediately got on his phone to my sister, to update her and Mr. X of the situation – hopefully including me in the conversation.

I kept to my post as the parade started to wander by, its young children playing their instruments, all dressed up and looking happy, proud to be part of this celebration.

Then, looking farther down the street, I saw a sight which made me cringe: it was Gavin, with his arm around a girl's shoulders; they were watching the parade and smiling.

Being this close to him again, almost exactly where we had first met, was enough to make a person believe in bad karma. But I remained where I was, hidden from view, and kept my focus on my own target.

I could feel myself returning to emotional control, as Terrence started to tuck into his meal, thinking how Biblical the moment was…

…the presence of death, and what could be a last supper.

# CHAPTER 30

## 10.25 a.m.

## Ravenfall – Uncle Harry's manor.

At the end of the day, we all come under the care of God. It is His design which decides our fate.

If we choose to accept this, then there is no harm done by any man; those who do will suffer God's wrath.

It is not for Him to remove these defects from our character; it is for each man to face and battle his own demons and, if need be, to ask for God's help, to give us strength.   Those who are too cowardly to admit their wrongs will find no forgiveness on the day of their judgement.   Only those who ask forgiveness, and repent their previous sins, shall be absolved and welcomed into the Lord's house.

Within only a few hours, through the broadcasts by the news stations, the people of Ravenfall had heard of the bomber's vehicle being discovered.

The city bomb techies had attended the scene out of curiosity, and discovered through an investigative process that there were components of interest from the blast which had occurred there. It was only through D.N.A. samples taken from the wreckage that the body had later been identified, through his military record, as an ex-bomb disposal specialist. The lieutenant from the city police unit had gone on record stipulating a theory that the bomber had lost control of his vehicle, and had been carrying one of his homemade devices. The accident had cost him his life and closed the case, as far as law enforcement was concerned.

It was inaccurate, but that didn't matter; the threat was now over. The city cops were finally packing up and leaving the village.

Uncle Harry's mind was put at ease for now, and hopefully my father could come up with some answers at his end, so this matter could finally be put to rest.


Uncle Harry turned off the television, feeling a great relief wash over him.

Now the danger was over, both Victor and Hector could stand down, and life could once again get back to normal – as soon as the person responsible for all this was dealt with appropriately.

The news of Terrence's possible involvement hadn't really surprised Uncle Harry, since Terrence had run the dark side of his business for years. He'd be capable of making the right contacts, and finding the bomber to take care of Uncle Harry – all so that he could get his hands on the trust money.

While we were covering our end of the investigation, Uncle Harry had done his own research into trustee law. Lawyers had translated the law for the layperson, who does not speak the native tongue.

And the language of the world these days was money; you either speak this language or you have it spoken for you. Otherwise, you get fucked by the translation, and soon find your wallet getting thinner. A man who understood this principle could make a lot of money playing both sides, manipulating the law to their financial advantage. When it comes to the law, any decent lawyer would come across some small loophole.

It appeared that a trust deed often has a clause set out, in regards to the change of a trustee procedure; if the trust deed has no change of trustee clause, the *Trustee Act* allows for the legal personal representative of the deceased trustee to appoint a new trustee – commonly, a solicitor with experience in trusts drafts a deed to ensure that a new trustee is appointed, and the assets of the trust are transferred from the deceased trustee to the new trustee.

"So, Terrence was probably going to appoint himself," Harry concluded, as he sat on the sofa, drinking tea with Mrs. Sykes. "Where Martin's brother fits in, I'm not sure; could be that he contacted Terrence and set this whole thing up."

Mrs. Sykes was bewildered at how darkly this was all playing out, especially since Uncle Harry had said that he wanted to change; now they were probably about to kill someone again. The bomber she could almost understand, but a promise was a promise.

Harry took her hand warmly; he really liked how she had turned his life around.

"I've told my people, if they get proof that Terrence is behind this, to bring him in alive." He patted her hand affectionately. "This time I'll trust the law to handle it."

It was refreshing that he was relying on a system he had worked around most of his life. But, he had promised her that he would change, for the good of his grandchildren, who were at that moment playing on the rug at their feet.

For the last couple of days, being back home, he had really enjoyed his time again with the twins. Unfortunately, work had ceased on the new mall, which was still a big blow to the community, who had counted on the development to bring prosperity and jobs. There would have been the usual department stores: menswear, with the best designer clothes, kids' toys, ladies' cosmetics and, of course, sporting goods for the outdoors lover. And, where would any mall be without its food court, with enough junk food to kill an elephant and send your dental bills through the roof?

"Man's most powerful instrument is the human mind: a tool with the power for creation or destruction, as history has shown." Harry was quoting his father. "But it's his legacy that really matters."

He looked to the tiny babies – so perfect; so innocent. They looked just like their mother had done when he had seen her as a child – on and off, when he wasn't being a crook. But, that was all now in the past.

Still, pain is not something you can always lock away in a box. And the worst imaginable is grief; it has no shelf life.

Now he could see that there was nothing wrong in honouring the memory of ones loved and lost. Even his daughter Laurie would not want her death to haunt him for the rest of his life.

Though, just how much of that was left, he wasn't sure.

"It's not always something you can have total control over. So, there comes a point when you have to take into consideration the future of one's family."

Mrs. Sykes smiled. He truly was changing – seeing the

bigger picture – and although it hadn't happened too late in his life, there was still time for him.

"But I cannot rely on that, or trust that the good Lord will give me any more extensions," he laughed, drawing nearer to her now. "I must take every opportunity, while it's in my hands."

He now gave hers a little squeeze, looking deeply into her eyes. "Would you do me the honour of being my wife? And, most importantly, my successor?"

She was immediately taken aback, and a little confused by the last question. "Harry, I'm not sure I understand," she said, a little flushed. "I admit that we've got very close over our time together, but marriage is a big step. And, your 'successor'?"

"It's an honour to be chosen as a successor trustee of a loved one's trust; you're just the sort of person I can leave in charge of wrapping up the trust, if anything were to ever happen to me in the future."

"But, Harry, I'm not family!" she said, growing a little flustered. Usually, the trustee was either a beneficiary of the trust, a close friend or relative.

"You could be. I already consider you trustworthy and responsible to keep me on the straight and narrow; someone who pays attention to detail and will get along with them when they get older," Harry nodded to the twins.

"They need a woman's – a *mother's* – touch!'

The last words made an impact, causing her breath to catch in her throat.

"I was nearly a mother once, but my uterus became infected." She lowered her eyes. "I always figured God didn't want me to be a mother."

Harry reached up and touched her cheek. "I think everyone deserves a second chance."

She smiled, feeling his warmth spread across to her now.

"Do you want the job? You don't have to take it," he said, earnestly, "but you'd be making this old man very happy."

She thought carefully for a moment, taking each question to mind. Being asked to marry, or serve as a trustee, out of sheer obligation, was a foolish act; both required a particular measure of love. The best thing she could do for all involved was politely decline the offers, if her motives were not genuine on both counts.

Harry could see she was reluctant to take on the roles, but remained quiet, hoping that she would give him a suitable answer or reason, either way.

Finally, she agreed – feeling a sense of loyalty, I suppose. She gave him a little peck on the cheek and stared down, with loving care, at the children she wished she'd had as a younger woman.

Parenting or guardianship requires time and attention, managing both people and money. There are never any guarantees that it's going to be easy, as guidance – particularly developing a good relationship with young or old people, over time – requires the building of trust. Partnerships mean equal responsibility, where just one party doesn't end up doing all the work. Challenges and complications have to be faced together, and hard decisions have to be made at the worst of times, perhaps leading to self-sacrifice. But, this is what you signed your life to, and you have a duty to maintain and defend what you promised, with all of your heart – or even with your own life.

# CHAPTER 31

### 10:45 a.m.
### The motel – Henry's room.

The best that life has to offer you is freedom, and the worst debt you pay is death.

But, everything has a cost; there's no getting around that. The simplest of pleasures, like alcohol and tobacco, are addictive, but terrible for our health. So, why do we deliberately poison our bodies and our souls?

Why are we so quick to throw our lives away on terrible sins?

One simple answer is that humanity has one common, fatal flaw: we are all helpless to deny our natures, even when they lead us to our own end.

Lying on his bed, looking through some exotic magazines, Henry was indulging in a fine brand of whisky. Looking to the side table, he reached over to get himself something special.

Holding the long tube in his fingers, he tried to aim for the artery, but a noise from outside made the needle miss and prick his flesh. Finally hitting the target, he was able to push down on the plunger, and could feel the rush stream through every cell in his body; it was a very welcoming sensation.

He was now looking forward to ordering a pizza, then just passing out on his bed again, for the rest of the day.

Unfortunately, my father had other plans.

Entering from the rear bathroom window, he stepped slowly down onto the floor, removing his gun, and slowly opened the door, seeing Henry lying sideways on the bed. He had come into the room quietly enough that he was on Henry before he even knew it.

Though surprised, he was not shocked to see my father holding a gun on him, with the look of a cold-blooded killer in his eyes.

In these moments, you would think the question of *why* was the most appropriate…

"Can I offer you a drink?" he asked, slurring, half out of his mind.

The junk on the bed told my father that he had arrived at an opportune moment; he needed answers fast, and he wouldn't have to apply too much pressure.

"I believe we have a mutual acquaintance: Mr. Terrence, the man you met with this morning. Though it was very brief and you didn't exactly part on the best of terms," my father said, cutting straight to it.

Henry now erupted with applause, clapping his hands together in a stylish compliment. "Every action has a consequence – a price, which needs to be paid sooner or later," he said, settling back on the bed.

My father kept the barrel focused, letting the man gloat – for all the good it did.

"I'm just surprised it's taken this long," he coughed, with a scratchy tickle in the throat; "I expected a visit on the first day of my release. But the man wouldn't have that; he wanted me to suffer. And now it all comes full circle."

My father wasn't sure what he meant by any of this. How had Henry been anticipating his visit – unless, of course, Terrence had been setting him up, and today Henry had discovered that he was being double-crossed by his partner.

"You're pretty smug for a man with a gun pointed at your chest," my father said, keeping the situation controlled. "Prison life didn't teach you anything at all."

Henry ran his palm over the surface of the bed, as though stroking a pet. "You wouldn't believe how hard a prison mattress is? Or how it feels to look out of a tiny window and see the outside world you are deprived of, all for protecting your family!"

The last word disgusted my father a little. "What family values does a lowlife like you have?" he said, keeping his voice low. "In all this time of your freedom, you haven't once visited your brother or sister-in-law's graves."

Henry shrugged, picking up the needle, which caused my father to direct the barrel, silently cautioning that his current actions could result in an unfortunate bullet to the knee.

"I never considered going back to Ravenfall and placing flowers over my brother, because he's as dead to me as I was to him, when I took our father's life," he said, dropping the needle.

"I figured it all out shortly after. My father didn't drag himself up onto that bed, and I didn't put him there, then just collapse in the bathroom," Henry looked miserably at my father; "it was all him: my brother did it all. He was a sick child, you know. He killed our father after I'd been knocked out."

My father listened, taking it all in, and started to build a picture in his mind. Everything Henry had done was for his mother and brother, and what did he get in return? All the birthdays and Christmases missed; never a single letter or card.

"He testified against me at the trial because he wanted to punish me, for leaving them both to that bastard. I should have just stayed away."

My father listened, unable to feel any sympathy for this

man. He was a professional, and emotions had no place there at this moment.

"Was I supposed to just walk back into town? And, for what; what family is there left for me? Just those two orphan infants I will never come to know, as long as that old man is alive."

My father agreed that he wasn't wrong regarding that last statement.

"I know he'll see me dead before he ever lets me get near them, so why don't you just do what you came here for, because honestly I don't give a shit!" Henry spat, picking up the bottle to take a drink, spilling it down his chin.

Nothing would have given my father more pleasure, but he still had a job to do.

"I need to know when Terrence contacted you, or you contacted him. Either way, whoever set this contract in motion is going to be disappointed to know your bomber is dead."

Henry's forehead wrinkled and his eyes narrowed. "Bomber...?! What are you talking about?"

My father didn't like having his patience tested, but he couldn't leave a mark on the man's body unless it was absolutely necessary. "Was it Terrence who contracted the hit on Harry?" he asked, impatiently. "What was your end in all this? Did he offer you money?"

Henry just stared for a moment, his expression unwavering. "You're not here to kill me!" Henry said, after a curious revelation. "Seems I'm not the only one who got played here."

My father wasn't sure whether to believe this man or not, but that didn't matter anymore.

What is the true measure of a man? Is it his ability to maintain control of his life? To be able to recognize and accept the truth when it is presented before him? What a life-defining moment was standing before him now.

There was nothing left to lose, because in these last moments he was left feeling empty. But he was surprisingly at peace; finally, his mind was clear, and there was only one choice.

Most people cannot control how they die, when or where; it could be any time, any place. It's simply inevitable, and there's nothing you can do about it. So, in the end, there's nothing else to do but accept it.

But, if Henry was going to go, it wasn't going to be quietly!

They say that reactions are the last thing to go, at the moment of your end.

When dealing with a man with nothing to lose, you are dealing with a sudden, unstoppable force; a rage rising up.

One now throwing a whisky bottle at my father's head.

It struck him, but only partially stunned.

He then felt the brother's hands grabbing for the gun.

They both struggled fiercely, but my father was the better fighter, delivering a well-aimed elbow to the ribs, following up with another strike. He was aiming for the nerves, so as not to leave too much visible damage. He sent Henry back into the bathroom, stunned but not ready to throw in the towel just yet.

Kicking out, he caught my father's knee badly, sending him to the floor, then took a face cloth and wrapped it tightly around his throat. They struggled again, and the pain in my father's knee made it difficult to lift himself up and maintain balance, giving Henry the advantage. The brother forced his face down into the bathwater.

Pulling back, he gasped for air, but the cloth was digging too deep to allow any give. My father, however, wasn't prepared to die – not like this, at the hands of a target. Looking around, he saw his salvation: the exposed cable, from which they had ripped the electric shaver in their struggle, was now hanging limply by the side of the sink.

Like any desperate man close to the extinction of their life, when the Lord throws you a lifeline, you reach out with everything you've got and take it.

Delivering a backward elbow to the ribs, he threw the brother sideways into the water, and quickly swung the bare live cord into the tub.

There was a short spark, as Henry's body twitched.

Then, it finally came to rest.

The breaker had tripped in the short, so the power was out and the water was now safe. Setting the brother's body in the right position, my father pushed his face beneath the surface, and waited for a while, to ensure that this was going to look like an accident.

We all know, only too well, how science is our greatest adversary these days. This is where a basic knowledge of forensics comes in handy.

Like ghosts, we appear then disappear methodically, never leaving the slightest trace behind. There were no serious marks on Henry's body.

My father had to respect the fact he had made his decision to fight. Being in his place, he'd have done no different. As a free man, he had chosen to die the way he wanted.

One thing still bothered him, though…

Henry had been telling the truth.

He had genuinely thought that my father had been there to kill him, under Harry's order – not Terrence's. That made no sense.

Unless Terrence had somehow manipulated them all.

Doing a quick sweep of the room, he found the letter Henry had been sent in prison from the parole board, and another letter with Terrence's company letterhead.

Everything was now falling into place.

Have the brother released to take the blame, and have us clean up everything. Nice and neat.

Only, he hadn't counted on us killing the bomber.

And now there were no loose ends, he was looking to cover his tracks.

But, no, there was still that photographer! Why had he been taking photos which implicated Terrence's connection with Henry? Perhaps there was yet another missing piece to the puzzle.

Limping back to the truck, my father took a tiny sip from his flask, and got on his phone to make a quick call to my sister Bethany, then quickly to me.

# CHAPTER 32

### 11.29 p.m.

### The express train to Ravenfall.

There are friends… and there are loose ends.

With the things you see and the knowledge you possess, sooner or later you are considered a liability. You can only stretch loyalty so far, before certain ties have to snap under the pressure!

The mind of a man who works in the establishment of law is like a crystal ball; it sees a lot and remembers many details.

Criminals, gangsters, lowlifes – these were the people who Terrence represented, and he had dirt and insight on all their business dealings tucked away. People like this he neither feared nor revered; at the end of the day, it was all about money.

Following him back to the train station, hanging back until he boarded one of the first-class compartments, I just managed to step through the door, before they automatically closed behind me.

Walking down the aisle to the first-class carriages, I

looked down at my own ticket; it was valid, but only for economy class. I took a seat near the door and waited until the ticket guard came through. It was then clear for me to go and find the correct compartment.

All of the blinds were down for privacy, but I could just make him out, sitting alone and reading his newspaper.

Returning to my own seat, I kept an eye on the passage through the door glass.

I'd been told by my father to keep an eye on Terrence. Bethany and Mr. X would be meeting us at the station, as Terrence had some explaining to do.

The bomber was dead, and now also the brother, Henry, yet we were still no closer to the truth. What if he got off before Ravenfall?

Suddenly I pulled back as Terrence came out, and walked down the carriage toward the toilet. Hopefully, he would be a while.

I decided to take the initiative. Entering his compartment, I took his briefcase down from the rack, finding it was of course locked, but I had my utility knife. Popping both locks, I received a welcoming surprise inside.

The man carried his own protection: a stylish, classic Glock pistol.

Sifting through the papers, I couldn't find any clues regarding the short meeting he'd just had with Henry; there were no specific signed documents.

The door suddenly opened behind me, and instinctively I snatched the gun and spun around, to see Terrence standing there, looking at me in the doorway. Without even thinking, I grabbed him by the tie and pulled him into the carriage, spinning and throwing him down onto the seat. Closing the door once again, I turned back to find him remaining where I had put him on the seat, his arms not reaching for anything.

But, a strange curl appeared at the corners of his mouth.

People smile when they're nervous, of course, trying to hide fear behind humour. But, when a gun is pointing at you, the only question you should be asking is whether it's loaded. Since he hadn't already rushed me, it was a certainty that it was.

"What the hell are you doing in here, going through my confidential papers?" he demanded, then looked to his own gun. "You should never pull a gun on somebody unless you intend to use it." He combed back his hair with his hand.

I didn't like his patronizing tone of voice, so I slugged him on the side of the head with the butt end of the pistol.

This would only work with the right intimidation, so I pulled back the slide to chamber the first round, reiterating that I was very serious.

"If it's money you want, I have my wallet in my jacket, but the credit cards will be no use to you," he said, clutching his head and sitting back in his seat.

It was clear that I wasn't the first to use this sort of tactic against him. But, how many times before had they really been prepared to follow through?

He looked behind me, though I knew already that nobody was out there. The blinds were still down and I had locked the door, anyway. The guard had already checked his ticket, so he wouldn't be back.

"I want to know why you were in Wallonfield," I said, not taking my eyes off of him for a second.

"What's that got to do with you?" he enquired, smoothing back his hair again, only to receive the same treatment as before – something I was starting to like the feel of.

"I hate people who answer a question with a question; such bad manners!" I said, now totally in character.

I caught him looking up briefly to the communication cord. What he was thinking was neither original nor a good idea.

The motion of the train made it challenging to keep my balance, so I held on to the luggage rack. "How did your meeting with Martin's brother Henry go?"

At this, he wasn't able to make eye contact with me. He was hesitant, as if unsure what to say next – a serious error for a lawyer! I myself wasn't sure where this was going yet, but this situation was going to get very unpleasant if he didn't start giving me answers.

"May I at least know who I am talking to, since you are in my compartment?" he asked.

Did the guy seriously not recognize me? Ironic, considering I had beaten his daughter in the karate tournament, not so long ago – though I suppose I had been wearing head protection at the time, which could have accounted for his lack of recognition.

"Let's just say I'm an associate of Harry's. Does he know about the meeting you've just had?"

His eyes shied away once more. Whether it was the gun, or that he was having a bad day, he wasn't in top form; usually his kind were able to maintain the persona, even under pressure.

Then, suddenly a sign of recognition appeared on his face. "I know who you are – at least, I know your family: you're the youngest of the butchers of Ravenfall. I've always found that ironic. I even had a visit from your sister not long ago."

"Let's stick with the subject at hand," I said, firmly: "why were you meeting with Henry?"

He now adopted his usual charismatic attitude. "You have that same manner as your sister," he shifted slowly in his seat: "direct and intrusive. I should really be getting authorization—"

I pulled back, as though to give him another whack, but he held up his hands.

"Start talking or this is going to the next level," I warned.

Again, the smile emerged; it was clear that he didn't think I was serious. He probably thought I was just a little girl, playing games.

Well, if you're not good at the game, you shouldn't play.

My finger was on the trigger, and the impulse from my wrist was tightening every few moments. My next decision would change everything; I would not be the girl I used to be, and I would follow in my family's legacy.

But, again my father's words came back to me from last night. And the memory of standing by Gavin's bed, unable to squeeze the trigger. I think Terrence could see it on my face: I didn't have what it took to kill.

This was now dangerous for me, but I still needed answers.

The impact of the gun to the face knocked his head back, and blood spurted out of his nose. Irony again: like father, like daughter! Smashing his face may have been harsh, but it made me feel a little better. His glasses had not broken, but they had slipped off his face. I hoped that he would be more choosy with his next comment.

Sadly, all that came from him were mumbled profanities, some of which I found extremely offensive to my gender. One shot to the leg quickly dropped him to the floor, where he cringed in pain.

The guy had tested my patience. Maybe I couldn't kill, but I didn't mind the sight of blood; he didn't know the half of what I was prepared to do to get answers. If he didn't start giving them up, as fast as humanly possible, I was prepared to cause him great pain, then leave him to bleed out.

"We're going to see just how good a lawyer you really are." I turned my wrist over, to look at my watch: "I'm going to give you a small amount of time to explain your involvement in all of this; by the time we reach the next station, I'd better have heard more than foul-mouthed retorts."

I took a seat and waited patiently, just watching the man, and felt no sympathy in the least.

Out of the window, we had the perfect view of the landscape.

"It's an interesting concept, this: seeing time slipping away so fast. The main difference between life generally and this moment, is that you know when this one is going to end."

Knowing certainly changes a person's perspective; no different really to those people who have an incurable illness – only, their time doesn't slip away quite so fast, right in front of their eyes.

He just kept moaning on the floor, so I started to get the ball rolling again. "I think I've got it all figured out, so why don't I run this scenario past you?" I lowered the gun and sat back, seeing that he was no longer a threat.

"You and Henry planned all this: get Harry out of the way, and you'd see to it he would become the new trustee, seeing as he was the only remaining family? Then, you could help him gain access to the money, and a generous commission for yourself?"

"No. I don't know what you're talking about!" he finally blurted, almost in tears.

As I pressed my foot down on the wound, he cried out again. I didn't want anyone to hear us, so I released it quickly.

"Oh? So, were *you* to be the trustee? Then, what was Henry's involvement; why did you have him released from prison? Did he set you up with the right contact: a certain contractor with no connection to you?"

Terrence looked up, his eyes pleading now.

"I truly have no idea what you're talking about; I had

never even spoken to Henry until I sat down in that café this morning; I didn't even know who he was until he told me. I received a letter, informing me to come along today, because someone was willing to sell information regarding Harry's situation."

I found this very far-fetched, but listened; we had time to spare until we pulled into Ravenfall – though, what I was going to do then, I wasn't sure.

"When I got there, he claimed to know nothing about it; he said he was expecting someone from Ravenfall. They had contacted him to come along today. He thought it was me, but when he mentioned something about parole and a sum of money arranged through my office, I didn't know what he was talking about. So, he got angry and walked out."

I smiled at his pathetic story. "You expect me to believe that two guys are told to go somewhere and meet, both have never met before and both have been told different stories?"

Terrence rolled onto his side, panting and sweating. "Maybe he did want Harry dead, but I never made any arrangement with him, to help him get the money. If I had, I certainly wouldn't hire a bomber to take Harry out like that; it would be far too suspicious! Particularly with the brother suddenly turning up, right after his death."

In many ways that actually made sense.  But, if it was not either of them, then who was behind all of this?

"I'm not so stupid as to even *think* a plan like that would ever be pulled off!" Terrence continued.  "Whoever wants Harry dead, I don't think even cares about the money! Vendettas of this nature are so emotionally deep they go beyond any subsidiary financial gain!"

I took it all in, and for some reason I was starting to see his point of view.  There was that man with the camera, who had been taking pictures of the two of them – he had not been sent by Henry, I wouldn't think, and certainly not Terrence.

A voice came over the P.A.: we would soon be arriving at Ravenfall.

I took my phone out of my pocket and phoned my father, who was currently questioning the photographer, after tracing him back to the pet shop where he worked.  It turned out that he was also a part-time private investigator, and he had been hired to be there that day, to take pictures of Henry and Terrence meeting together.  The man simply said that he'd been sent photos of the two men and paid by someone going by Harry's last name, but the description given had not been him.

The rest of what he said was a revelation of unimaginable proportions…  I listened carefully.

The instant the train began to pull into the station, I jumped straight out of the door and bolted toward the exit. I found my sister Bethany and Mr. X waiting outside.

Jumping into the back of the car, I told them to make straight for Uncle Harry's manor; I'd fill them both in on the way.

If we were lucky, we could still be in time to save Uncle Harry!

# CHAPTER 33

### 12:20 p.m.
### Ravenfall – Harry's manor.

There is never a hundred per cent protection; no room which can't be walked into. Whatever threat exists on the outside world can reach you once in close proximity. No true sanctuary exists outside the Kingdom of Heaven – not on Earth nor in space. Anywhere, at any time, anyone can be reached.

And, whatever – or whoever – wishes to harm you, will not be deterred at the door by some fleshy wall.

Victor was saying goodbye to his brother Hector, outside. Their time together had been brief, but the men shared a special bond, always relying on each other, whenever needed.

Returning to the house, as his brother drove off through the gate, Victor immediately came into contact with Mrs. Sykes, who was coming down from upstairs, and no longer startled by his presence.

"I'm going to miss having the both of you sneaking around this house," she smiled, pleasantly. "Harry's in the lounge; I was just going to take him some tea. Can I get you anything?!"

Where do hatred and spite stem from? Nobody is completely free of these emotions; they fester and hide behind the masks we create over our faces, so nobody ever truly sees our transformations.

But, you are never truly invisible in this world; you are always a part of it, in one way or another. We are interconnected as beings; strangers coming together one moment, then parting just as quickly.

Mysterious and enticing, we can be whatever we wish to be, and act however we choose to act. But anonymity does not always cloak a person's trail; anyone can be found, and any secrets unearthed and brought to light.

Harry was in the living room, sitting on the couch looking over some papers, when the clock on the wall suddenly chimed. It was twelve twenty-five exactly.

"Your time is up, Harry," a voice spoke.

He looked around, to see a gloved hand holding a tiny revolver, which was pointed directly at him with the hammer pulled back.

It comes so easily to some people: hiding a dark entity, which resides deep in the human soul. No matter how respectably they dress to hide this dark monster, you can still see it, seeping through their eyes.

"The most dangerous and volatile terror to be found in nature is the creature which coils its way around others, unsuspected, before crushing with sheer magnitude of violence, until it chokes its prey." Mrs. Sykes spoke with a cold tone to her voice.

Harry was taken aback for a moment, then placed the papers on the coffee table in front of him, settling back once more, comfortably on the couch. "I must admit, I never would have suspected you. But, I suppose it makes sense, the car going off so early, while you were at a safe distance." He remembered everything so vividly now: she had put her hand in her pocket; her own phone must have set off the explosion.

"I came into town to watch you get into your car, but you surprised me by coming out of the flower shop. I missed one opportunity and my associate failed a second time. I was very disappointed; a man with his reputation!" she said, moving to her right, while keeping him in her sights.

Harry could have kicked himself for never considering her. How can a person be so soft in the head as to think that people are not capable of having different sides to their personality?

"Am I at least allowed to know why?" he asked.

She slowly reached into her pocket and removed a newspaper clipping, which displayed Martin holding his winning Euro Lottery cheque, along with his obituary. Harry took it in, but still didn't clearly see how this was anything to do with her, until she turned it over and brought it closer to his eyes.

The article read: *"ELDERLY MAN MURDERED, NO SUSPECTS IN CUSTODY."*

Looking at the picture of the man, Harry did not recognize the face, but he realized the connection now.

It was the man whose wallet Martin had stolen, containing the winning lottery ticket.

There isn't anybody in this world who hasn't lost a loved one at some time. When seeing them go right in front of you, or being told of their passing, it's like the whole world around you just stops – as if you've just died at the same moment, and everything around you no longer seems real.

"They say that life is about moving on, even when it's difficult to accept the fact that they are gone from this world. The clock ticks for all of us, but it hadn't been his natural time; just cold-blooded murder!" she said, screwing the article up in her fist.

When she had learnt of her husband's death, and the theft of his wallet, she had looked up all the details of the winning lottery ticket on the website. There had been only one reported win on the system – only one lucky picker of all seven numbers. Then, right out of the blue, a newspaper article about Martin cashing in the winning ticket led her to only one conclusion. But, what could she do about it?

"Try going to the police and explaining how your husband always picked the same winning numbers using our birthdates! It was not conclusive enough evidence!" she said, in disgust.

Seeing the numbers, she was certain that the ticket had belonged to her husband, and Martin had taken his wallet off of her husband's body. But, even the news of Martin's death had not brought any comfort.

"I didn't know your husband. My son-in-law stole from the people of this community – good people; I just wanted to make things right. I only learnt about the ticket after the fact."

Harry had known there was no real evidence that Martin had attacked the old man. Martin told my sister Bethany, when they'd been on the run in a church, but it didn't really matter: justice had been served.

"You could still have told the truth. He killed my husband! He was bludgeoned to death, his wallet stolen, and your son cashed in the ticket!" she spat, fiercely. "There was brief mention of a certain amount being paid to a second party: a family member who resided in Ravenfall."

Harry nodded, seeing the pieces finally coming together, all fitting nicely. "My son-in-law paid for his crime, and I paid back what he owed. My daughter left me her children, and I only wanted what was best for them; the money was the means to give them a good life—"

"Paid for with my husband's blood! You can't twist this to make it all so noble."

She had only learnt of the death of Martin's wife after she had arrived in Ravenfall and paid a visit to the local library, collecting information from the historical local tabloids. Discovering that Harry was just as much a criminal as Martin, she did not think it right for her husband's rightful winnings to go to him; all his life he had managed to get away with something. So, learning of the two twins, she had made enquiries at the local job centre, securing herself the position she guessed would be vacant, at Harry's house.

There wasn't a day that passed when she hadn't been able to look into his face and feel a terrible wrath building, and today was no different – especially after the marriage proposal and offer.

"It took me a while to put together this little red herring: writing letters to the brother in prison; pretending to be your lawyer, Terrence; setting up the photographer to take pictures of them together – all so perfect."

Harry had to hand it to her: it *was* perfect. All the evidence pointed toward the non-existent conspirators, turning his own people against each other, when all the time they couldn't see what was in front of them: the housekeeper, free to move around and manipulate the situation, right in the open.

"You are the one who has to live with the blood on your hands – that is what you told me. I have to live out my days knowing that my husband was murdered, and you allowed that fact to be covered up, taking the money which rightfully belonged to us!"

Harry had no excuses; everything she said was true, and he regretted deeply all that had befallen her. In some ways, she was entitled to her revenge.

But nobody wants to die at the hands of an executioner. The only true dignity in death is lying in a bed, with your loved ones around you. There was no one left to see him off on his final journey; all that was before him now was a hideous death.

But he wasn't about to sit there, in his own home, and beg for his life.

In a way, it was inevitable having death stare him in the face. "We all have to go, sooner or later, and it's every man's choice how we meet our end. I choose the way of the Samurai – the ancient Japanese warriors who embrace their fate with honour," he said, slipping down to his knees. He placed his palms together and began to pray, with all of his heart.

When you put a lot of people in body-bags, it's difficult to imagine yourself in one. Then again, you can't afford to allow yourself any delusions of immortality. You can only pray for so long, but sooner or later you run out of words... And then, all that follows is the sound of a single shot, followed by – one hopes – everlasting peace. You can either accept it's your time, or you send the Grim Reaper packing!

A noise was suddenly heard out in the hallway, startling Mrs. Sykes.

Harry acted quickly, snatching a concealed revolver from under the coffee table and squeezing the trigger.

The first shot rang out in the room, just as I came running through the door. I was still holding Terrence's gun in my hand.

I was glad Uncle Harry was still alive.

You probably expected me to come in and save the day. Well, that is the classic climax in most books and movies, isn't it?

Mrs. Sykes's body hit hard against the wall. Her eyes were wide and mouth gaping; the gun had fallen to the ground at her feet. Looking across to Harry, who was now returning to his feet, she looked somehow appreciative, as though her own suffering was coming to an end. As she slid down the wallpaper, a dark, smeared trail stained the colourful patterns.

A second shot, this time to the heart, made her head flop forward and her eyes close, dead.

Uncle Harry lowered the gun. He looked sorrowful at first.

Then, straightening himself, he addressed me as though I were a guest, turning up out of the blue. "To be honest, she wasn't much of a housekeeper!" Uncle Harry said, looking down at the gun in his hands, thoughtfully.

I looked back into the hall, and found my sister Bethany and Mr. X standing over Victor, who was lying unconscious in the hall, with a broken glass by his hand. Mrs. Sykes must have drugged him, so that she could have her private time with Harry, who was now coming out to join us, concerned for his man – but more so for the children.

Darting up the stairs, he headed straight for the nursery, pushing the door open, urgently, and striding over to the crib, happy to find both twins still awake, lying next to each other.

Coming up behind him, I smiled as he lifted one out and held him in his arms – something he would be forever grateful for, from that day onward.

There were not many questions asked about Harry's housekeeper. In passing, he would tell people she'd gone back home to take care of her sister, and he'd written her a very good reference.

When it is necessary to make a person just disappear, you have to have the right methodology for disposing of the body, so it is never found. No body, no police investigation relating to a possible homicide. Though, when it came to Ravenfall, the cops weren't big on asking too many questions, anyway; after it was all over, nobody queried what had happened or why. Everyone probably guessed that the bombs were just the work of a maniac. I suppose it all depends on your own point of view.

I asked Uncle Harry quietly, one time, if he had been heartbroken, learning that everything Mrs. Sykes had told him was a lie. He said no, because in the end he'd told her the truth – and so had she; now they were even.

As for the little twins, he took on a new nanny and housekeeper: Laurence's mother, in fact. She had always been there in the past, and she was a good, kind friend.

Now that she had a job and a comfortable place to live, Laurence was free to move to The Big City, to start taking his training and future boxing career to the next level. It was sad to hear that we were losing him; he was, after all, one of the good guys.

On his last night, he invited me out for dinner. We sat and spoke together, whilst eating a good meal.

The subject of my own future finally, inevitably came about.

He offered to share an apartment with me; we'd go halves on the rent and I could find a part-time job, while attending university. It sounded good, and the thought of being with him was tempting, but as he reached across and touched my hand, and I looked into his eyes, something just didn't feel right.

"I don't want to be alone, and to love someone is not the hardest thing. But, to have them love and accept me, for who I am... that might be a challenge!" I said, pulling back regretfully.

Ravenfall was my home, and I had decided to stay and help the family business, and continue with my training. I wasn't going to give up my legacy.

"All you can do is live in hope that you'll find somebody, someday," he conquered disappointedly, shying his eyes away.


We still remain in contact, and he has done very well for

himself since his boxing career came to an end; he became a Close-Protection Officer in the corporate industry. It is a dangerous job, but then few things these days don't involve some risk, in one way or another.

Such as my sister Bethany getting engaged to Mr. X!

Yep, I don't know about you, but I didn't see that coming, either.

She too moved to The Big City, and moved in with Mr. X.

But, as for what came next, that's for another time!

# CHAPTER 34

**One year later.**

**The Big City.**

There are two types of people: those who feel and those who don't.

The world is full of good people and bad people. We all have our reasons to love, and we all have our reasons to hate. Most never question if what they do is right, but also never admit it is wrong, even to themselves.

As for society, people don't know what, how or who these people are, truly.

When you are at home with your loved ones, you're actually content not knowing. You feel safe when you turn out your lights, because you feel you are one of the good ones, and somebody is watching over you.

It is only the people on the other side who should fear people like us.

But, it isn't always that way, because even those who appear innocent wear a mask. Then again, don't be too quick to judge; even the good guys wear a mask, too, now and then.

Pulling the car over to the side of the road, I climbed out of the back seat of the cab and tipped the driver, asking him to wait; I wasn't going to be long.

As I smiled pleasantly to the doorman, he opened the door leading into the Kitty Kat Club – a high-class, exotic dance club to be found in The Big City.

It was my first solo contract and it was simple. Our services had come highly recommended, and the client had wanted a woman for this particular job.

It may sound strange, I know, but it is quite common that a client will ask for a male or female contractor; either might be more understanding of the client's reasons. And, as I've already explained, this is of particular importance to us.

On this occasion, it wasn't one of those horrible situations where a lot of research had to be carried out, or a great deal of debate on whether to take the contract. The hardest thing for me was to try and keep my emotions in check, throughout. How and where was the easy part: somewhere he would least expect and would have his guard down.

The man was something of a predator, of his own nature. This guy was the most hated kind, but the law couldn't touch him without any hard evidence. The client was his most recent victim, looking for justice. She had survived his attack somehow, but had not been able to secure any proof of his involvement to the police: no witness; no D.N.A.   Long hours of talking to a psychotherapist had done little to give her peace of mind.

But then, you can't always be sure that therapy is the best cure.

The D.J.'s voice broke through the room, as I moved to the bar area, taking in the scenery of wonderful high heels, already working the stage area.

I quickly found my target, sitting by himself at a table, apparently bored by what was on offer.  He looked at the tiny figure pouting her lips and shaking her hips, whilst wearing a stylish, fluffy, two-piece bathing suit.  Her curly, red hair playfully danced off the shoulder line.  They were all very attractive, but tonight he was looking for a special treat.

His eyes immediately lit up with interest as I approached.

There is a certain freedom which comes from being human, which is awarded to every person on the planet; everyone has their own particular vice.

While love was only for idealists, pleasure, pain and death were for the strong-willed; summoning their darkest natures makes them feel more than human.

Gavin was so incapable of true empathy, even his smile

appeared false in the eyes now.

Resting forward on his elbows, he took me in: the ravishing delight who had immediately taken a liking to him, over everyone else. Of course, the suits were known to be the best moneymakers, and they weren't shy when it came to splashing out on a little evening company.

I hadn't applied too much cosmetic, as it hurt the tips when a girl got too sweaty, and ended up with a stream of dark mascara running down her face.

Not that this was the main point of attraction to a man's wallet.

"Buy a girl a drink, and you can whisper whatever fantasy you want in my ear," I purred, offering my hand.

I led him out back to a private-show room, helping to make him feel comfortable, by slipping him a small bag of a special white mix.

So often the male wants their fantasy to come true. The only problem with getting swept up in a fantasy is that it can lead to bad choices. And, sooner or later, every fantasy has to come to an end, and everyone has to pay the price. The cost can be severe... If not to say... dream shattering.

Straddling his lap as he sat in the chair, I knew that his hands would eventually work their way up to my throat, wanting to hold me tightly enough to feel the life leave my body. He would want to look me in the eyes until they went back into my head, and his face would be the last thing I would ever see.

But, he hadn't seen my hands reaching up behind him, to remove a tie-back hanging from the wall. His eyes had gone hazy, due to the extra spice I added to the cocaine; soon, his arms would go numb and he would be defenceless.

Suddenly, there came a look of familiarity in the eyes. Gavin finally recognized me...

...but I had already tightened the rope around his throat.

He made a grab for my hair, but found that it came away in his hand – I had heard he had a particular obsession with brunettes, so the wig had been a perfect enticement.

Twisting my grip, I found that all the energy had vanished from his arms now, and he was helpless in this death grip. I watched his eyes roll back into his head.

Some die quickly, while others hold on for as long as they can, but I never leave my target until they stop breathing; only then is the contract complete.

Standing over him, I controlled my breathing and took it all in, finding no emotional response to the action I had just carried out.

Hanging him by the neck from one of the hooks, I redressed myself. Then, like a ghost, I vanished through the main room without anybody paying me any mind.

Sitting back in the cab, I just stewed in my own thoughts while the radio played. At that moment, it was too early to tell how this would affect me.

It had been almost a year since I'd last seen Gavin, and each day since I'd learnt how to disconnect from the past a little more; I only held onto the fond memories now, while others faded to black.

It's amazing how fast we grow and change. To my parents, I may seem like their little girl, but inside I no longer consider myself that innocent anymore.

Arriving home and entering the kitchen, I removed my jacket and came to sit by my mother, who was already serving her fine cuisine onto a plate for me.

I looked across at my father, but no questions came; he didn't ask if I had been successful. It was probably self-evident; if I hadn't, I would have not come in the way I had.

Besides, we were at the kitchen table, where such business did not belong, in family time.

Taking each other's hands, we bowed our heads, as my father said the prayer. Whilst my eyes were closed, the images from the club were revisiting me, playing out in a loop, as my father recited the blessing:

*"Lord, we give thanks…"*

I could now see it clearly; the answer had finally come, at the cost of a life.

I *was* capable of killing a human in cold blood.

True life hung not by a thread, but by a rope – one which I'd held with both hands.

It was not a chain that bound me to my destiny; this was the way it had to be, to be able to carry on my family legacy. My fate can still be changed, if I so choose, but instead I embrace what is in my blood, and now I walk the path of no return; there is nothing more to do than accept my destiny.


So, now everything has been laid out, and all the pieces put together to make a clear picture. I've given you enough, hopefully, to reach your own conclusions.

You might not want to admit it, but I'm guessing you've picked up something from our time together, about the world and maybe how you see it now.

We are not forced against our will; it is for each to choose their path in life – make the decision to become what they are and will forever be.

When I think about the words I choose to put down here, I wonder what people will come to think of me and my family.   Writing these words is by no means a confession, intended to set me free of any demons, as there are none to speak of.  And, like me, I'm sure you'll lose no sleep.  This is just a story, after all.

Maybe these are spoken lies, or perhaps I have told them as best I could, without them meaning to appear so.  Whatever, there are still those of you who have chosen to keep reading.  I have talked and you have listened – just as before – by your own free will.  If your interest is purely entertainment or fascination, I will not judge.

In truth, you have languished on these words too long now to even doubt that what I have written isn't mere fabrication.   Does it bother you to have witnessed such atrocities?

There are worse things in this world than those who kill for money, such as those who cause suffering and death for pleasure – to those we come a-calling.   Maybe you appreciate that we maintain a suitable balance, to punish those the law cannot?  If we receive recompense for our hand striking a deadly blow, is that not only fair, to do what others cannot or will not?

What we do is not heroic, but then it is not necessarily evil, either.  We are not inhuman – though you may argue, or may not even care.  It has already been decided, and what *is* is meant to be, regardless of your – or anyone else's – opinions.    Still, feel free to form your own judgment.

# ABOUT THE AUTHOR

## ACKNOWLEDGMENTS

The publishers and authors would like to thank Russell Spencer, Matt Vidler, Susan Woodard, Leonard West, Lianne Baily Woodward and Laura Jayne Humphrey for their work, without which this book would not have been possible.

## ABOUT THE PUBLISHER

L.R. Price Publications is dedicated to publishing books by unknown authors.

We use a mixture of both traditional and modern publishing options, to bring our authors' words to the wider world.

We print, publish, distribute and market books in a variety of formats including paper and hardback, electronic books, digital audiobooks and online.

If you are an author interested in getting your book published, or a book retailer interested in selling our books, please contact us.

www.lrpricepublications.com

L.R. Price Publications Ltd,
27 Old Gloucester Street,
London, WC1N 3AX.
020 3051 9572
*publishing@lrprice.com*